DARK OF NIGHT

SHADOW SECURITY BOOK THREE

RAMONA GRAY

EK PUBLISHING INC.

DARK OF NIGHT

Eleanor loves being a personal driver for the stoic, deliciously sexy lion shifter, Wes Masters.

And she's had a crush on him since day one.

Unfortunately, Wes isn't looking for a relationship, and he's made it clear he won't make an exception for her.

Wes's attraction to the smart, beautiful human grows daily. But even if his traumatic past hadn't broken him and his lion, he can't get past their fifteen-year age gap.

But when Eleanor is targeted by a violent, unstable shifter bent on destruction, Wes and his lion are determined to keep her safe.

Even if it kills him.

CHAPTER 1

"We have a problem."

He glanced up at Hoyt, his face serene. "What is it?"

"Whitman rabbited."

He blew his breath out and scrubbed a hand across the two-day growth sprouted on his jaw. "Fuck. I knew that asshole was losing his nerve. Find him. Check his house and -"

"There's more, Chad."

Double fuck. Hoyt only called him by his first name when it was really bad. "What?"

"He destroyed the serum in the lab."

"All of it?"

"Yeah. Walters found the vials smashed in the lab on sixth. Nothing is viable."

"How the fuck did he take the vials from the lab when there are cameras every two fucking feet in that place, Hoyt?"

"He hacked the system, ran a loop of the video feed."

"He's a fucking biochemist, not a hacker!" Chad sucked in a deep breath. Losing his shit wouldn't help the situation.

1

"Okay, have Simpson and Edwards start cooking up a new batch of juice. The team is due for their next shots in twelve hours. It'll be close but -"

"He took the formula."

The storm brewing in Chad's chest became a category five hurricane. "What do you mean he took the formula?"

"He deleted it out of the system, but Edwards is confident he took a copy of it. He saw him earlier this morning at the computer with a flash drive."

"He had a fucking flash drive, and Edwards didn't think that was worth telling me about?" Chad's blood pressure climbed to stroke levels. "What the fuck, Hoyt?"

Hoyt shrugged. "He didn't think twice about it. Whitman is the lab head, and Edwards is just a peon hired to make the juice."

"Fucking hell." Chad leaned back in his chair. "I told Bradmore we needed to have copies of the juice formula offsite. I fucking told him, but he refused to listen. Too fucking worried that outside sources would get a hold of it."

He stared at the ceiling, his guts churning. "Whitman will take this public."

"You don't know that for sure," Hoyt said.

"Like fuck, I don't!' Chad snapped. "We need to find him before he blows the whole program out of the water. Take a team to his home."

"It's been five hours since he left the lab," Hoyt said. "He told Edwards and Simpson he had a doctor's appointment."

"What the fuck, Hoyt? You're the head of security, and you had no idea any of this happened for five fucking hours?"

Hoyt's face reddened. "This isn't my fault, Chad. Whitman has high-level clearance. He's allowed wherever the fuck he wants in the lab."

"Christ, this just gets worse and worse. Take a team to

Whitman's house. Maybe they can find a clue to where he's hiding."

"You want me to take Rourke and the others?" Hoyt said.

Chad shook his head. "No. They need to conserve their energy. Take a human team."

Hoyt headed toward the door, pausing in the doorway when Chad called his name.

"All I need is the juice formula. Whitman can be cleaned and tossed. Let Jasper know where to pick up the body. Clear?"

"Crystal," Hoyt said.

HOYT'S RETURN ONLY A FEW HOURS LATER DIDN'T SIT WELL with Chad. He motioned the man into the chair across from his desk. Hoyt sat, and when he didn't say anything, Chad said, "Well?"

"Whitman's dead," Hoyt said.

Relief swept through Chad. He leaned back in his chair. "Thank Christ. Okay, we get Edwards and Simpson started on a new batch of juice, and I'll -"

"It wasn't us," Hoyt said.

"What do you mean?"

"I mean, we didn't fucking clean him. He died of a heart attack, I think."

Unease slithered down Chad's spine. "Do you have the juice formula or not, Hoyt?"

"No," Hoyt said.

"Fuck," Chad said. "Tell me what happened."

"We went to his place first. His neighbour was outside watering her flowers. I sent Jacobs in to talk to her. You know the ladies can't fucking resist him."

Chad waved his hand impatiently. "What then?"

"The neighbour saw Whitman leaving a couple of hours earlier. Said he looked like he was in a hurry. He had a suitcase and a package."

"What kind of package?" Chad said.

"A box. The neighbour said he was on his way to mail it."

"How did she know that?"

Hoyt shrugged. "I guess Whitman dropped it as he headed toward the car. She picked it up and saw a mailing address on it."

Chad sat forward. "Did she remember who it was addressed to?"

"Nah. Anyway, Whitman told her he was going on vacation for a few weeks. Said he was visiting friends upstate. The neighbour told Jacobs that he didn't look so hot, though. Pale and sweaty, and he looked scared, she said."

"So, we don't actually know if he mailed the box," Chad said.

Hoyt snorted impatiently. "Am I telling the fucking story or not, Chad?"

Chad seriously considered pulling his gun from his desk and putting a bullet between Hoyt's eyes. Instead, he gave his head of security a thin smile. "By all means, finish your fucking story, Hoyt."

"We didn't know for sure he went to the post office, but we figured it couldn't hurt to check. We went to the post office closest to his house."

"And?" Chad said.

Hoyt made a face. "The coroner was just loading Whitman's body to take him to the morgue. We talked to a few of the lookie-loos, and they all said the same thing. Whitman came out of the post office, pale and sweaty and rubbing his chest. He climbed into his car, drove about twenty feet, and rammed the car into a tree. He most likely had a heart attack while driving."

"Shit," Chad said. "Did you get the parcel from the post office?"

"No."

"What the fuck, Hoyt?"

"There were police in the post office, taking statements," Hoyt said. "I couldn't exactly waltz in there and bribe the post office for the package. The fucking truck showed up while we waited for the police to leave, and they loaded the packages for the day. Whatever Whitman sent is gone."

"Whatever he sent? He obviously sent the fucking formula to someone."

"It's more likely that he emailed it," Hoyt said. "Probably to every newspaper in the country."

"He didn't. The package he sent has the formula," Chad said.

"How do you know that?"

"He won't have sent it by email because he's not a stupid man. I'll have Angston confirm it by checking his work and personal computers, but I'm confident he won't find any electronic evidence of it being sent. And as far as making the formula public? He'd never do that."

"Why are you so sure?" Hoyt said.

"Because Whitman believed he could fix the formula. He wanted more time to work on it than the Board was willing to give him. He wouldn't expose the formula to the public, not when he believed he could fix it," Chad said. "But he was smart enough to send it to at least one person because he knew we'd fucking find him sooner or later."

Hoyt cleared his throat. "We went to the morgue. Bribed the morgue attendant into letting us see the stuff Whitman had on his body when they brought him in. There was a receipt from the post office. He sent it priority and on priority receipt slips -"

"They show the address," Chad said.

"That's right." Hoyt pulled out his phone and tapped the screen. "Whitman sent the parcel to a woman named Eleanor. Eleanor Whitman. His daughter."

Chad jerked in his chair. "Whitman doesn't have a kid. He has a dead wife but no kid."

Hoyt shook his head. "He has a kid. I called Angston and had him do a deeper dive into Whitman. The old man hid her well, but he definitely has a kid."

"Fucking Angston, I should have him fucking cleaned for missing that," Chad said. "Tell me about the kid."

"Eleanor Whitman. She's twenty-seven years old, lives in Bridgedale, worked at a few restaurants in her teens, then worked for Uber for three years. She started her own trans-portation company two years ago. She's been driving rich assholes around ever since."

"So, she's not a brilliant scientific genius like her father, is what you're saying," Chad said.

Hoyt shrugged. "Maybe she's just unmotivated."

Chad tapped his fingers on the desk. "He was right to hide her from us."

"I'm sending a team in tonight to search Whitman's house," Hoyt said. "Likely, he sent the flash drive with the formula to his kid, but we'll do a sweep just in case. How long do they have?"

"Their next dose is needed in six hours." Chad stood and walked to the bar fridge tucked at the far end of the credenza. He opened it and stared at the vials of serum on the top shelf.

Hoyt joined him. "You have extra."

"Not enough for all twelve," Chad said. He brought out a

vial, staring at the way the blue liquid gleamed in the light coming through the window.

"So, we're gonna lose the whole fucking team," Hoyt said.

Chad shook his head. "No. We keep dosing Rourke. There's enough juice to keep him going for a couple of weeks if we only use it on him."

"What about the others?"

"They'll either die or wish they were dead as the serum wears off," Chad said.

"You should dose all of them. We'll have the juice back within a day or two," Hoyt said.

"And if we don't? I'd rather keep one than lose all of them."

"You're making a mistake choosing Rourke."

"He's the fastest and the strongest of them," Chad said.

"And the most aggressive," Hoyt said. There was a touch of disgust and fear in the big man's voice.

"It works to our advantage," Chad said.

"Does it? He shows no remorse over the people he's killed," Hoyt said. "Hell, none of them do, but he fucking enjoyed it, Chad."

"They completed their mission. There's nothing wrong with them being happy about that."

"Innocent people died on their mission," Hoyt said. "At their hand. That wasn't supposed to happen."

"Mistakes were made, but we tweaked the juice to lower the aggression."

"It didn't work, and you know it. They're dangerous, Chad. You think you can control them, but you can't. The whole program needs to be scrapped."

"You losing your fucking nerve, Hoyt?" Chad said. "You thinking about rabbiting like Whitman?"

"You know I'm fucking not," Hoyt said.

"Good." He returned to his chair and opened his laptop. "Put a man on Eleanor. Once she has the parcel from her father, he goes in and takes it from her."

"You want her left alive or cleaned?" Hoyt said.

Chad didn't hesitate. "Cleaned."

CHAPTER 2

"You don't need to be nervous. You've done this hundreds of times. Hell, maybe even thousands of times. Nothing has changed," Eleanor said to the Eleanor in the rear-view mirror.

Rear-view Eleanor's face didn't believe a word she said.

Eleanor couldn't blame her. No matter how many pep talks she'd given herself on the drive over to Wes's office, it didn't negate the fact that, while yes, driving Wes home from work was a completely normal occurrence, this time it was far from normal.

Last week she'd kissed Wes.

Kissed the man who'd had a leading role in every single one of her sex fantasies for the last year. And not only had he kissed her back, but he'd said things to her. *Dirty* things that he certainly didn't say in her fantasies. But to be fair, despite seeing her twice a day, nearly every day for over a year, Wes barely spoke to her in real life. The lion shifter was the quietest man she'd ever met. Why would she suspect he indulged in dirty talk with the women he had sex with?

"Whoa, take it down a notch, Eleanor," Rear-view

Eleanor said to her. "You kissed, and he mentioned your lady parts were greedy for his dick. That's not even close to having sex with him."

"My lady parts *are* greedy for his dick," Eleanor said. "Ridiculously greedy. And now that I know what a great kisser he is and how good he is at the dirty talk, I haven't had a dry pair of underpants since."

Rear-view Eleanor had nothing to say on the subject of damp underpants.

Eleanor slumped in her seat, staring at the steering wheel. She was losing it, right? It was the only explanation for why she just had a five-minute conversation with herself.

The car door opened, and she sat up straight as Wes slid into the back seat. He nodded to her, buckled his seat belt, and stared out the passenger window.

Like he always did.

As if he hadn't had his tongue down her throat.

As if he hadn't said he'd give her his cock as soon as she showed him her pretty tits.

As if she hadn't felt his erection against her pussy.

Great, there went her underpants again.

She cleared her throat. "Hey, Wes."

"Hello, Eleanor." He glanced at her, and the hope in her chest died a sudden and violent death. Wes looked at her the way he always did. Polite disinterest and nothing more. As if that moment on Thursday night had never happened between them.

She waited for a beat, her hands clenched tight around the steering wheel, her heart fluttering around her chest like a trapped hummingbird, but Wes didn't say anything. Not even when the silence became awkward.

"Straight home?" she finally said.

"Yes, please."

She checked over her shoulder and pulled out into traffic. For a Monday, the rush hour traffic was weak, as if everyone had decided to take a vacation simultaneously. It only took her twenty minutes to drive to Wes's place, even with easing off on her habit of speeding.

She slowed to a stop and parked in front of Wes's house, trying not to be hurt over his silence and failing miserably. He really was going to act like what happened between them last week had never happened.

She bit down on her urge to say something, to force him to at least acknowledge the kiss they shared. But what good would that do? If he wanted to pretend it didn't happen, then it meant he had regret.

Or he hated the way you kissed.

She cringed inwardly. Oh, God. She hadn't even thought of that possibility.

Wes unbuckled his seat belt before reaching into the inside pocket of his leather jacket. The motion brought the scent of his aftershave to her. He smelled so good. He always smelled good, and he always looked good. He was over forty, but my God, the man kept himself in good shape. She supposed it was partially his lion shifter genes and partly his job. Working at a security firm, you needed to be in shape, right?

Wes was definitely not like some of the other forty-something men she drove to appointments. He wasn't going soft around the middle or thinning on top, and the little laugh lines around his eyes and mouth only enhanced his good looks. Wes's body was... in a word – delicious. He was tall and lean and muscular as hell. Her mouth dried out, just remembering the feel of his thick thigh between hers and the pressure of his hard chest against her tits. His coppery brown eyes had a weird way of making her feel just the slightest bit off-kilter, and his thick dark hair with the silver at the temples was cut short the way she liked.

Sure, but not short enough that you couldn't get a good grip on it when he has his face buried between your legs, am I right?

Her face flamed red as lust and embarrassment jostled for the number one spot in her body. Wes inhaled, and the slightest hint of red tinged his tanned cheeks.

Perfect. Just perfect. He could smell her lust.

"Take this, Eleanor," Wes said.

She stared at the black can he held out to her, the words "Mace Pepper Gel" written in white and red on the side of it.

"Mace," she said. "You got me Mace?"

He nodded, and she said, "Why?"

"Because that pocketknife you carry for protection wouldn't cut a loaf of bread," Wes said. "Take the pepper spray, Eleanor."

"If I use this in the car, it'll hurt me too," she said. "The knife is better."

"Do you even know how to use that knife?" Wes said. "Have you had any training?"

"Does a person need training?" Eleanor said. "I mean, I've seen *Psycho* a few times. It's your basic stabby-stab motion." She pretended to stab an invisible shower curtain as Wes's face turned into a dark cloud.

"The Mace is better protection," Wes said.

"Not if I'm inhaling it, too," Eleanor said. "I can't run away if I'm blinded by pepper spray."

"Better to be hit with a bit of pepper spray than raped or murdered." Wes's voice was tight, and she couldn't quite suss out the look on his face. It was a cross between irritation and worry.

The irritation she got – eventually, she irritated the shit

out of almost everyone she met – but the worry was a mystery. The kissing last week aside, Wes had spent over a year rejecting every attempt she made to be his friend. Why would he care so much about her safety?

There was only one way to find out.

"Why do you care so much about my safety?" she said.

Surprisingly, hurt joined the worry and irritation. "Do I have to have a reason?"

"No, but my safety isn't your concern. We're not even friends," she said.

His lips thinned out, and he dropped the can of Mace into the front passenger seat before shoving open his door, climbing out of the car, and slamming the door shut. She watched him stalk toward his front door, his movements as graceful as... well... a cat.

Great. Now she'd hurt his feelings. Her stomach churning, she stared at rear-view Eleanor. "I didn't mean to hurt his feelings. But we're not friends. Right?"

Rear-view Eleanor nodded. "You most definitely aren't friends."

That made her feel even worse. She glanced at her phone. She had precisely thirty-two minutes to get to the post office before it closed and then drive to the pub for dinner with Daisy.

"ELEANOR! ELEANOR, OVER HERE!" DAISY WAVED FROM A booth near the back of the pub.

Eleanor walked through the nearly empty pub and slid into the booth across from the tiny woman. "Hey, Daisy. How are you?"

"I'm good," Daisy said. "Better."

"You sure?" Eleanor eyed the faint bruising around Daisy's throat. "It's only been four days since a cheetah shifter nearly murdered you."

Daisy paled, her fingers tearing at the napkin in front of her.

"Shit. Daisy, I'm sorry. I'm… well, fuck, I'm an idiot," Eleanor said.

Daisy smiled at her. "You're not."

"I am. I shouldn't have brought it up. Or at least not so bluntly. My mother always said if tact were a sin, I'd be innocent."

Daisy's smile turned into a laugh, and she tossed the shredded napkin aside. "It's okay, honestly. I mean, it was one of the most terrifying moments of my life, but my mate rescued me, and both Anna and I are safe, and Xander is behind bars. He'll never hurt Anna or anyone else again."

"Are you still tutoring Anna?" Eleanor said.

"Yes. Cooper doesn't want me to, but the danger is over, right? Cooper thinks I'm doing it for the extra money, but now that I'm living with him, I don't need the extra money. I just really like Anna. She's a good kid."

"So, you're living with Cooper permanently now, huh?" Eleanor said. Cooper owned the security firm Wes worked for, but Eleanor knew he and Wes were friends. Good friends.

"Yes," Daisy said with a soft smile. "I am."

"Is it weird because he's your boss?" Eleanor asked. Daisy worked at the security firm as the receptionist.

"No," Daisy said.

Their server arrived, a tall thin man with brown hair tied back in a ponytail. He sniffed at Daisy, a weird look crossing his face before he took a step back and cleared his throat. "What can I get you ladies to drink?"

They gave him their drink order, and when he'd walked away, Eleanor said, "What's with the look and the sniffing?"

"He must be a shifter. Cooper marked me again before I left," Daisy said.

"Right, the marking thing. It makes you smell like Cooper," Eleanor said.

"That's right," Daisy said.

"You know, you've never actually told me how he marks you. Does he pee on you, Daisy?" Eleanor said.

Daisy laughed so hard that the woman sitting alone at the bar turned around and gave them a brief look before gazing into her drink again.

"He doesn't pee on me, Eleanor. Why would you think that?"

"Because my childhood best friend had a dog named Shaggy who marked everything by peeing on it. It's plausible that cat shifters mark the same way, right?"

"I guess, but no, that's not how they mark," Daisy said. "Cooper rubs his face over my neck and," her face flushed prettily, "other spots sometimes, and it transfers his scent to my skin."

"Kinky," Eleanor said, but even she could hear that it lacked her usual enthusiasm.

Daisy studied her as the server returned with their drinks. Eleanor hadn't opened her menu, but this was one of her favourite pubs, and she didn't need to look at the menu. She ordered her usual as Daisy quickly made her decision. The server left, and Daisy sipped at her beer. "Eleanor, I haven't had the chance to say thank you."

"For what?" Eleanor took a drink of beer.

"For what?" Daisy echoed. "If it hadn't been for you and Wes, I would have been hurt or dead, and Xander would've kidnapped poor Anna."

"I didn't do anything," Eleanor said. "I was only there because Wes doesn't drive and needed my car to do the stakeout."

"I know that's not true," Daisy said. "Grayson and Wes were over on Sunday, and Wes told Cooper exactly what happened. You spotted Xander, and you convinced Wes to break into Xander's apartment, and you saw the picture of Xander and Tabitha on the fridge."

"Wes told you I did that?" Eleanor said.

"Yes. Did you think he would take the credit?" Daisy asked.

Eleanor shrugged. "I don't know him that well."

Daisy leaned forward. "Will you tell me what happened with you and Wes that night?"

"Nothing happened." Eleanor set her bottle of beer down with a thump. Her nerves were suddenly wrapped up tighter than a ball of elastic bands. "Why do you think something happened? Did Wes say something, uh, happened?"

"No, but you seem sad tonight. And both you and Wes were acting weird at the house Thursday night after Cooper saved Anna and me from Xander."

"We weren't acting weird. You'd had a traumatic experience and weren't seeing things clearly," Eleanor said.

Daisy just stared at her. Eleanor's palms itched, and she scrubbed them against the thighs of her jeans. She was dying to tell Daisy what had happened. She had a hard time making and keeping friends, and as sad as this was, even knowing Daisy for less than a month – she was the closest friend Eleanor had.

Daisy reached out and took her hand. "You don't have to tell me. But I think we're starting to be friends, right? And you look like you could use a friend right now."

Eleanor took a deep breath. "Wes and I kissed Thursday

night in the hallway of Xander's apartment because Xander was coming out of his apartment and there was no place to hide, and I kind of panicked and grabbed Wes and started kissing him."

"Oh, okay," Daisy said.

"He kissed me back," Eleanor said. "Like, with tongue, and his hands were… and he said… stuff. Stuff that I didn't expect him to say."

She knew her face was bright red, and thank God, Daisy didn't ask her to elaborate. She just nodded and said, "That explains the weirdness."

"I was already attracted to him, okay? Like, super attracted to him, but I was one hundred percent positive that he wasn't into me. Partially because of the age difference, but also I never shut up, and I know it drives him crazy, and plus, he told me he's into tall blondes with blue eyes, which is the exact opposite of me. Only…"

"Only what?" Daisy said.

"He was very… enthusiastic about the kissing," Eleanor said.

Daisy laughed. "I think that probably indicates you're wrong about him not being into you. Have you talked to him since Thursday night? I know he didn't go into work on Friday, and he drove in with Grayson this morning."

"I picked him up after work. I thought he was avoiding me, especially when he didn't book me for this morning's drive into work, but at noon today, he sent me a text and booked me for the rest of the week, like he normally does."

"What did Wes say when you picked him up after work?" Daisy said.

"Nothing. He was the same as he always is. He acted like we hadn't made out in a hallway, like he hadn't had his tongue in my mouth, or felt up my ass, or told me he'd give me his cock when… oops. Sorry. That's way too much information," Eleanor said.

Daisy shrugged. "I don't mind. Maybe he was just embarrassed or didn't know what to say. I mean, Wes barely talks at the best of times, right?"

"Yeah, but it was more than that. When Wes looked at me tonight, it was like I was just Eleanor. The same ditzy girl who's driven him to and from work every day for over a year and nothing more. Like he didn't even remember kissing me. I spent the entire weekend obsessing over every moment between us on Thursday night, and it was more than clear that he didn't give it a second thought. It meant nothing to him."

"Well," Daisy said carefully, "that might be true. But it might not be either. Wes has a really good poker face."

Eleanor blew out her breath. "Maybe, but it doesn't matter anyway. I hurt his feelings."

"How?" Daisy said.

"He gave me a can of Mace for protection, and I argued with him. I said my safety wasn't his concern because we weren't even friends." She poked at the peeling label on her beer bottle. "I didn't mean it. I was just kind of pissed that he was acting so… normal. You know? But it was obvious that it hurt his feelings, and now I feel bad, and then I got that stupid parcel."

"What stupid parcel?" Daisy said.

"It's from my dad," Eleanor said. "I haven't talked to the guy in two years, and out of the blue, he mails me a box."

"What was in it?" Daisy said.

"I don't know. I got the notice that I had a parcel at the post office almost six days ago. I kept forgetting to pick it up. I finally remembered today, and now… now I wish I hadn't. I wish they'd sent it right back to him. Anyway, it's in the trunk of my car. I'm not in the right headspace to deal with whatever my emotionally distant father sent me. I'll look at it in a day or two."

"Are you close to your mom?" Daisy said.

"I was. She died two years ago."

"I'm so sorry," Daisy said. She reached for Eleanor's hand again, and Eleanor stared at the ring on Daisy's finger.

"Hold the phone… is that an engagement ring?"

The brightness of Daisy's smile could have powered the entire pub. "It is."

"You and Cooper are engaged?"

"We are. He asked me to marry him on Saturday."

"Holy shit," Eleanor said. "That's fast. You've known him, what? A few months?"

Daisy cleared her throat, and Eleanor said. "Shit. Sorry. There's that lack of tact again. What I meant to say is – congratulations."

Daisy laughed and admired the diamond in the dim light over their booth. "Thank you, Eleanor. I know it's quick, but Cooper is my mate. I love him and can't imagine being without him."

"And he can't be without you, or he'll go insane," Eleanor said.

Daisy nodded, and Eleanor said, "It's so weird that if a shifter thinks you're his mate, he'll go insane if you don't feel the same way."

"It is kind of weird, but luckily, I love Cooper," Daisy said.

Their food arrived, and Eleanor unfolded her napkin and placed it in her lap. "I'm happy for you, Daisy. Do you know when the wedding will be?"

"We haven't made any decisions yet," Daisy said. "Can I ask why you don't talk to your dad?"

Eleanor ate some of her rice. "He and my mom divorced

when I was eleven. I went to his apartment every other weekend for the next few years, but there was no real point to it. All my dad cares about, all he's ever cared about is his job and his work."

"What does he do for a living?" Daisy said.

"He's a biochemist," Eleanor said. "The guy is brilliant, a serious genius, but he has the emotional capacity of a fish. I don't know why my mom ever married him. He barely acknowledged her existence or mine even when we all lived in the same house."

"I'm sorry," Daisy said.

Eleanor shrugged. "I'm over it. I had a phase in my teenage years where I tried everything I knew to get him to pay attention to me. I even got myself arrested, but it was pointless. His first love is science, and it'll always be that way. When Mom was alive, she made me check in with him at least once a month. I'd send a text or email him, but after she died, we just stopped communicating. He came to Mom's funeral, we had an awkward dinner the next night, and I haven't talked to him since."

"That's terrible," Daisy said.

"Nope, that's just my dad. He doesn't care about me and never has," Eleanor said. "I've made my peace with it."

"Have you?"

"Yes. It took some therapy, but I can't make the guy love me, right? Just because we share DNA doesn't mean he's required to be a dad."

"So, then why are you upset about the parcel?"

Eleanor opened her mouth, stared at Daisy, and then closed her mouth. "I don't know. I just… it's been two years since I've talked to him, six months since I've even thought of him, and now out of the blue, he mails me a parcel. On top of everything that happened with Wes, it's ... maybe a little too much?"

"Understandable," Daisy said.

"I'm afraid that it'll be some of my mom's stuff that she left behind at the house," Eleanor said abruptly. "Dad was always a bit of a packrat and too focused on his work to care about cleaning, so it's not surprising that he's just finding some of her stuff now. And while I don't care that Dad doesn't give a shit about me, I miss my mom. I miss her a lot, even now, and the thought of getting a box of her stuff after I did the hard part of cleaning out her apartment two years ago... it breaks my heart. Dad won't know that, or even if he did, he wouldn't care."

"If you want me to be there when you open the parcel, I'm happy to do that," Daisy said.

Eleanor smiled at her. "Thanks, Daisy. I appreciate that, but I think I'll be okay. As I said, I'll give it a day or two and then open it."

"Okay, but if you change your mind, just let me know," Daisy said.

"I will." Eleanor smiled at her. I'm happy we're friends, Daisy."

"Me too, Eleanor."

CHAPTER 3

This was ridiculous. He was a damn lion shifter, and being nervous around a human was fucking embarrassing.

Wes paced back and forth in his front hall, peeking out the side window next to the door every couple of minutes like a teenage girl waiting for her prom date. His lion growled at him, and Wes muttered, "I *know* I'm acting like an idiot."

He leaned against the wall and made himself take a deep breath, hoping it would calm his jangled nerves somewhat. His lion was worked up, pacing restlessly inside him and every few minutes or so making a loud growl that set Wes's teeth on edge.

He didn't know what was worse, the usual silence from his lion or this weird growling thing he'd been doing since the moment – the very fucking moment – Eleanor had left their side last Thursday. Wes had fully planned on begging Grayson for a ride to and from work this week. Being close to Eleanor after what happened between them on Thursday was a terrible idea, but he had texted her and booked her driving services for the week by Monday at noon.

He had to. His lion barely spoke to him anymore, so when he'd demanded this morning that they see Eleanor this week, Wes couldn't deny him. His lion had always been on the quiet side, just like Wes, but in the last four years, he'd spoken less and less, until sometimes Wes went days without talking to him.

His stomach twisted, and he stared at the picture hanging on the wall in front of him. It was small, only a five by seven framed photo of Wes, Cooper, Grayson, Boone, and, his eyes lingered on the laughing man's face... Derek, but the photo could have been the size of the wall for the amount of hurt it brought on.

His stomach knotted tight, and his lion made a low and mournful cry before falling silent again. He closed his eyes, the sweat beading up on his forehead and the sick feeling intensifying until he was dangerously close to vomiting up the toast he'd forced down for breakfast.

It wasn't your fault, he told his lion. *Please believe me. It wasn't your fault. I'm the one to blame.*

His lion didn't reply. He never did when Wes tried to talk to him about the accident.

His lips curled up in a bitter smile. The accident. He could call it an accident. He could pretend that it was nothing more than being in the wrong place at the wrong time, but the truth of the matter was – he'd lost focus, and a man died because of it.

Take down the picture, then. For fuck's sake... stop torturing yourself.

He couldn't. Staring every day at the man whose death he caused was a small price to pay for his sins.

Like all lion shifters, his hearing was excellent, and he heard Eleanor's car as she neared his house. His lion sat up, not quite purring, but close to it. Wes could almost feel his lion's sorrow dissipating.

Don't get that excited. She doesn't even think we're friends.

His lion snarled at him, and Wes winced. It was true that Eleanor didn't consider him a friend, but he didn't need to remind his lion of that.

Or maybe her feelings are hurt because you acted like you never kissed her, you asshole.

Wes wanted to ignore his inner voice, but it made an excellent point. But pretending he'd never kissed Eleanor, pretending he didn't know how she sounded when she moaned or how fucking good she smelled when she was aroused, was necessary. If he didn't, he'd be trying to coax her into his bed so he could finish what they'd started in that damn hallway.

This time his lion did purr. He thought mating with the human was a fine idea. He didn't care that they were old enough to be Eleanor's father or that a woman in the prime of her life wouldn't want someone as broken and fucked up as they were.

There's nothing wrong with us, his lion growled.

He'd be thrilled his lion was talking to him if the beast wasn't so clearly angry with him.

He stepped outside, locking the door behind him and walking down the sidewalk toward Eleanor's car idling in front of his house. He slid into his usual spot in the backseat and buckled his seat belt.

Eleanor pulled out onto the street without her regular greeting. After a moment, his lion growling unhappily, Wes said, "Good morning, Eleanor."

"Hello, Wes." Her voice was almost painfully formal. He could smell her discomfort and under that a lingering scent of sadness. Was that because of him? It had to be. Why else would she be a ghost of her usual happy, chatty self?

Comfort her, his lion demanded.

I can't. She doesn't want our comfort.

You lie! His lion roared so loudly, he winced.

"Wes?" Eleanor stopped at a red light and stared at him in the rear-view mirror. "Are you okay?"

"Yes, why?"

"Your eyes were yellow, and your pupils were slits."

"I was talking to my lion," Wes said.

"I know what it means," she said. "But I've never seen you talk to your lion before."

"He doesn't talk much," Wes said.

"Shocking."

His hope that Eleanor had returned to her usual self died when she lapsed back into silence and stepped on the gas.

Fuck it. He had to say something. He couldn't be with Eleanor in the way she and his lion wanted, but he couldn't stand the idea that she didn't think they were friends.

"Eleanor, I -"

Her phone rang. She had it clipped to the dashboard, and Wes could see the "unknown caller" on the screen. She glanced at him again. "What were you going to say?"

"Nothing that can't wait. Answer your call," he said.

"I don't take calls when I have clients in the car," she said.

He winced inwardly at the client comment but kept his face stoic. "I don't mind."

She shrugged and hit a button on her steering wheel. "Hello?"

"Yes, I'm looking for Eleanor Whitman."

Wes stiffened. He knew a cop's voice when he heard one.

"This is Eleanor Whitman." Eleanor turned left. A strip

mall was coming up on their right, and Wes unbuckled his seat belt and leaned forward.

"Ms. Whitman, my name is Detective Howards. I'm with the 57th precinct in Emerton."

Wes tapped Eleanor on the shoulder and pointed to the strip mall. Pitching his voice low, he said, "Pull over, Eleanor."

Frowning, Eleanor did as he asked as the detective said, "Is your father Solomon Whitman?"

Eleanor parked in front of a falafel place. "Yes. Why?"

"I'm afraid I have some bad news regarding your father. He was in a serious car accident eight days ago."

Eleanor's hands gripped the steering wheel. "Eight days ago? What hospital is he in?"

"I'm sorry, Ms. Whitman, but your father didn't survive the accident."

"He didn't... what? What did you say?" Eleanor stared blankly at Wes, her look of confusion heartbreaking.

Before he could say anything, Eleanor grabbed her phone off the dashboard, unbuckled her seat belt, and slid out of the car. Wes followed her, leaning against the hood of the vehicle as Eleanor paced back and forth in the empty parking spot beside them, her phone smashed up against her ear in a death grip.

Her face grew steadily paler as she listened to the detective. After almost ten minutes, she said, "No, I understand. Yes, I... no, I... okay. Thank you, detective. Right. Okay. Thanks."

She ended the call and stared at the phone in her hand as if she'd never seen one before.

"Eleanor?" Wes said. "Are you okay?"

He could have kicked himself. Obviously, she wasn't okay.

She raised her gaze to him. "My father is dead." Shock covered her features in a thick haze, and she stared wide-eyed at him. "He died eight days ago."

Comfort her, his lion demanded.

He walked toward her and opened his arms. "Come here, Eleanor."

She stepped into his embrace. He wrapped his arms around her and kissed the top of her head when she rested her cheek against his chest. "I'm so sorry, Butterfly."

Her arms crept around his waist and locked behind his back. He stroked the length of her back as she took a shuddering breath. "It took them a while to find me because he… because he didn't have me listed anywhere as his dependent. Not at work, not in his will, not anywhere. It was like I didn't exist to him."

To his surprise, she laughed bitterly. "Fuck, I don't know why I'm so shocked by that."

"How did they find you?" he said.

"They only knew I existed because they tracked down a third cousin of my father's, a woman named Patricia – I don't even know who she is - and she told them he had a daughter.

She leaned back and stared up at him. "We weren't close. I hadn't talked to him in two years, and now he's dead. He had a heart attack while driving, and he drove off the road and straight into a tree. He died immediately."

He stroked his thumb across her cheekbone. "I'm so sorry, Eleanor."

Her dark eyes were still full of confusion. "I didn't… I haven't spoken to him in two years, and now I'll – I'll never talk to him again. My mom is dead, and now my dad is dead, and I'm… I'm alone."

Tears slid down her face, and he pulled her close, rubbing

her back and kissing the top of her head again. "You're not alone. I'm right here with you, Butterfly."

She drew in a hitching breath. Already her tears had slowed, and she wiped at her damp cheeks self-consciously. "I'm sorry for what I said yesterday. I didn't mean it. I... we're friends, right?"

"Yes," he said. "We are."

"But only friends, huh?" she said with another hitch in her breath.

He wanted to be more. Fuck, did he want to be more. But he couldn't do that to Eleanor. He couldn't drag her down with him. "Yes, only friends."

She didn't reply, but her sorrow intensified, and the look on her face cut him as sharply as a blade. He glanced around them. "There's a coffee shop at the far end of the strip mall. Why don't I buy you a coffee, and we can talk about your dad?"

"You have to work," she said.

"I can be a little late."

She hesitated. "I can't. I have another client to pick up at nine-thirty."

"Can you reschedule?" He was almost desperate to spend a little more time with her. To stay with her until the confusion and the sorrow he could smell on her was gone.

"No. I'm driving her to the airport. She can't miss her flight."

"Maybe we can find someone else to drive her to the airport," Wes said.

"No, I need to do my job. I don't drive, and I don't get paid, you know?"

"I know," he said.

She sucked in a shuddering breath before backing away from him. His lion whined like an angry kitten, but what was

Wes supposed to do? He couldn't force Eleanor to stay in his arms. She sniffed and then wiped the last trace of tears from her cheeks. "Sorry, I, uh, I got your shirt damp."

"It's fine," he said. "Eleanor, maybe you should consider taking the day off after your nine-thirty client. I can rearrange my schedule today. We can go for coffee or have lunch and -"

"Thank you, but no. I'm fine now," Eleanor said.

"You're not fine. You're in shock."

She shrugged before ducking around him and opening the driver's door. "Get in, Wes. I might still get you to work on time if the traffic gods are feeling generous this morning."

His lion grumbled and whined again. Wes couldn't blame him. He hated the way Eleanor was distancing herself from him, but it was for the best. He couldn't be the man she wanted him to be.

"Fuck me sideways!"

Wes stood and peered over the cubicle wall at Boone. The tiger shifter looked like he was about to lose his shit as he dropped his phone onto his desk and rubbed at the back of his neck.

"What's wrong?" Wes said.

"You about to Hulk out on us?" Chase, the newest member of their security team and the youngest at only twenty-six, peered over the other cubicle wall. He wore a "Shadow Security" golf shirt, and his light brown hair stuck up at odd angles like he'd been running his hand through it while he worked.

"Spare me the comic book shit, kid," Boone said. "I've got a fucking crisis on my hands." He sniffed in Chase's direction. "You smell funny."

"No, I don't smell at all," Chase said.

Wes inhaled in his direction. It was true. Not only did Chase not have his usual scent, he had no scent, period.

"Why are you using the Scent B Gone spray?" Wes asked.

"Stupidest fucking name ever," Boone muttered.

Wes grinned slightly. Boone wasn't wrong. The spray worked well to neutralize a shifter's scent but covering yourself with a spray called *Scent B Gone* felt a little juvenile.

"The Scent B Gone company sent us samples. It's their new and improved version. You read what happened with their last version, yeah?"

Wes nodded. He'd seen it a few weeks ago, just happened to catch the tail end of the story on the news. "Yeah, the scent blockers in the formula wore off if you even sweated a little."

"That's right. They shouldn't have messed with the original formula," Chase said. "Anyway, Coop asked me to test it out, make sure the new formula works this time before we order a case. I'm going for a run in about half an hour. You wanna join me, Boone?"

"Does it look like I'm in the mood to watch you kick my ass in a run?" Boone said. He grimaced and swiped a hand across his face. "Fuck. Sorry, Chase."

"What's wrong?' Wes repeated.

"Maria just quit," Boone said. His pupils turned to slits as he went inward and talked to his tiger.

"Shit," Chase said, "that's the second nurse in two days, right?"

"Third," Wes said as Boone's pupils rounded out. "The first one only lasted six hours."

Boone's grandmother had broken her hip last week. Although the tiger shifter was in her late eighties, she was probably the toughest shifter Wes had ever met. And while she loved Boone a great deal, she didn't have the sweetest personality.

Boone stared at Wes. "What the fuck am I gonna do? She hasn't even left the hospital yet, and that's the third private nurse I've hired who's quit, and they aren't even fully responsible for her. She comes home from the hospital on Thursday, and I can't stay at home with her while she heals. It'll be at least a month, probably longer. She's not healing as quickly as they'd like. I thought Maria could handle her. She's a cougar shifter, and she did four tours when she was on active duty, but she just called me in hysterics. Nan wanted Maria to take her outside in her wheelchair, but the doctor said bed rest until tomorrow, so Maria refused. Nan got mad and told Maria to sleep with one eye open from now on because Nan would rip out her throat while she slept and let Alfie bathe in her blood."

"Question," Chase said. "Who's Alfie?"

"Nan's poodle," Boone said.

Chase snorted laughter, and Boone glared at him. "Swear to fucking God, Chase. I'll superglue your laptop to your desk."

"Can you talk to Nan's doctor?" Wes asked. "Maybe she knows a private nurse who -"

Boone shook his head. "I already asked her before I found Maria. She said she refused to torture a fellow medical professional then hung up on me."

Wes would have grinned if it weren't for the clear waves of misery coming off of Boone.

"Maria was my last hope. I'm so fucking fucked," Boone groaned.

"I might know someone," Chase said hesitantly.

Boone stared up at him. "Seriously? Why didn't you say something when I was scrambling to hire Maria?"

"Um, because I've met your grandma?" Chase said. "She came by with cookies last month, remember? I introduced myself, and she told me I smelled like cheese and looked like someone who had back acne. When I told her I didn't have back acne, she said that's exactly what someone with back acne would say. And she wouldn't let me have a cookie because she said I hadn't proved my worth to the office yet."

Despite the worry for Eleanor that had sat in his gut all day, Wes laughed. Chase turned to him. "She had my cheetah whimpering like a damn cub. She terrified him."

"She terrifies everyone," Wes said. "But she has a good heart."

"Who's the person you know?" Boone said.

"My cousin. She just moved here from Rosehaven a couple of weeks ago. She worked as a nurse at Saint Mary Hospital, but she didn't want to work in a hospital again. She's applied at doctor's offices, but no luck yet. I could give her your number, see if she wants to meet with you about taking care of your grandmother."

"You must really hate your cousin." Grayson, a tiger shifter and Cooper's best friend, joined them.

Boone growled at him, and Grayson shrugged. "Hey, you know I love your grandma, but she also scares the shit out of me. Besides, I thought you found a nurse for her."

"She quit," Wes said.

"Already?" Grayson leaned a hip against Boone's desk. "Didn't you just hire her?"

"Yes," Boone said with another defeated look at Chase. "Give your cousin my number."

"Seriously though, do you hate your cousin?" Grayson asked Chase.

Chase laughed. "No. But she's getting kind of desperate

for work, and she's living in a motel right now, so she would be cool with doing the live-in thing for Boone's grandma."

"What kind of shifter is she?" Boone said.

"Oh, she's not. She's human. My uncle married a human."

A surprised growl escaped Boone's mouth, and the burgeoning hope on his face died a swift and tragic death. "Shit."

"What?" Chase said.

"I can't hire a human to look after my grandmother," Boone said. "Nan will eat her for breakfast."

"Literally," Grayson said with a grin.

Boone growled at him before staring at Wes again. "What the fuck am I gonna do, Wes?"

"Hey, my cousin is tough," Chase said. "My uncle and aunt have five kids, and Hedra is the only human. She grew up with four older cheetah siblings, and she doesn't scare easily. I'll give her your number, okay? You can at least meet with her."

Boone continued to stare at Wes, who said, "I don't think you have much of a choice at this point, Boone."

"Fuck me," Boone said before dropping his head into his hands. "Give her my number, Chase."

"Will do." Chase sat down at his desk.

"Wes? Do you have time to chat about the Wilton's security detail for next week?" Grayson said.

"Yes." Leaving Boone sitting at his desk with his head in his hands, Wes followed Grayson toward the boardroom.

CHAPTER 4

Eleanor stared blankly at her phone screen. She'd been scrolling through Facebook for the last five minutes while she waited for Wes to finish work for the day, but she couldn't remember anything she'd just looked at.

Hell, she could barely remember her day. It had passed by in a haze of disbelief and numbness and a curious lack of grief. Her father was dead. Shouldn't she be feeling something? As selfish as this sounded, her tears this morning had been more for herself, for the weird and immediate feeling of terror at being utterly alone in this world. No parents, no siblings, no aunts or uncles or cousins. No... friends.

She swallowed hard. She'd gone her entire life yearning for that connection that most people felt with another person – whether it was a lover or a partner or a friend – and she'd never found it. It was her fault. She talked too much. She was too blunt. Too weird. Too... Eleanor.

She'd tried over and over to change herself, but it proved impossible. She was only twenty-seven, but her hope that she would eventually find her person – the one who loved her for who she was even with all her faults and flaws, grew dimmer with each passing year.

She leaned her head against the headrest and closed her eyes. Immediately, she was back in Wes's embrace, his hands stroking her back, his low voice calling her butterfly, and his scent washing over her. Wes's smell was as comforting as freshly baked cookies.

A strained giggle escaped her mouth. What would Wes say if she told him that he smelled like cookies to her? He'd probably look at her like she was insane.

He doesn't smell like cookies to you, idiot. He gives you the same happy feeling as cookies.

She lifted her arm to her nose and took a long sniff. Did she smell like Wes to other shifters now? Daisy said Cooper rubbed his face against her to mark her. Wes had kissed the top of her head… was that almost like marking?

The idea of being marked by Wes was also comforting. Not that she was terrified of shifters like Daisy was, but she wouldn't mind if other shifters knew she belonged to Wes.

Uh, Eleanor? He made it clear that he just wanted to be friends this morning.

Right. Friends only. She didn't belong to Wes Masters, and she never would.

That thought filled her with more grief than the news of her father's death, and just what the fuck did that say about her?

She jerked in surprise when the car door behind her opened, and a blond man wearing a long dark coat and aviator shades sat behind her. He slammed the door shut, and Eleanor stared at him in the rear-view mirror. "Are you drunk? I'm not a cab, buddy. Get out."

She froze, her heart first stopping and then kickstarting back into life like an overtaxed engine when the man pressed a gun to the back of her head. "Give me what your father sent you."

"What?" Eleanor said. The gun barrel dug into her skull, and a soft whimper escaped her throat.

"Give it to me, you stupid bitch," he said.

"My father is dead," Eleanor said.

"I know. But I also know he sent you a package. I want it."

"Why? It doesn't belong to you. He sent it to me, not you."

His upper lip curled, and he smacked her upside the head with his free hand. "What the fuck? Just tell me what you did with the fucking package. It's not in your house."

"How do you know that?" she said.

"How the fuck do you think? A woman living alone should get better fucking locks on her doors. Is it still in the car? I couldn't tell last night if you brought it inside," he said.

"Have you been watching me?" she asked.

He cuffed her across the head again. "Just give me the package, for Christ's sake."

"Then what?" she said.

"Then I'll leave you alone," the man said.

She couldn't see his eyes behind the mirrored sunglasses, but she knew he was lying. The minute she handed over the box from her father, this man would put a bullet between her eyes. Of course, if she didn't hand it over, he really would kill her.

"It's in the trunk," she said. "You can take it. I won't say anything."

The man shook his head. "Start driving, Eleanor."

"To where?"

"Somewhere quiet and less crowded. Outside of the city," he said.

Her stomach crash landed somewhere around the brake pedal. The tiniest bit of hope that he might let her live faded.

"Why?" she said. "You can just take the package and leave. I swear I won't say anything to anyone. I don't even know what's in it."

"Drive, Eleanor," he said and prodded her head with the gun. The cold detachment in his voice sent fresh terror rampaging through her system.

Trying not to panic, she said, "I... I'm waiting for my client."

"That's too fucking bad. He can find a new ride. Start driving before I -"

The bruising pressure against the back of her head disappeared, and the man cursed under his breath. Wes leaned down and stared at her through the open window of the front passenger seat.

Terror and joy shot through Eleanor. As much as she wanted to believe Wes would save her, a bullet would kill him as easily as it would kill her.

Shit. Wes was going to die because he didn't fucking drive.

WES'S LION WAS GIDDY THE ENTIRE ELEVATOR RIDE TO THE main floor. His lion's excitement boosted Wes's mood too. He couldn't remember the last time his lion had been this happy. If he'd known that deciding to invite Eleanor out for dinner would cheer his lion up this much, Wes would have done it months ago.

This isn't a date, asshole. You're taking Eleanor for dinner so she can talk about her dead father. This is about her grieving and you being a supportive friend.

Both he and his lion ignored his inner voice. He would take Eleanor to his favourite restaurant. He paused and slapped his hand down against his ass, muttering a curse when he didn't feel his wallet in the pocket. Shit, he'd taken it out at lunch and shoved it into his desk drawer.

He took out his phone, stopping in the foyer of the office building and ignoring the humans and shifters who exited the bank of elevators and headed for the front door. He started to text Eleanor before glancing out the expansive windows that flanked the front door of the building. He could see Eleanor's car, and he decided he'd tell her in person that he had to run back upstairs.

It was faster than texting, right? He wasn't doing it because he and his lion were dying for even just a quick glimpse of Eleanor.

He pushed open the front door and walked down the sidewalk to Eleanor's car. The passenger window was open, and he leaned down and stared at Eleanor. "Hey, Eleanor, I have to -"

He stopped talking. The thick and tangy scent of Eleanor's terror filled the interior of the car. She gripped the steering wheel so tightly he could see the veins standing out in the back of her hands.

He stared at the human sitting in the backseat behind Eleanor, then opened the passenger door and slid into the front seat. He slammed the door shut as the man said, "Get the fuck out."

"Excuse me?" Wes craned his head to stare at the man. His lion growled and snarled. Eleanor's fear had worked him into a frenzy.

"I said get the fuck out."

"I paid for this ride, and I paid extra not to rideshare. So, if anyone is 'getting the fuck out', it's you," Wes said.

Beside him, Eleanor was practically hyperventilating. He knew why she was so terrified. The man's left hand rested on his leg with the fingers tapping out a nervous rhythm, but his other hand remained tucked inside his jacket. No doubt holding the gun that Wes could smell.

"She double booked us by mistake," the man said. "But I booked first. Isn't that right, Eleanor."

"Yes," Eleanor said. Her voice was soft and faint and so un-Eleanor-like that his lion whimpered in alarm. "Sorry, Wes. I double booked. You should get out of the car."

He didn't move, and she stared pleadingly at him. "Leave, Wes. Find another ride, okay?"

"No," he said.

The scent of her fear deepened. Wes hated that he made it worse for her, but there was no fucking way he'd leave Eleanor.

"Are you kidding me? She said to get out," the blond man said. The scent of his anger overtook the smell of Eleanor's fear.

Before Wes could say anything, Eleanor said, "It's fine. It's all good. Wes's house is, uh, on the way to your destination, so I'll just drop him off first. Easy squeezy, lemon peasy." Her voice nearly broke on the last syllable, but she tossed a large and false smile at the man. "It won't take any extra time, I promise."

The man glanced at his hidden right hand before studying the crowds of people walking past them on the sidewalk. The building that housed the Shadow Security office was downtown. While Wes and his lion usually hated the large number of people that crowded the downtown core, right now, he could have fucking kissed every single one of them.

"Fine," the man said. "Just drive."

Eleanor pulled out into traffic. Her usual smooth and

effortless driving had morphed into a jittery, tension-filled ball of anxiety. Twice she nearly slammed into the back of the car in front of them, and she came dangerously close to side-swiping a parked car as she took the turn leading out of downtown.

Wes hadn't buckled his seatbelt like he usually did, and he seriously reconsidered his decision when Eleanor sped down the freeway like a driver in a bank heist B movie.

"Slow down, Eleanor," he said in a low voice. The last thing they needed was to be pulled over by the cops. The human in the backseat would likely kill all of them if that happened.

Still white-knuckling the steering wheel, Eleanor eased back on the gas. They rode the twenty minutes to his house in silence. Eleanor's fear increased with each passing mile, and his lion's anger soared right along with it. By the time she parked in front of his house, he could barely hear anything over his lion's growling.

He reached for the door handle, and his lion roared so loudly, Wes thought his eardrums might shatter from the pressure.

We are not leaving her!

No, we're saving her. Trust me.

His lion stopped pushing for control, and Wes said, "I'll see you tomorrow morning, Eleanor."

"Yes." Her bottom lip trembled, but she smiled gamely at him. He could smell her shock and confusion that he was leaving her, but under that was an undercurrent of relief. Later, when he wasn't focused on saving Eleanor's life, he'd make it clear to her that she never needed to worry about him.

Every part of him screamed to stay in the car. His body stiff with tension, he got out of the vehicle and slammed the door shut.

SHE WAS SHOCKED WHEN WES LEFT HER. SHOCKED BECAUSE she knew he smelled her fear, and he didn't seem like the kind of guy to abandon a terrified woman.

But under that shock, there was relief. Deep, intense relief that left her weak and shaky. The idea of Wes dying because of her – the idea of Wes dying at all – was almost as terrifying as knowing she was about to die.

"Let's go, Eleanor," the man said.

"Listen," she said as Wes passed by her peripheral vision. "You don't have to -"

She screamed when the back window shattered. Wes, his body swelling, his eyes glowing bright yellow, and vicious snarls falling from his mouth, reached inside and grabbed the man by the upper arms.

Covered in broken glass, the man squealed with ear-piercing panic. Wes roared, his mouth opening impossibly wide to reveal thick, sharp fangs. Eleanor clapped her hands over her ears, watching in wide-eyed disbelief in the rear-view mirror as Wes dragged the man out through the broken window.

She sat in stunned bewilderment for nearly fifteen seconds before ripping open the glovebox and fumbling out the can of Mace. She opened the door and fell out of the car, landing on her knees with a hard thud.

She scrambled to her feet, holding the Mace as she stared at Wes and the man. Wes hadn't entirely shifted, but his body still swelled, and golden hair covered most of his face and exposed skin. He shook the man like a ragdoll. The man screamed again, and Eleanor panicked when he pulled the gun out from under his jacket.

"Wes! Gun!" she shouted and charged forward, fumbling

to get the lid off the Mace as Wes made another angry roar. The gunshot was shockingly loud on Wes's quiet neighbourhood street.

She felt an immediate burn in her arm, so intense and painful that the Mace tumbled from her suddenly nerveless fingers. She stared at the blood sliding down her arm from beneath her t-shirt sleeve.

"Wes?" she said. "Wes, I'm bleeding."

The man screamed again. Eleanor watched as Wes tore the gun from his hand and threw it into the street. He let out a third roar, he was more lion than human now, and the man shrieked in terror as all along the street, front doors opened, and neighbours ran out of their houses.

"Wes," Eleanor said. "I think I've been shot."

She barely spoke above a whisper, but Wes's head twisted to look at her, his dark yellow eyes glowing with harsh light, his skin completely hidden under a thick layer of golden fur.

"Eleanor." The voice was Wes's voice, but not Wes's voice. Thicker, deeper. More animal than human.

He tossed the man aside like a broken toy and strode toward her. He pulled her into his embrace, his body returning to normal and the fur fading from his face. "You're all right. I have you. You're safe, Butterfly."

———

"Sir, if you cannot control yourself, you'll need to leave hospital grounds."

Wes growled at the nurse standing in front of him in the emergency room waiting area. She growled back, her eyes turning to jade as the humans in the waiting room gave each other nervous looks.

43

"You don't frighten me, lion shifter," the nurse said. "So, knock it off with the growling."

He growled again, his ability to control his lion entirely out the window. "If you'd let me see Eleanor, I wouldn't be -"

"I've told you three times, sir, you can see your friend when the doctor is finished with her."

"Is she a damn prisoner back there?" Wes snapped. "She's not allowed even one visitor?"

His body swelled even more, and the nurse looked to the security guard standing near the entrance. The guard ambled over, and although he was a cougar shifter, he was at least seventy, and Wes could smell his cougar's apathy toward the situation.

"I want to see Eleanor, and I want to see her now," he snarled. "If you think you're going to stop me from -"

"Wes, chill out, man." A hand clamped around his arm, and Boone's scent filled his nostrils.

He growled at Boone. The tiger shifter squeezed his arm hard and gave him a pointed look before smiling at the nurse. "Sorry. My friend will behave himself from now on."

"See that he does," the nurse said with a sniff of disdain.

"He will, I promise, gorgeous." Boone laid on the charm like thick honey. The Boone charm was notoriously effective. Usually, it had women – human and shifter alike – ready to drop everything for him. The nurse only looked him up and down this time, rolled her eyes, and walked away. The security guard returned to his entrance post as Boone guided Wes to a quiet corner of the waiting area.

"Calm down, Wes."

Wes bared his fangs at him, and Boone said, "I know you're worried about your driver friend, but if you shift, they'll kick you out, and you won't get to see her at all. So, take a fucking breath, buddy."

Wes snarled but then closed his eyes and took four deep breaths. His lion growled, and Wes soothed him quickly.

She's okay. I promise she's okay. We'll see her soon.

His lion quieted, and Wes stared at Boone. The younger man clapped him on the back. "There you are. Better?"

"Yeah, thanks."

"Don't mention it."

"What are you doing here?"

"Nan's at this hospital. She's up on the fourth floor. Cooper called me and asked me to come down to emergency."

"Why? Cooper said he was on his way."

"He is, but apparently, there was something in your voice that made him think you were on the verge of freaking the fuck out," Boone said.

Wes flushed as the entrance doors opened and Cooper, his mate Daisy clinging to his hand, strode into the emergency room. He headed toward them, clapping Wes on the back and nodding to Boone. "How is she?"

"I have no fucking idea," Wes said. "She's been shot in the arm. That's all I fucking know. The ambulance took her away, but I had to stay behind to talk to the police and give them a description of the guy. I took a cab to the hospital as soon as I could leave, but they won't let me see her."

His voice turned plaintive. "They won't let me see her because I'm not family or her mate. I should have lied and said I was her mate. Why didn't I say I was her mate?"

"It's okay, Wes," Cooper said. "I'm sure she's all right."

"There was a lot of blood," Wes said, his voice cracking a little.

"Is she in surgery?" Daisy said.

"No, I don't think so." Wes slammed his fist against his thigh. "I don't know for sure. They won't tell me a fucking

45

thing. She's all alone, and she's in pain, and she… she's alone."

"Okay, let me try," Daisy said. "Maybe they'll give me some information."

She headed toward the nurses' station as Cooper said, "Tell us what happened."

Wes ran through the events quickly, his voice doing that weird cracking thing again when he got to the part where he turned and saw the blood flowing down Eleanor's arm.

"Holy shit," Boone said.

"What?" Cooper asked.

Boone pointed to where Daisy was being allowed past the security door leading into the emergency room. The door closed behind her, and Cooper grinned. "That's my girl."

He turned to Wes. "Daisy's with Eleanor now. She's not alone, okay? Tell your lion to chill."

Wes nodded. He still wished it was him with Eleanor, but at least his lion might settle the fuck down now.

"Did you get a good look at the guy?" Cooper said.

"Not great. He wore sunglasses, and my lion was pretty fucking angry. I could probably pick him out of a line up though." Wes hit his thigh again. "I can't believe I let him get away. Fuck, I'm an idiot. But my lion saw the blood on Eleanor, and he… he didn't care about the guy anymore, and he was in control enough that I couldn't stop him from going to Eleanor."

"It's all right," Boone said. "You saved Eleanor's life. You did good, buddy."

"No, I fucked up," Wes said. "I fucked up, and now Eleanor is still in danger."

His lion was riled up again and pushing for control. Cooper squeezed his shoulder. "Hey, it's okay. Just relax. We'll keep Eleanor safe. It's what we do, right?"

"Yeah," Wes said. "She won't be able to afford it, but I'll cover the cost for security."

Cooper shrugged. "We'll worry about that later. Any idea why this guy went after Eleanor?"

"No," Wes said.

"Maybe a carjacking gone bad?" Boone said.

"Maybe," Wes said.

"But it doesn't feel that way to you," Cooper said.

"No, it doesn't. I know that's stupid, but…"

"It isn't. What are you always telling us? Trust our instincts," Boone said.

"Yeah, you're right. I just think that -"

His lion roared with happiness when he caught Eleanor's scent. Wes looked past Cooper's wide body, relief coursing through him when Eleanor and Daisy walked out of the emergency room.

He ran across the waiting area, stopping in front of Eleanor and scanning her face anxiously. "How do you feel?"

"Okay," she said as she touched the bandage that covered her upper arm. "It's just a scratch."

Daisy frowned. "It's more than just a scratch, Eleanor."

Cooper and Boone joined them. Cooper took Daisy's hand. "How did you get past the nurse, my mate?"

Daisy lowered her voice. "I told her I was Eleanor's sister."

Cooper grinned and pressed a kiss against her mouth. "Very clever, little mate."

"Hey, I'm Boone," Boone said to Eleanor. "I work with Wes and Cooper."

"Hi, Boone," Eleanor said. She smiled at him, but Wes could smell her weariness.

"Cooper, I told Eleanor we'd give her a ride to the pharmacy to pick up her antibiotics and pain meds and then a ride home," Daisy said.

"Of course," Cooper said. He gave Eleanor a small smile. "How many stitches did you need?"

"Only ten. I got lucky. The bullet only grazed my arm," Eleanor said, but she didn't look like she felt lucky.

Wes could barely stop himself from putting his arms around Eleanor. Ignoring his lion's demands to do just that, he shoved his hands into his pockets and said, "Why was the guy in your car, Eleanor?"

She swallowed hard. "He was looking for the package my dad sent to me."

"Your dad sent you a package?" Wes said.

"Yeah. I picked it up last night from the post office. It's still in the trunk of my car. I was going to open it tonight, but then... you know."

Wes nodded. "Okay. We should get Eleanor home."

"I'm gonna head back upstairs. Call me if you need me." Boone clapped Wes on the back and headed toward the elevator.

His lion growled at him to take Eleanor's hand. Wes kept his hands shoved firmly in his pockets and headed toward the exit with the others.

CHAPTER 5

"Thank you for the ride home," Eleanor said. She unbuckled her seatbelt, staring at Cooper and Wes in confusion when they unbuckled their seat belts as well. "Um, what's happening?"

"Give me your house keys, Eleanor," Wes said.

"What? Why?"

"Cooper and I will check your house while you stay in the car with Daisy," Wes said.

"I'm sure it's fine," she said. "The guy probably doesn't know where I live."

That was one enormous lie, and she hoped like fuck they couldn't see it on her face. The guy knew where she lived, had been in her damn house. As soon as Wes and the others left, Eleanor was grabbing the baseball bat from her closet and shoving chairs under the doorknobs of both doors.

Eleanor, that's not good enough. Wes works for a security company. He can help you. Protect you.

Yeah, well, as appealing as the idea was to hire Wes as her private bodyguard, she didn't have that kind of money. She barely had money to stay in a cheap motel, not unless she wanted to go without groceries for a few days. A baseball bat would have to do.

"Eleanor?" Cooper stared at her in the rear-view mirror.

"Uh, sorry. What?"

"I said how do you know?" Cooper said.

"Well, I… I mean, I guess I don't," Eleanor said.

"Exactly. So, stay in the car while we take a quick look around." Wes held out his hand for her keys.

"I think this is a little overkill, but okay." Eleanor dug around in her bag to find her keys. A paramedic had returned the Mace to her bag before leaving for the hospital, and she dropped it on the seat next to her. "I tried to use this, but I couldn't get the lid off of it."

Eleanor! Could you try any harder to let Wes know how stupid you are?

"It's okay," Wes said.

She handed over her keys. "It's the silver one."

"Sit tight. We won't be long," Wes said.

Cooper leaned over and pressed a kiss against Daisy's mouth. "Stay in the truck with the doors locked, my mate. No matter what you hear."

She flushed a little. "Don't get shot, and I will."

Cooper laughed and opened the driver's door. "I'll be right back."

Wes and Cooper headed toward the front door of Eleanor's small bungalow. She peered out the window, her anxiety level cranking up to def con red when Wes opened the front door and disappeared inside.

"He'll be okay," Daisy said. She'd twisted in the front seat so she could look at Eleanor. "Our guys are tough."

"Wes isn't my guy." Eleanor scratched at the tape holding the bandage to her arm.

"He's acting like he is," Daisy said. "He was freaking out at the hospital."

She shrugged. "Because he's a nice guy, that's all."

"It seemed more than that to me."

"Well, it isn't," Eleanor snapped. "He told me just this morning that we were only friends, so can you lay off the 'he's your guy' thing?"

She immediately felt guilty for snapping. "Shit. I'm sorry, Daisy. I didn't mean to be a bitch."

"You're not," Daisy said. "I should have minded my own business."

"You didn't do anything wrong." Eleanor glanced at Daisy before returning her gaze to the front of her house. "I really like Wes, and after the kiss we shared, I thought maybe... anyway, it doesn't matter. He just wants to be friends."

"I'm sorry, honey," Daisy said.

Eleanor shrugged. "What are you gonna do, right? Fuck, what a shitty day. I found out my dad is dead, the guy I'm kind of obsessed with gave me the 'I only like you as a friend' talk, and I got shot. I need ice cream. I *deserve* ice cream, right?"

"Wait... your dad is dead?" Daisy stared wide-eyed at her.

The door to her house opened, and Cooper stepped outside, followed by Wes. Eleanor's relief was short-lived when they returned to the truck, and she got a good glimpse of Wes's face.

"Your place was broken into and ransacked," Wes said. "Obviously, the guy came here looking for the package from your dad."

"Maybe, or maybe there's more than one guy," Cooper said.

Eleanor rubbed the spot just above her right eyebrow. The headache starting there would only worsen if she didn't get some Advil into her body. Oh, and the entire tub of Rocky Road in her freezer.

"Why do you not look surprised?" Wes said.

"I'm surprised," Eleanor said.

Wes stared at her, and she muttered a curse. "Fine. The guy might have said something about being in my house."

"Jesus Christ, Eleanor!" Wes's frustration with her was palpable.

She didn't know what to say, so she did what she did best – she babbled. "Okay, well, thank you for doing, uh, a sweep of my house first. That's what you call it, right? A sweep? Do you guys have a book of all the lingo I need to learn now that I'm caught up in some crazy shit? Because I feel like it would be helpful to know the phrases I should be using. I mean, in case some rando tries to kill me again or whatever."

Lord, could she look any dumber in front of Wes? Her attraction to Wes and terrible social skills meant that she habitually babbled in front of him. However, the combination of her exhaustion and worry that she was still in danger meant she was really making an ass of herself tonight.

That's not worry you're feeling, Eleanor. It's terror.

She opened the truck door, but before she could slide out, Wes blocked her way. She stared at him. "Uh, Wes? You wanna get out of my way, big guy?"

He shook his head. "You can't stay at your house tonight."

"I've got a baseball bat, my pocketknife, and a can of Mace," she said. "I'll be fine. He knows the package isn't in my house, right? He's not gonna come back. He's probably too busy cleaning the poop out of his pants after you nearly killed him."

52

She was proud of how normal she sounded. Like she wasn't on the verge of wetting her pants just thinking about being alone in her house tonight.

"It isn't safe," Wes said. "You're not staying here."

Embarrassed by the admittance, she said, "I don't have any friends or family I can stay with, okay? And even if I did, I wouldn't put them in danger like that. I'll shove chairs under my doorknobs and call 9-1-1 if I hear any weird noises."

"Wes is right," Cooper said. "There's a good chance that the guy could come back to your house tonight looking for you."

She tried not to shudder and failed miserably. "Yeah, okay. I won't stay here."

Stupidly, she waited for Wes to say she could stay with him. The silence dragged out. Wes cleared his throat but didn't say anything. Hoping no one could hear the disappointment in her voice, Eleanor said, "Cooper, can you drop me off at a motel? Nothing too expensive. There's a Motel 8 not too far from here."

She'd have to go a couple of days without eating to afford even a night or two at a cheap motel, but it was better than being dead, right?

"Don't be silly," Daisy said. "You can stay with us. Right, Cooper?"

He nodded. "Yes. You should pack a bag with enough clothes for a few days. It's probably best you don't stay here for a while. Your car is still at Wes's, right? We'll swing by his place to drop him off and grab the package your dad sent you. Okay?"

She rubbed above her eyebrow again. "Maybe I shouldn't stay with you. I don't want to put you or Daisy in danger like I did with Wes, and -"

"You didn't put me in danger," Wes said before a growl escaped his throat.

"I did," Eleanor said. "It was my fault that -"

"No, it wasn't." Wes growled again before a pained expression crossed his face. He took a deep breath. "It wasn't your fault, Eleanor."

"Still, I don't want to put Cooper and Daisy in danger."

"You won't," Cooper said. "I'm more than capable of keeping you and Daisy safe, even if this asshole figures out where you are and comes after you again." He glanced impatiently at his watch. "I don't mean to be a dick, but I haven't had dinner yet, and I'm starving over here. Can we stop arguing about this so I can get some food into me?"

Daisy grinned at him. "You're cute when you're hangry."

"I'm adorable when I'm hangry," Cooper said. "But I really do need food, so Wes, maybe you could move your ass so Eleanor can get out of the truck?"

Wes moved aside, and Eleanor slid out of the truck, wincing when even the slight jar from her landing made her arm ache.

Wes frowned at the way she rubbed her arm and said, "I'll come in with you."

"So will I," Daisy said. "You'll need my help to pack because of your arm."

Cooper rolled his eyes. "Christ, I guess I'm going in too. Anything to make this happen faster."

With a low grumble, he reached in and lifted Daisy out of the truck. Acutely aware of Wes's gaze on the back of her head, Eleanor headed toward her house.

ELEANOR STARED AT THE SMALL BOX ON COOPER'S KITCHEN table. Her father's neat handwriting was sloppy, like maybe he'd been in a hurry. She traced the lettering before glancing at the postmark. "He mailed this the day he died. This might have been the last thing he wrote before dying."

She winced at how melodramatic she sounded. Christ, what was wrong with her?

Daisy rubbed her back. "You don't have to open it tonight if you don't want to."

Cooper added the last of the dinner dishes to the dishwasher and closed it. "But you probably should."

"Coop," Wes said with a scowl. "Don't push her into doing this."

To her surprise, Wes had come with them to Cooper's house. When they arrived at Wes's house, he'd instructed her to stay put, then taken the parcel out of her car and climbed back in beside her. He'd slammed the truck door shut, and a look passed between him and Cooper before Cooper pulled back onto the street and driven them to his house.

"I know it's difficult, but the sooner we know what it is that guy is looking for, the sooner we can figure out a way to track him down," Cooper said.

Eleanor stared at the big lion shifter as he sat down next to Daisy. "I thought you were a security firm, not private detectives."

"We are, but we've been known to do a little extra for a client from time to time," Cooper said.

"Client? I'm not a client," Eleanor said. "I can't afford to hire your firm for security, let alone for extra services." She pushed her chair back and stood. "I'm sorry. I think there's been a misunderstanding about me staying here for the night. Um, I'm gonna go."

Wes's hand wrapped around her wrist, and even in her

exhaustion and her worry, his touch made goosebumps prickle to life, and she immediately felt too warm.

"Cooper's not charging you to spend the night here," Wes said.

"Okay, but I still can't afford private security or -"

"I know," Cooper said. "Don't worry about it. Just open the box, and let's see what we're dealing with."

"Don't worry about it?" Eleanor said. "What do you mean, don't worry about it?"

"I mean… don't worry about it?" Cooper said. He gave Daisy a look that clearly said, *is she always this stupid, or is it just the trauma?*

"Okay, but just so we're clear, I haven't hired you for security," Eleanor said. She knew she was harping on it, but she wasn't wealthy. As much as she didn't want to die, she also didn't want to suddenly find herself with a bill she had no hope of paying.

"Yes, you haven't hired us for security," Cooper said.

"Because I have a pocketknife and Mace, so I'm good," Eleanor said.

"Neither did you much good tonight," Cooper said.

Wes muttered a curse, and Daisy squeezed Cooper's arm. "Honey…"

"It's the truth," Cooper said. "I'm not trying to frighten her, but -"

"Well, you are, so knock it off, Coop," Wes said. Eleanor stared at him in fascination when a low growl drifted from his throat, and his eyes turned yellow.

Cooper inhaled and glanced at Daisy before growling at Wes. "You're scaring my mate."

"It's okay," Daisy said. "I'm not afraid."

"You are." Cooper pulled her out of her chair and into his lap. "It's all right, my mate."

He purred to her, and Daisy smiled and pressed a kiss against his cheek. "Thank you, honey. That's better."

Cooper glared at Wes even though he still purred. Wes glanced at Daisy. "Sorry, Daisy. My lion is... upset right now."

"It's fine," Daisy said. "I get it."

Wes still held Eleanor's wrist, and he tugged lightly on it. "Sit down, Eleanor."

She sank back into her chair. Wes released her wrist and said, "If you want to wait until tomorrow morning to open it, you can."

"No, I'll open it now."

They'd ordered Thai food for dinner, and the small amount she'd managed to eat now sat like a rock in her belly. Hoping she didn't throw up, she peeled away the tape on the box and opened it.

She picked up the faded t-shirt that sat on top and stared at it. "Wittica Summer Camp" was etched across the front with a graphic of a cartoon sun smiling down on a half dozen tents pitched along a river's edge. She ran her fingers along the faded and peeling graphic.

"Does this mean anything to you?" Wes said.

"It's mine," she said. "I used to wear it every night to bed. I guess I left it at his place during one of the weekends he was forced to spend time with me."

She cringed at how angry she sounded, but it was too late to take it back. It was out there now.

She set the t-shirt aside and pulled out the picture frame. She caught her breath and blinked back the tears as Wes scraped his chair closer and made a soft sound that was almost a purr as he stared at the picture with her.

"Is that your mom and dad?" he asked.

"Yeah. This picture used to be on my dad's desk in his

home office. Mom is eight months pregnant with me." She traced her finger over her mother's stomach as Daisy slid off Cooper's lap and sat on the other side of Eleanor.

"They look happy," she said.

"They do," Eleanor said. She studied her mom's face, that thousand-watt smile that Eleanor missed so much beaming out. Her mother had one hand on her belly and the other arm slung around her father's waist. Her father, usually so solemn, also had a giant smile and his arm was around her mother's shoulder. They looked impossibly young and impossibly happy.

"This was my favourite picture of them. Probably because it's one of the very few where my dad looks happy and... present. You know? Like, he's right there with my mom, not off in his head thinking about work."

"It's a wonderful picture," Daisy said quietly.

Eleanor set the picture aside and peeked into the box. The only other item was a small cardboard storage box, the kind you might get at a dollar store. She took off the lid and stared at the pressed rose inside before carefully lifting it out.

"Does the rose mean anything to you?" Wes asked.

She shook her head and set it aside before taking out the key under the pressed flower.

She turned it over and over in her hand. The light above the table made it gleam dully.

"Does the key look familiar to you?" Daisy asked.

"No, I've never seen it before," she said.

"It's a bus station locker key," Wes said.

"Really?" Eleanor studied the number etched at the top of the key.

"How many bus stations are there in Emerton?" Wes said.

"I don't know an exact number, but it's a big city, so... a lot?" Eleanor said.

"So, obviously, the guy is after the key," Cooper said. "Any idea what might be in the locker?"

"I don't have a clue," Eleanor said. "I guess I'm making a road trip to Emerton tomorrow."

"Like hell you are," Wes said. "It's way too dangerous. Whatever is in that locker, the human was willing to kill you for it."

"Which is why I need to find it," Eleanor said. "I can't have men trying to kill me every freaking day. I'll find whatever is in the locker and hand it over to..."

"Who exactly would you hand it over to? You don't even know what it is. It could be a bomb, for all you know," Wes said.

"A bomb?" Eleanor said. Despite her exhaustion, she couldn't help but tease him. "Take it down a notch, Wesley. My dad was a biochemist, not James Bond."

"The point is you don't know what you're walking into. What if this guy knows he's looking for a bus station key? What if he has other men planted at the bus stations in Emerton, just waiting for you to show up in case he can't get the key from you?"

"Man, you've put a lot of thought into this," Eleanor said. "Probably why you're so good at saving people's asses." She glanced at Cooper. "You should give him a raise."

"Noted," Cooper said with a grin. "He is right, though. Checking out a bunch of different bus stations on your own is dangerous."

"I'll watch for suspicious looking men in aviator glasses," Eleanor said. "They probably got a group discount on them."

"This isn't a joke, Eleanor," Wes said.

"You think I don't know that?" She turned on him, anger sparking its way through her body like wildfire. "I almost died today, Wes. *You* almost died today. Trust me. I know this isn't a fucking joke. But I drive people around for fucking peanuts most of the time, and I have bills and rent, and I can't afford to hire a security consultant to search a bunch of bus stations for a parcel my dead father left in a locker that may or may not be a fucking bomb!"

She'd run out of breath and anger. Exhausted and feeling sick over her outburst, she said, "I'm sorry, I shouldn't have yelled. But it's been a long day, and I'm tired. I need some sleep."

Daisy stood when she did and said, "I'll show you to the guest room."

"Thanks, Daisy."

Eleanor paused in the doorway of the kitchen when Wes said, "You can't go to Emerton on your own tomorrow. Promise me, Eleanor."

"Yeah, I know," Eleanor said. "Thank you again for saving my life, Wes."

CHAPTER 6

"Thanks for the ride back to my car, Cooper," Eleanor said.

"Don't mention it," Cooper said.

"Are you sure you slept okay last night, Eleanor?" Daisy twisted in her seat to stare at her.

"I look that bad, huh?" Eleanor said.

"No," Daisy said.

"Your mate can't lie worth crap," Eleanor said to Cooper.

Cooper grinned at Daisy, who poked him in the thigh. "Don't agree with her. I'm good at lying."

"No, my mate, you are not," Cooper said with another grin.

"You just look a little tired and worried," Daisy said. "Which is understandable."

"I'm okay," Eleanor said as Cooper turned onto Wes's street.

"What's your favourite food?" Daisy said. "I can make it tonight for supper."

"Oh, um, can I get back to you on that?" Eleanor said. "I don't have much of an appetite right now."

She sounded guilty as hell, but, man, she was just as bad at lying as Daisy. She hated lying to Daisy, but she couldn't tell her that last night after she was alone in the guest room, she'd cancelled all of her clients for the next two days, mapped out the bus stations closest to her father's house, and booked herself a motel room. The minute she dropped Wes off at work, she was driving the eight hours to Emerton. She'd text Daisy once she got there and let her know she was safe but wouldn't be staying with her and Cooper tonight.

Cooper stopped in front of Wes's house, and Eleanor muttered a curse. Her car was gone.

"Somebody stole my damn car," she said.

She wanted to cry.

She wanted to scream.

She wanted to kick something.

She settled for saying 'fuck, fuck, fuck' under her breath.

"It's not stolen," Cooper said. "My friend Abe owns an auto repair place. I texted him last night and he agreed to come in early to the shop to fix your window, so you wouldn't have to cancel your clients today. I asked Grayson to drive your car over to the shop this morning. Abe said it would only take an hour, so Gray should be back any – oh, there he is."

Grayson parked in front of Cooper's truck, shutting off the engine and climbing out as Eleanor stared at Cooper. She felt decidedly weepy, and she cleared her throat and blinked hard to hold back the tears. "Cooper, thank you so much. That was incredibly kind and thoughtful of you."

"You're welcome," he said.

"Wait, how did you get my keys?" she said.

"I took them out of your purse earlier this morning when Gray stopped at the house," Cooper said. He paused, "I just grabbed the keys, I didn't, like, snoop around in your purse or anything."

She laughed. "Coop, you could have stolen all the contents and worn my purse like a hat if you wanted. You just saved me so much time."

"No big deal," he said.

Eleanor didn't know how to explain to him that, yes, it was a very big deal. Used to taking care of everything herself, to have Wes, and now his friends too, helping her was an unexpected and wonderful gift.

"How much do I owe you?" she asked.

He just shrugged. "I don't know. We'll settle later. Have a good day at work, Eleanor. We'll see you tonight."

He stared steadily at her in the rear-view mirror. If Eleanor didn't know better, she'd swear he knew what she was planning.

"Great, thank you again. See you tonight." She hopped out of the back seat of Cooper's truck, tossed her bag over her shoulder, and slammed the door shut before he or Daisy could say anything else.

She walked over to Grayson and held out her hand. "Hi, I'm Eleanor."

"Nice to meet you, Eleanor. I'm Grayson." He shook her hand.

"Thank you so much for helping with my car. I really appreciate it."

"No problem. Any friend of Wes's, as the saying goes." He smiled at her before standing next to Cooper's window. "Hey, Coop. I have an errand to run before I come to the office. I'll be back in time for our ten o'clock meeting."

"Sounds good. Thanks again for your help this morning," Coop said.

Grayson nodded and waved to Wes as Wes stepped out of

his house. He climbed into a silver SUV parked across the street and drove away with a final wave to Cooper.

She stuck her bag in the trunk of her car, as Wes walked toward her. "Hold up, Eleanor."

She paused in shutting the trunk, watching as Wes tossed in a leather overnight bag next to hers before nodding to Cooper.

"Hey, Wes," Cooper said.

"Hey. Thanks again for the ride home last night."

"Don't mention it. See you later."

"Oh hey, since Cooper is right here, why don't you drive with him?" Eleanor said. "It'll save you some money, right?"

"I booked you for this morning," Wes said.

"Right, yeah, I know, but I mean… I'm cool with you cancelling this morning. I get it. It's silly for me to drive you to work when Cooper's right here and going to the office."

She didn't relish losing the only income she'd make for the day, but if Wes went with Cooper, she might be able to beat the morning rush hour traffic getting out of the city.

"No, thank you." Wes opened the back door of her car and climbed in, shutting the door behind him.

"No… thank you?" Eleanor echoed.

Cooper laughed. "See you, Eleanor."

He drove off, and Eleanor closed the trunk and slid into the driver's seat. She shut the door and waited for a minute or so. Yesterday, she'd sat in this seat while a man held a gun to her head. She thought maybe she'd feel different, that maybe the car wouldn't give her the sense of comfort it always did, but she felt okay. Felt… normal.

"You okay?" Wes said.

"Yeah," she said. "I am."

"Good. How's your arm?"

"It's all right. Sorer than I thought, but the pain meds have made a difference," she said.

"Did you take your antibiotics this morning?"

The concern in Wes's voice brought on a wave of emotion. Since her mother died, she hadn't had anyone who was concerned about her. It was kind of nice to have someone worrying about her again.

"Yep, I did." She started the car and buckled her seat belt. As she pulled out onto the street, she said, "So, what's with the overnight bag? You going out of town?"

"You should take the Henderson freeway," Wes said.

She frowned. "That'll take me twice as long to get to your office."

"But it'll get us out of the city before rush hour traffic gets terrible."

She immediately pulled over and put the car into park before twisting to face him, the seatbelt digging into her neck. "What the hell, Wes?"

He stared calmly at her. "I'm going with you to Emerton."

"I'm not going to Emerton."

He didn't reply, and she scowled at him before slamming her hand down on the steering wheel. "How did you know?"

"You can't lie worth shit, Eleanor. I knew last night you were going to go. Even after you promised me."

"I never promised," she said. "And I'm an excellent liar."

He snorted. "No, you are not. And even if you were, as soon as Cooper texted me and said you had your overnight bag with you this morning, it was a clear sign you weren't planning on staying at his place tonight."

She opened her mouth, paused, and then said, "Fuck, this spy shit is a lot harder than the movies make it out to be."

"This is not some movie spy shit," Wes said. "This is

65

dangerous and reckless, and you thinking it's like a movie is exactly why I'm going with you."

"I don't need your help," she said. "I'm driving you to work, Wes."

"Are you going to drag me out of your car?" he said. "Because that's the only way I'm leaving this vehicle."

"I'll call the police and have you arrested," she said.

He grinned, and his pupils turned to slits as he talked to his lion. "I know," he murmured, "she's stubborn."

"I'm not stubborn," she said when his pupils went back to normal. "You can tell your annoying lion that." She leaned a little further over the seat when he didn't say anything and yelled at Wes's face. "I'm not stubborn, lion!"

Wes laughed, and, just like the first time she heard his laugh, she was both delighted, and a little turned on by the sound of it.

"You don't have to yell," Wes said. "He has excellent hearing."

"Wes," she said, her voice turning serious, "I don't want to put you in danger, okay? Yesterday, I almost got you killed and -"

Her voice cut out when Wes leaned forward and cupped her face. His thumb stroked her cheek, and goosebumps rose on her skin when he purred to her and then said, "Eleanor, you don't have to worry about me. Ever. I am more than capable of taking care of myself. Do you understand?"

She nodded, her throat too dry to speak. When Wes's gaze dropped to her mouth, she parted her lips, hoping against hope that he would kiss her. She missed his taste, his tongue, his touch.

His nostrils flared, and she almost moaned with disappointment when he dropped his hand, his purring cut out, and he shoved back into his seat until he was as far from her as possible.

"Drive, Eleanor," he said hoarsely.

"Wes," she said, "I don't..."

"I'm going with you," he said. "End of discussion."

She turned around, catching with the edge of her vision the way Wes immediately adjusted the prominent bulge in his jeans. A perverse pleasure went through her. At least she wasn't the only one turned on as fuck right now.

CHAPTER 7

"Seriously, Wes?" Eleanor stopped beside the driver's door, juggling her purse, a can of Dr. Pepper, and a sandwich that Wes was confident would give her food poisoning.

"What?" he said.

"You don't have to sit in the back seat. You're not a client right now," she said.

He hesitated, and a brief look of embarrassment flickered across her face. "I promise I won't, like, grope you or something if you sit in the front seat."

"I know," he said and opened the front passenger door. He pushed the seat back and sat down before clicking his seat belt into place and setting his bottle of water in the cup holder next to Eleanor's Dr. Pepper.

She put on her seat belt and started the car before tearing open the wrapping on the sandwich. He cringed when she took a big bite. "You know," she said when she finished chewing, "if I'd known my insistence that I buy lunch meant you wouldn't eat, I would have let you pay. I'm not completely broke, Wes. I can buy you lunch."

"I know," he said, "but I've never eaten a gas station sandwich in my life, and I'm not about to start now."

"Never?" Eleanor stared at him, her sandwich starting to drip what he hoped was mustard – Christ, let it be mustard and not some weird yellow fungus – down her hand. "You've never eaten a gas station sandwich ever?"

"Never," he said.

"Gas station burrito?"

"No."

"Gas station hot dog?"

He visibly shuddered, and she laughed before licking the mustard away. "Wimp."

"Do you want food poisoning, Eleanor? Because this," he pointed to the sandwich, "is how you get food poisoning."

She grinned at him before taking another huge and deliberate bite. He rolled his eyes and opened the bottle of Dr. Pepper for her before opening his water and taking a drink. "I reserve the right to say I told you so when you're puking along the side of the road in half an hour."

"Not gonna happen," Eleanor said before taking a swig of soda. "I have a cast iron stomach. When I was sixteen, I joined a competitive eating team. I once ate thirty-seven hot dogs in less than thirty minutes and won us the state championship."

"You're kidding," Wes said.

"I'm not," Eleanor said. "I beat out a guy named Big Gene. He was 6'6", weighed close to four hundred pounds, and been state champion for three years running."

"How many hot dogs did he eat?" Wes said.

"Thirty-one," she said with a grin.

"Do you still do competitive eating?" Wes said.

"Nah, it's a young person's game."

"Yeah, because you're so old," he said with a snort.

She just shrugged. "I'm not that young. I'm twenty-seven."

"Compared to me, that's young."

"How old are you?" she said.

He hesitated, and she pointed the second half of her sandwich at him. "Don't turn back into a mute now, Wes. I gave up my age. You can do the same."

"Forty-two," he said.

"That's not old," she said.

He didn't reply, and she finished the last of her sandwich before wiping her mouth with a napkin and drinking some Dr. Pepper. She reached into her jacket pocket and produced a package of beef jerky. "Here, I bought this when you weren't looking. This will stop you from passing out from hunger, and I'm pretty sure beef jerky never goes bad."

He grinned and opened the package, his stomach rumbling. "Thank you."

"You're welcome." She pulled out of the gas station and back onto the highway. They drove in silence for a while. His lion made a low whine that Wes ignored. Eleanor had been quiet all morning which wasn't like her at all, but she'd just lost her father, and someone had tried to kill her. He couldn't and shouldn't expect her to be her usual self. Still, he missed the sound of her sweet voice, and the thought of driving another four hours with nothing but the radio made him and his lion miserable.

"Exactly how much does your company charge clients per hour anyway?" Eleanor said.

His lion purred happily, and Wes swallowed down the sound before saying, "You're not being charged for this."

"So, Cooper's just giving away his company services for free? Pimping you out like you're some kind of security gigolo?"

She laughed at her own joke, and he rolled his eyes, but he was happy to hear her silliness and her laughter. The last forty-eight hours had been terrible for her, and he was beyond relieved that maybe she was bouncing back to her usual self.

"I took a few days off," he said.

She glanced at him, and he wanted to smooth the little lines that appeared between her eyebrows. "So, now you're losing out on pay because of me?"

"I took a few vacation days," he said.

"Right. I've forgotten what it's like to have the option of getting paid for days off."

"Running your own company is a lot of work," he said.

"It is, and yeah, I miss paid vacation days and health insurance that didn't cost me as much as a car every month, but the good still outweighs the bad. I like being in charge of my own destiny." She laughed. "That sounds stupid. Anyway, I worked for Uber for a few years before branching out on my own. And, for the most part, it's been great. Most of my clients are people like you. I mean, you book me the most out of all my clients by far, but -"

"Sorry," he said.

She frowned at him. "Don't be. Half the time, I can only afford groceries because of you and your daily bookings."

"Christ," he said, "are you deliberately trying to worry me, Eleanor?"

She just shrugged. Wes wanted to keep questioning her on exactly how often she went without eating, but afraid of sounding like a fucking father, he kept his mouth shut.

If she lived with us, she'd have more money. Like Cooper's mate, his lion said.

She's not moving in with us. Don't be ridiculous.

His lion growled and retreated, but not very far. Wes could feel him right at the surface, listening intently to every word Eleanor said. He didn't mind. In fact, it filled him with a deep sense of relief. He hadn't realized just how disengaged his lion had become until he'd suddenly become fascinated with Eleanor. His lion was attracted to Eleanor, just like Wes, but not to the same depth and obsession. At least, he hadn't been. But ever since Wes had kissed Eleanor, ever since he'd heard her moan and smelled her sweet arousal for him, his lion's interest had skyrocketed.

That in itself wasn't surprising. Their cats were led by the most basics of needs – food, shelter, and fucking. Breeding too, but that wasn't a possibility for Wes, so his lion showed no interest in it.

Still, his lion hadn't shown this much interest in a woman since Wes left the military and joined Cooper's security firm. Not that there'd been many women to show interest in. He'd slept with three women in the last four years, and all of them had been a casual one-night-only thing.

And he hadn't slept with a single woman since the day he'd climbed into Eleanor's car and seen her for the first time.

He studied her, hoping she'd be distracted by driving enough not to notice his stare. She wore a pink t-shirt with a faded graphic of 'Free Britney' and a pair of jeans. Her dark hair was in a ponytail, and he could just make out the tattoo on the back of her neck. A vine of white daisies that disappeared under her t-shirt. He'd give his right arm to know precisely where that vine of daisies ended on her body.

He swallowed hard as he continued to stare at her. Her skin was soft, her hair like silk, and her lips were sweet. He knew that now. Knew it because she'd kissed him. She'd kissed him, and he'd almost lost control and fucked her right there in the damn hallway. Would have fucked her if they hadn't been interrupted.

His cock swelled at just the memory of touching Eleanor. He could deny it, but he wanted her even more now. He masturbated nearly every fucking night to that moment in the hallway. In his fantasies, he took what he wanted. He stripped Eleanor naked and mated with her... claimed her.

His lion purred with pleasure and need. Wes had a fucking semi, and if Eleanor looked over, if she glanced at his crotch, she'd see exactly what she did to him. How much he truly wanted her.

Would that be such a bad thing?

"Why are you staring at me? Do I have mustard on my face or something?" Eleanor didn't look away from the road.

He studied the passing landscape out his window. "I wasn't staring at you."

"Yes, you were."

He cleared his throat. "So, feel free to tell me to fuck off for asking personal questions, but how long were you and your dad estranged?"

She shrugged. "We weren't close even when he and my mom were still married, but once she divorced him and we moved out of the house, that was pretty much it. He was always so wrapped up in his work that it didn't leave a lot of space for Mom or me."

She took a sip of her drink. "Mom stuck it out for way longer than she should have. She stayed because she wanted me to have both my parents, but Dad wasn't there even when he was there, you know?"

He nodded, and she took a deep breath. "I feel guilty that she stayed so long. If she hadn't, maybe she could have found someone else to love, someone who saw her for the incredible person she was. But she never did. First, she was too busy being a single mom to me and then..."

"Then?" he said when she didn't say anything.

"Then she died," Eleanor said softly. "She missed out on so much, and that's partially my fault."

"It isn't," Wes said. "Don't let the brain weasels tell you it is."

Eleanor glanced at him and grinned. "Brain weasels... I like that."

"Derek said that all the time whenever one of us doubted ourselves or felt guilt over something that was out of our control," Wes said. "One time, Boone was -"

He stopped abruptly. He couldn't remember the last time he'd said Derek's name out loud.

"Who's Derek?" she said when he didn't continue.

"He was in the military with Coop and me and Gray and Boone," Wes said.

"Oh," she said. "So, all five of you left the military and started the security firm?"

"Cooper left first and started the firm, then six months later Gray and Boone got out and started working with Cooper. Six months after that, I left the military and joined them."

"Derek didn't want to join the security firm, too?" she said.

"He died overseas." He could hear the pain and sorrow in his voice. His lion had retreated again like a small child hiding from the monsters in the dark.

Eleanor glanced at him before reaching out and taking his hand, linking their fingers together. "I'm sorry, Wes."

He shouldn't be encouraging the hand-holding, but it felt good to touch her. Just the feel of her hand in his had brought his lion right back to the surface, purring eagerly as the depression and sadness that mired down his lion was knocked back.

"Was Derek your best friend?" she asked.

"We were all good friends, but Boone was closest to Derek," Wes said. "But it was my fault he died."

What the fuck?

In four years, he'd never once spoken those words out loud.

Eleanor squeezed his hand, her voice sympathetic when she said, "Was it your fault? Or is that the grief over losing your friend telling you lies?"

His throat and eyes burned, and he wasn't sure he could even speak past the golf ball sized lump in his throat. "No, it was my fault."

"How did he die?"

"I don't want to talk about it," he said.

He waited for her to either try to coax him into telling her or get pissed that he wouldn't. To his surprise, she squeezed his hand again and said, "Okay. Do you have any siblings?"

He was more grateful for the change of subject than he could say.

"No siblings," he said.

"Do your parents live here?"

"No, they retired to Florida a few years ago. It's where my mom is from, and my dad promised her when he finished working, they would move back."

"Are you close with them?"

He nodded. "Yeah. Pretty close. I fly to Florida every few months to see them. My mom would -"

He stopped and stared at their linked hands.

"Your mom would what?" Eleanor said.

"She would love you." He made himself let go of her hand.

She grinned at him. "Oh yeah? So, you're saying she's an ultra-cool lion shifter then, huh?"

He laughed. "Yes to the ultra-cool, no to the lion."

"She's not a lion?" Eleanor said in surprise.

"Nope, she's a lynx. My dad is the lion."

"So, are you a lynx lion hybrid?" she said.

"No. When two different shifters mate, their offspring is one or the other. It's a fifty-fifty chance."

"Neat," she said. "I knew that when humans and shifters mated, it would be one or the other, but somehow just assumed that there would be a hybrid thing happening with two shifters."

"Actually, with humans and shifters, it isn't a fifty-fifty split," he said. "More like seventy thirty."

"Seventy percent chance human?"

"Seventy percent chance shifter," Wes said.

"That's kind of cool," Eleanor said. "So, you ever been married?"

He nearly crushed the water bottle he held. "What?"

"Sorry, was that too personal of a question?" she said. "I'm terrible at knowing where the line is at small talk."

"It's fine. It just... took me by surprise," he said.

"You don't have to answer. I know you're a private person."

He was a private person, but he liked the intimacy of sharing with Eleanor. "Never married. Engaged once."

"Ooh," she said. "Intriguing. Is it recent and still too painful to talk about? Or can I ask for details?"

"It was a long time ago," he said. "I ended the engagement when Juliet cheated on me while I was overseas."

"She's a dick," Eleanor said. "She didn't deserve you."

He shrugged. "I had done back-to-back tours, and just before I left for the second one, I told her I planned on doing a third. She was angry and upset."

"Doesn't mean she should cheat," Eleanor said. "How did

you find out? Oh God, did she send you a 'Dear John' email?"

"No. When I'd finished my tour and came home, she was pregnant," he said.

"Are you kidding?" Eleanor's face was almost adorable in its shock. "She does realize you have to be home to impregnate her, right?"

"She told me she got pregnant when I was on leave."

"Oh," Eleanor said. "So, you had to wait until the baby was born to find out who was the actual dad?"

"No," he said. "I knew I wasn't the father. The timing was off, only by a week or two, but she couldn't get away with the lie like she thought she could."

What he told Eleanor was the truth, although there was more irrefutable proof of why he couldn't have been the father. When their relationship started to become serious, Juliet had told him she didn't want children. He'd been relieved. He didn't want children either, but more importantly, he was medically incapable of having them. He hadn't bothered to tell Juliet about his low sperm count diagnosis. There hadn't seemed to be a point. She was adamant about never wanting to be a mother.

When she'd tried to convince Wes he was the father and discovered the truth that he couldn't have kids, she was beyond pissed that he had never told her and accused him of lying to her about it. Of course, considering she was pregnant with another lion shifter's child, she hadn't had much of a leg to stand on when it came to the lying thing.

"So, what happened to her and the baby?" Eleanor said.

"She married the father, and they went on to have six more kids. As far as I know, they're still married," he said.

"Seven kids? Holy cannoli," Eleanor said. "I'm sorry she cheated on you. That was a shitty thing for her to do."

"How about you? Ever been married?" he said.

"No. Not even engaged," she said. "Hell, I've never really had any serious relationships either. The longest I ever dated someone was a year and a half."

"So, you're not looking for a relationship?" he said. Selfishly, he was kind of happy about that. He wasn't sure he could sit in Eleanor's car twice a day while she talked about her boyfriend.

"Oh, I totally am," Eleanor said. "I'm ready for the long-term commitment thing and have been for a while. It's just…"

"It's hard to meet people," he said.

"Actually, no. I'm signed up to a couple of different dating sites, and not to brag, but guys usually swipe right on me." She grinned at him. "The problem is the first date. I don't make a great first impression, and if by some miracle, the guy does want to see me again, by the third or fourth date, he usually bails. My friend Andrew says I have the looks but not the personality to keep a man's interest."

"He's not a very good friend," Wes said.

Find out where this Andrew lives so I can kill him, his lion urged.

You are not killing a human because he's an ass to Eleanor.

"What did your lion just say?" Eleanor asked.

Wes cleared his throat. "He agrees with me that Andrew is a bad friend."

"He isn't. Just very blunt. Besides, he's right. I try hard to be likable, but, as you're well aware, I always talk too much, and I'm socially awkward. As much as I try not to be like my dad, I inherited his habit of being a total weirdo in social situations. Even as a little kid, I had a hard time keeping friends. Part of the reason I do the job I do is that I thought it might help improve my social skills. Talking to strangers all day, you know? Only, it hasn't worked. At least not in the boyfriend department. I'm too obnoxious for a long-term relationship."

"There's nothing wrong with your social skills," Wes said.

"Says the man who before a few days ago, hadn't said more than a hundred words to me in almost a year and a half," Eleanor said teasingly.

"Are you trying to say I'm socially awkward too?" Wes said.

"We make quite the pair," she said. "I talk way too much, and you don't talk enough. Maybe it's why we're friends?"

"Maybe," he said. He wanted Eleanor to think of him as her friend, so why did it piss him off so much to hear it?

"See," Eleanor said with a sigh, "there I go again. Screwing up and saying the wrong thing."

"You didn't," he said. "We are friends."

"Then why do you look so annoyed?"

"I don't," he said.

"That's your annoyed face."

"I don't have an annoyed face."

"Buddy, you have an annoyed face."

"Eleanor," he said.

"Look, there it is again," she said.

He laughed, and her look of delight made his lion purr happily.

"You have a great laugh, Wes."

"Thanks, you do too," he said. "And you're not obnoxious. You'll find your mate, Eleanor. One who loves you for who you are."

"Thanks, but I'm not holding my breath," Eleanor said with a grin, but he could see the pain lurking just below the surface of it. "Why didn't you find someone else? Do you have trust issues because of what your ex-fiancée did? If you do, that's understandable – I know what it's like to be cheated on, and it sucks hairy monkey balls – but you should know that you're a total catch. You've got a steady job, you're smart, you have a fantastic body, and you're good looking."

His lion purred loudly at the compliments, puffing out his chest and preening like a bird. Wes contained the urge to roll his eyes. He didn't think he was traumatized by the cheating. It had sucked, and he didn't ever want to go through that again, but the affair itself wasn't what stopped him from pursuing a relationship.

At first, it'd been his job. Then the death of Derek and his guilt over the role he'd played in it. The one time he'd stayed the night with a woman, he'd scared the hell out of her by screaming in his sleep. The nightmares about the day Derek died still happened occasionally. And, although the bad dreams were far less frequent, they were no less intense. Sometimes they were bad enough that his lion freaked out and took control, forcing Wes to shift so he could better defend them against an invisible enemy.

"Sorry," Eleanor said. "I'm prying too much."

"It's not the trust issues," Wes said. "I just…"

"Just what?" she said when he didn't continue.

"I don't have a lot of free time for a relationship," he finally said because he had to say something and confessing that no other woman did it for him since the moment he'd climbed into this car and seen Eleanor's beautiful face was madness.

"Oh," she said. He could hear the skepticism in her voice.

He watched as she rolled her shoulders and cracked her neck. "Ooh, that was a good one," she said before cracking her neck again. "Does this gross you out?"

"No, should it?"

"This guy I dated – the one who made me wear a blonde wig while we had sex because he was cheating on me -"

"I remember the story," Wes said.

"Right. Anyway, he hated it when I cracked my neck. Said it was disgusting and unladylike and that I needed to try harder to be a lady around him. I said I'd try my best to be more ladylike in the future. Then I spent the next five days crop-dusting him every time we were in the same room together."

Wes roared with laughter. He laughed until his stomach hurt and his eyes watered, and he had to gasp in gulps of air. When his laughter finally tapered off, he could smell Eleanor's delight and happiness and… lust.

He took a deep breath and a drink of water, trying to ignore the lust that made him want to direct her to pull the car over so he could fuck her in the back seat until she screamed his name.

"I know it was immature, but he deserved it," Eleanor said.

"He did." Wes took another drink of water as Eleanor rolled her shoulders again.

"Man, my shoulders and neck are stiff today," she said. "The hazards of holding a steering wheel ten hours a day."

Feeling weirdly guilty, he said, "I'm sorry I can't give you a break from driving."

"Oh, it's no problem," she said. "I love driving. It doesn't bother me that you can't drive."

"I can drive," he said as his lion grumbled in annoyance. "I just *don't* drive."

"Why not?" she said.

His lion's good humour and happiness disappeared immediately, and so did Wes's. "That's none of your business."

He was brusque when he hadn't meant to be, but even just thinking about why he didn't drive made both him and his lion miserable.

"Sorry, Wes," Eleanor said as the scent of her guilt and embarrassment drifted to him. "I shouldn't have pried like that. I have no excuse for my rudeness other than the afore-mentioned social awkwardness."

"It's fine," he said. "I'm being a dick."

"You're not. I'm just being... well, Eleanor." She laughed, but there was no humour in it. She turned the radio on and turned up the volume, smiling gamely at him. "Let's listen to some music for a while, yeah?"

He nodded and stared out the window as his lion retreated with a low whine.

CHAPTER 8

"It doesn't fit." Eleanor could hear the discouragement in her voice. But considering it was the fifth bus station locker number 732 they'd tried, she had the right to be discouraged.

She stared at the key in the palm of her hand before slipping it back into her pocket. "Why do these stupid things not have, like, an identifying mark for which station it is. This is ridiculous."

Wes studied the people milling around them, his big body on alert, his gaze sweeping from side to side. "How many more bus stations are on your list?"

"Another four." She rubbed at her shoulders, trying to ease the tension from them. "If Dad even chose a bus station somewhere remotely close to his house. What if he chose one on the other side of the damn city? What if it isn't even in this city? This is like looking for a needle in a haystack."

"We'll find it," Wes said. His voice was calm, and it reassured Eleanor even though she knew he had no idea if they would find the right locker or not. He held out his hand. "Let's go."

She slipped her hand into his, the feel of his hard palm against hers bringing on those delightful shivers that made her feel warm and weirdly gooey inside. He'd held her hand in every single bus station. Although she knew he was only doing it to keep her close to him and therefore easier to protect, she'd been indulging in a sweet little fantasy that Wes was her boyfriend, and they were just casually…

Casually what, Eleanor? Looking for some mystery item that your dead father left in a random bus station locker before some nasty men with guns decide to kill you for it?

Casually running errands. Just casually running errands with her very handsome and very protective boyfriend, Wes, who didn't mind that she talked too much or said whatever she was thinking at the most inopportune times.

Wes led her outside and into the warm night air. It was close to ten, and she was exhausted. She had barely slept last night, and the lack of sleep had caught up to her. She wasn't someone who could miss a night's sleep and power through. She needed her eight hours and was grumpy and non-functioning if she didn't get it.

She unlocked the car as they approached it, and Wes opened the driver's door for her. Man, she loved how sweet he was. "Where to next?"

"Um…" she took her phone out of her pocket and tried to focus on the list of bus stations. "Uh, I think if we…"

She covered her mouth as a yawn threatened to split her head in half.

"Maybe we should call it a night," Wes said.

"No, I'm okay. We can do one more," Eleanor said.

"It can wait until tomorrow," Wes said. "You need sleep, Eleanor."

She sighed and rubbed the back of her neck. "Yeah, I do. C'mon, let's head to the motel."

"Do you want to grab something to eat first?" Wes said.

"Maybe they'll have a restaurant nearby," she said. "I'm more tired than hungry, but if you're starving, I could swing by a drive-thru, or -"

"I'm good," he said. "Let's just go to the motel."

***

"ARE YOU FUCKING KIDDING ME?" WES LITERALLY GROWLED in frustration. The sound made Eleanor's insides shivery, despite her exhaustion. Was it weird that she desperately wanted to hear Wes growl while he was balls-deep inside of her?

"This cannot be our only option," Wes said as he stared at the motel and then at his phone again. Eleanor could see the latest hotel where he'd just tried to book a room on the screen.

Eleanor studied him in the dim light of the motel parking lot. "Is this where I get to tell you 'I told you so'?"

She popped her pain meds into her mouth and swallowed them with a swallow of water before gently rubbing at her arm below the sutures. Fuck, did her arm hurt tonight. Who knew sort of being shot would hurt this much?

"What the fuck even is a funko pop convention anyway?" Wes said. "And why is it so popular that every hotel that isn't potentially rat and bug-infested is completely booked?"

"People like their funko pops," Eleanor said. "Look, do you think I would have booked this murder motel if I'd had any other choice? I might be poor, but even I have standards. This was the only choice left. C'mon, let's go check in. We've been sitting in the parking lot for nearly twenty minutes. The manager's gonna call the cops on us."

"Like a cop's ever been to this place," Wes muttered as he followed her to the lobby.

"My room has two double beds, but I can book you a second room," Eleanor said. "I'll pay for it."

"No, you're not," Wes said in a tone that clearly suggested it would be best she not argue with him.

They stepped inside, and the smell of mildew and mold made Eleanor want to gag. God, she hoped the rooms were cleaner than the lobby, or she'd have to sleep in the car. She didn't care how uncomfortable it was.

"What?" The manager sat behind the desk, his feet up while a small television blared some late-night game show that involved people dunked into tubs of green goo.

"Hi," Eleanor said. "I have a room reservation under Eleanor Whitman."

The man didn't take his eyes off the television. "You didn't tell me you'd be a late check-in. Almost gave your room away."

"What a shame," Wes said before moving away to study the rack with postcards stuck haphazardly into it.

Eleanor smiled at the hotel clerk. "So sorry about that. A pack of koala bears attacked me, and I had to fight my way free. It took longer than I thought – they're wirier than they look."

"Uh-huh." The man finally tore his gaze away from the TV to stare at her. A different light shone in his eyes, and she tried not to shudder when he ogled her tits. Dating a man who worked at a murder motel was a bad idea to begin with, but the man's greasy mullet, stained yellow teeth, and scraggly beard would have made even the most desperate of women think twice.

She stuck her hand into her pocket, feeling the reassuring bulk of her pocketknife as the man stood up and leaned against the counter until she could feel his gross breath on her face. He was big, and there was a hardness to him that made her knees watery and her stomach churn. Fighting the urge to back away - men like him liked it when women were intimidated - she stared blandly at him like she wasn't afraid as her heart thumped and bumped, and her flight instinct screamed at her to run.

Of course, if the guy were a shifter, he'd know right away that she was afraid of him. Shit, maybe she should casually show him the Mace in her purse or -

Wes's hand landed on the back of her neck and cupped it firmly as he made another one of those low growls. This time the sound sent relief rushing through her instead of lust. He stared unblinkingly at the clerk as the man backed up a step.

"You one of those shifters?" the man said.

"Is that a problem?" Wes asked calmly.

"Don't see many of them around here, that's all," the man said. His gaze drifted to Eleanor again. "She ain't no shifter. Those females are some big bitches."

Wes growled again, and the man swallowed hard before picking at a pimple sprouting near his nose. "I'm just saying. She's too little." His gaze dipped to her chest for a second time.

Eleanor stared up at Wes when he bared his teeth. His fangs looked very large and very white in the fluorescent lighting. "Stare at her tits one more time, and I'll rip your fucking eyeballs out of your head and make you eat them. Do you understand?"

The man turned a shade of green that Eleanor hadn't thought skin could turn. "Yeah."

"Say it." Wes's whole body swelled, and golden-coloured fur sprouted across his cheeks.

"I understand." The man's voice dropped to a whisper. "I

don't mean no disrespect. I didn't know she was your woman."

"Apologize to her," Wes said.

"I'm sorry, Ms. Whitman," the man said without looking at her.

"Um, okay, thanks." Eleanor didn't object when Wes drew her close to him before putting his arm around her waist in a possessive grip.

The man fumbled at the laptop's keyboard for a few minutes before handing them a card key. Still refusing to look at her, the clerk said, "It's room one twenty - fourth door after the vending machine. The parking spot in front of it is yours to park in. Just need your license plate number, ma'am."

He shoved a piece of paper and pen toward them. She wrote down her license plate number and picked up the card key. "Thank you."

"You're welcome, ma'am," the clerk said with another furtive glance at Wes. "Maid service is gone for the day, but the room has fresh sheets and clean towels. You can call me here at the front desk if you need anything at all."

Wes stared silently at him until the man returned to his seat and stared at the laptop screen. Trying not to smile, Eleanor linked her fingers with Wes's when he took her hand, and she followed him out of the lobby.

"Man, you're a way better personal defense system than a pocketknife or a can of Mace," Eleanor said with a laugh. "If I had the money, I'd hire you just to scare off the gross men who leer at me."

Wes's hand tightened around hers. "How often does shit like that happen to you, Eleanor?"

She shrugged. "Probably no more than it happens to any other woman. We just learn to deal with it, you know?"

"Fucking men," Wes muttered. "We're the worst."

"Oh shit!" Eleanor stopped abruptly. "I forgot to book a second room. I'll go back and -"

"It's fine," Wes said. "There are two beds. It's safer for you if we stay in the same room." He studied the darkness around them before pulling her a little closer. "C'mon, let's get the car parked and get into the room before we're murdered."

She moved the car to their parking spot and popped the trunk. Wes grabbed both of their suitcases and brought them over as she unlocked the door, and they stepped inside. She fumbled for the light switch, her stomach doing a weird flippy thing when she saw the beds. Or rather – bed.

"Where's the other bed?" she said and then winced at how foolish she sounded.

Wes sat the suitcases on the bed. "They must have made a mistake in the room booking."

"I'll call the front desk and get us switched to a room with two beds." Eleanor headed toward the phone, stopping when Wes took her wrist.

"It's fine. I can sleep on the floor."

She scowled at him before pointing at the carpet. "You really want to lie on a carpet that hasn't been cleaned in decades? You'll probably get, I dunno, flesh-eating disease from it."

"Doubtful," he said.

"It'll take me two minutes to call and get the room switched," she said.

"As my mate, you wouldn't demand a room with two beds," he said. "It'll look odd if you do so."

"I'm not your mate," she said as her stomach did that flippy thing again.

"He believes we are. I want it to stay that way." Wes dropped her wrist and walked over to the window. He pulled the curtains closed. "Do you want to order something to eat?"

"Wes, you can't sleep on the floor. Seriously," she said. "It's so gross. I have to call him."

"No, Eleanor." He opened his suitcase. "Are you hungry?"

"I won't call for a different room if you agree to share the bed," she said.

"It's only a double," he said. "I'm not a small guy, Eleanor."

"It's fine. I'm small, and I like to sleep on the edge of the bed, and I don't cuddle," she said. "It'll be fine."

He stared at her, and she said, "I'll put up a pillow barrier. Make your choice, Wes. Pillow barrier or a room with two beds."

"Fine. Pillow barrier," he said.

"Good."

"What do you want to eat?" he said.

"Honestly? I'd rather just have a hot shower and go to bed. I'm exhausted," Eleanor said. "But you go ahead and order some food."

"I can wait until morning to eat," Wes said.

She felt like he was probably lying, but too tired to keep arguing, she grabbed her toiletries and clothes from her suitcase and headed toward the bathroom. She flicked the light. "Oh my God."

"What's wrong?" Wes said.

"The bathroom is actually clean. And the towels look clean too."

"Great. Maybe we won't be infected with the flesh-eating disease after all," Wes said.

She grinned at him before closing the bathroom door and leaning against it. She was about to share a bed with Wes.

She stared at herself in the mirror over the sink. This was fine. Everything was fine. She could share a bed with Wes without trying to coax him into having sex. No problem. No big deal.

ELEANOR HUNG HER DAMP TOWEL ON THE HOOK. SHE smoothed her t-shirt, tugged self-consciously at her shorts, and ran her hand through her wet hair.

Stop stalling and just go out there already.

She stared at her chest. It was apparent she wasn't wearing a bra, but she'd be damned if she put one on to go to bed. She had to wear the torture device all day. She wasn't wearing it all night too. Besides, Wes had made it more than clear that he wouldn't exactly be seducing her tonight. Hell, she'd be lucky if he didn't decide to sleep in the car.

She balled up her dirty clothes, tucked them under her arm, and opened the bathroom door. Wes sat at the small table, staring at his phone, and he didn't look up as she stuffed her clothes into the side pocket of her small suitcase.

She sat cross-legged on the bed, plucking her t-shirt from her chest. "Bathroom's all yours."

"Thanks." Wes grabbed his toiletry bag and clean clothes from his suitcase and disappeared into the bathroom still without looking at her.

She shoved her pillow behind her back and leaned against the headboard. Her stomach growled loudly. Already, she regretted her decision to skip eating in favour of sleep. Especially since she was sure she wouldn't get much sleep, not with Wes lying in bed next to her.

The shower turned on, and she immediately had a vision of a naked Wes in the shower. Not that she knew what a naked Wes looked like, but she could imagine it. Could imagine it in lust rattling detail, as a matter of fact.

She studied the bathroom door. What would Wes do if she popped into the bathroom and offered to wash his back for him?

So, now you want to be arrested for sexual harassment?

Wes wanted her. There was no way a man could kiss a woman like he'd kissed her, no way a man could say the dirty, delicious stuff he'd said to her if he didn't want to have sex with her. He just needed the tiniest push in that direction.

Eleanor, no. You're acting desperate and gross. Wes has made it clear he's not going to sleep with you.

The reminder that Wes had rejected her rather soundly killed her lust. She scrolled through Facebook for about ten minutes before closing the app. She couldn't sit here and listen to Wes in the shower, knowing she'd never see him naked. She wasn't into that kind of mental torture. Feeling sorry for herself, she slid off the bed and rooted through her purse for some money. She'd grab them some food from the vending machine. It was better than nothing.

Holding the cash and the door card key, she stuck her feet into her sandals and left the room. The vending machine was near the office, and she walked past the other first-floor rooms, the warm wind blowing her wet hair back from her face.

She studied the vending machine contents before buying a couple of sodas, two packages of those crackers and fake cheese abominations, and a couple of chocolate bars for dessert.

Eleanor walked back to their room, juggling the drinks, the food, the card key, and change. She stood in front of the door, trying to decide the best way to get the card key to the lock without dropping everything.

The door suddenly whipped open, and she squeaked in surprise, stumbling back when a wild-eyed and dripping wet Wes shouted, "Eleanor!"

"What?" she said. The sodas started to slip, and she squeaked again when Wes pulled her into the room, slamming the door shut. The food and drinks tumbled to the floor, and she stared at him in confusion. "What's wrong?"

"You can't just leave the room like that, Eleanor." Wes's voice was weird. Higher than usual, like it was on the verge of cracking. "Where were you?"

"Getting us some dinner." She pointed to the food on the floor. "Why are you freaking…"

Her voice died in her throat, and her irritation that the soda would probably be too fizzy disappeared.

"Wes," she said.

He ran a hand through his wet hair, pacing with short jerky strides back and forth in front of her. "You can't leave the room without telling me. Do you understand? It's late and dark, and who the fuck knows what type of people are lurking around this place."

"Wes," she said.

"You could have been kidnapped," he said. "Did you think about that possibility? Did you even take your Mace with you?"

"Wes," she said.

"I gave you that Mace for a reason, Eleanor. You're supposed to always carry it with you, not just when you feel like it or when it's convenient for you. Even if you're -"

"WES!"

"What?" He stopped pacing, annoyance on his face and hands on his hips. "What, Eleanor?"

"You're naked."

CHAPTER 9

Wes stared blankly at Eleanor. He'd thought he heard the door close when he was in the shower but told himself Eleanor wouldn't be so crazy to leave the room without him. Still unable to shake the worry that she'd left, he'd quickly finished showering and called her name as soon as he shut off the water. When she hadn't answered, panic had flooded both him and his lion, and his ability to think rationally had been lost. He'd immediately run for the door.

Eleanor's face was flushed, and she stared unabashedly at his dick. His cock hardened, and Eleanor's answering moan and the way her hands clenched into fists sent a rush of need through him.

He backed up a step or two when Eleanor walked toward him. His naked ass hit the wall, and he stared down at Eleanor as she stopped a few inches away from him.

"Eleanor," he said, trying to maintain some semblance of control, "you can't leave the room like that. I was worried, and -"

"Your dick is so pretty," she said. "I want to touch it. May I?"

The purring escaped before he could stop it. A soft smile crossed Eleanor's face. "Is that a yes?"

"We can't do this," he said.

"Yes, we can."

"We shouldn't do this," he said.

"Shouldn't and can't are two very different things, Wes." She placed her soft hand on his stomach, her fingernails tracing just above his navel. "See how easy this is? I can touch you without any effort."

He moaned, trying to keep his hips still when those beautiful fingers of her touched the dark hair just above his cock. "Please may I touch you, Wes?"

"Yes," he rasped. "Touch me, Butterfly."

Her hand wrapped around his dick and rubbed with long, firm strokes that sent pleasure rocketing through every part of his body. His purring increased in volume as his hips rocked against her.

Her smile grew big. "I love the sound of your purring."

He cupped the back of her head, threading his fingers through her damp hair and pulling her forward until their lips met. He kissed her hard, demanding entrance immediately, groaning when she parted her lips and let him in. She tasted so fucking good. He angled his mouth over hers and slid his tongue deep into her mouth, asking for her total surrender.

Kissing her, touching her, had consumed his thoughts for what felt like decades. As she pumped him with a slow rhythm, he cupped both her breasts and ran his thumbs over her nipples. He growled at how hard they were and pulled free of Eleanor's mouth.

"Don't stop," she said. "I want more kisses, Wes."

He purred to her and tugged at the hem of her shirt. "Show me your pretty tits, and then I'll kiss you."

She let go of his dick, and he tugged her shirt over her

head and tossed it on the bed. He was momentarily distracted by the sutures in her arm. He pressed gentle kisses against them. "How does your arm feel?"

"Better. The pain meds have kicked in and it barely hurts now," she said. "I'm showing you the girls, live up to your end of the deal, mister."

He laughed and gave her a fleeting teasing kiss before dropping his gaze to her chest. He stared at her perfect breasts, their nipples a dusty pink colour and as hard as pearls. She made a startled yelp when he picked her up and carried her over to the bed, dropping her onto it before pushing her thighs apart and kneeling between them.

"Beautiful," he said and then purred to her before he bent his head and kissed between her breasts. Her hands clutched at his wet hair, and she moaned when he nipped at the underside of one breast before circling her nipple with his tongue.

"Wes," she moaned, "please."

He kissed the tip of her nipple then laved at it with his tongue. Her hips bucked, and he ground his cock against her fabric-covered core before sucking hard on her nipple. Her skin was silky soft, and he teased her nipple with his tongue and lips as he plucked gently at the other with his finger and thumb.

Her soft cries and moans of need set his veins on fire with lust, and he purred to her again before kissing her. She sucked eagerly at his tongue, making a small cry of protest when he pulled back and then kissed and nipped his way down the column of her throat.

Wes! What are you doing? You can't do this. It's not right. You know it isn't.

He ignored his inner voice. What the fuck did it know anyway? He wanted Eleanor, and she wanted him. He was tired of denying what they both wanted.

"Butterfly," he licked the hollow of her throat, "I'm going to eat your pussy until you come on my face, and then you're going to ride my dick."

"Sure, yeah, okay. Sounds like a neat plan," Eleanor moaned.

He laughed and nipped at her collarbone. "Neat?"

She cried out, rubbing herself furiously against his cock when he sucked hard on her nipple. "Fuck, I can't think straight when you do that, Wes."

"You don't need to think, Butterfly," he said. "Just let me make you feel good, okay?"

"A-okay," she panted.

He smiled and kissed his way down her body, taking his time tasting the smooth, silky skin of her stomach before he tugged on the waistband of her shorts with his teeth. He curled his fingers around the waistband. "Lift your hips."

She lifted her hips just as something loud and heavy hit the wall to the left of the bed. Eleanor made a startled cry when there was another heavy thud, and the piece of nondescript art hanging on their side of the wall fell off, and the glass exploded with a jagged cough.

"What the hell?" Eleanor said as Wes stood and the muffled sounds of two men screaming at each other drifted through the wall. Another hard thud and Eleanor cringed when the drywall cracked.

"Stay here," Wes said. He threw on his jeans and shoved his feet into his shoes as Eleanor sat up, her arms crossed over her naked breasts.

"Wes, maybe we should call the hotel clerk?"

Wes shook his head as he grabbed the card key off the floor next to the forgotten food. "He's useless."

The screaming grew louder, and Eleanor slid off the bed.

"It's too dangerous. What if they have guns or are shifters or -"

"Stay in the room, Butterfly. I'll be right back." His balls aching and his temper flaring, Wes left the room.

"I don't want you ever doing that again." Eleanor glared at Wes when he returned to the room nearly ten minutes later. "Do you know how ridiculously dangerous that was? What if they had guns?"

"They didn't," he said. "I spoke with them, and they'll be quiet from now on." He avoided looking at her as he set the card key on the table and double-checked the locked door. She decided his refusal to look at her didn't bode well for them picking up where they left off.

She held out her hand. "Come back to the bed."

"Eleanor, I can't," he said. "Not until you put on a shirt."

He stared resolutely at the wall. She sighed and said, "You didn't seem to mind ten minutes ago."

"That was a -"

"Don't you dare say I was a mistake, Wes," Eleanor said.

"You're not a mistake." He raked his hands through his hair and glanced at her. A pained expression crossed his face. "Butterfly, please. Put on a shirt."

She relented at the real agony in his voice and tugged the shirt over her head.

"You're not a mistake," he repeated. "But what we're doing isn't right. I'm," he swallowed hard, "old enough to be your father for fuck's sake."

"Barely," she said. "I have never and will never look at you in that way, Wes. Don't insult me by pretending that I do."

"Your relationship with your father wasn't great. Naturally, older men would be a -"

"Are you fucking kidding me?" Eleanor planted her hands on her hips as hot anger surged over her skin. "Why is it that when men fail as fathers, when they do everything fucking wrong and can't be bothered to be there for the daughter they helped create, the woman is treated like there's something wrong with her? That she's the one with the issues – fucking *daddy issues* – when she hasn't done a single goddamn thing wrong? Don't stand there and tell me I have daddy issues because my father was a piece-of-shit dad, Wes. It is not my fault that he was a bad father, and I'm not into older men because of it. I'm into you because, up until this fucking moment, you seemed to be one of the good guys. I didn't give a fuck how old you were. I just liked you for who you are."

"Shit," Wes said. "You're right. You're absolutely right, and it was a real dick thing for me to say. I apologize for implying you have daddy issues."

Her anger faded at the sincerity in his voice and face. She blew out her breath. "Look, I get that this feels weird to you, but I swear the age thing is no big deal, okay?"

"It isn't just that," he said.

"Then what is it?" she said.

"You're looking for a relationship," he said. "I'm not."

Fuck, why had she admitted that to him? She could punch herself right in her big mouth. "Okay, but that doesn't mean I wouldn't be up for some casual sex with you."

"In the hopes that it would turn into something more?" he asked.

"No," she said.

He didn't reply. Her stomach heaving around like a hurricane, she said, "Look, I already know I'm not relationship material and that I drive you crazy, but -"

"The men you dated were the issue, not you," Wes said. "Don't let them convince you that you wouldn't be great in a relationship. You're sweet and kind and funny, and you don't hold anything back. That's a good thing, Eleanor."

"See, you say all these sweet things but then straight up say you won't date me," Eleanor said.

"You're too young for me. This age gap means we're at different stages in our lives, and dating me would be a waste of time for you," Wes said.

"Then we keep it casual," she said. "I'm good with casual sex."

"No, you're not," he said.

"Stop it," she snapped. "Don't act like you know me better than I know myself just because I happened to tell you that I'm looking for a relationship. I can have casual sex with you while still dating and looking for Mr. Right."

He growled, his pupils turning to slits and the blue becoming yellow in a heartbeat. She stared fascinated at him until he finished talking to his lion and returned to her.

"What did your lion say?" she asked when his pupils rounded.

"He doesn't like to share, and neither do I… not when it's our mate, not when it's a casual sex partner," Wes said. "If you're fucking me, you're not fucking anyone else."

Her cursedly short temper burst at the seams. "That's not how casual sex works with someone, Wesley."

"It's how it works with me," he said. "Which is why you and me fucking is a waste of time for both of us."

"Well, I guess it's a good job we're not fucking then. Now I can get on with finding my mate."

Wes growled again, and she put her fists on her hips. "Stop growling at me. I'm not afraid of you."

"I don't want you to be afraid of me," he bit out.

"Good, because I'm not." She climbed into the bed and shut off the bedside table lamp, plunging the room into darkness. She yanked the covers to her chin and turned on her side, away from the pillow barrier. "Make sure you stay on your side of the pillow barrier. My interest in fucking you has dropped to 'never gonna happen in a million fucking years'."

Wes didn't reply, and she busied herself punching her pillow into a more comfortable position as she listened to him unzip his jeans and take off his shirt before he climbed into his side of the bed.

She didn't care that he was mostly naked and within touching distance, she told herself grouchily. Wes Masters was a jerk, and she had no interest in sleeping with him. Ever.

Keep telling yourself that. Maybe eventually, you'll believe it.

She told inner Eleanor to shut the hell up before closing her eyes. She was exhausted, and she needed to stop thinking about Wes and get some sleep. Once they returned home, she'd simply tell him she was no longer available to be his driver, and she'd never have to see his stupid gorgeous face again.

ELEANOR'S DECLARATION THAT SHE DIDN'T LIKE TO CUDDLE was complete bullshit. Wes knew it was bullshit because not only had Eleanor breached the pillow barrier ten minutes after she fell asleep, but she'd plastered herself to his back like a baby koala to its mother.

Not that he minded being the little spoon to Eleanor's big spoon. In fact, despite how things had ended with Eleanor last night, and despite being in a murder motel with two unstable humans right next door, he'd slept better last night than he had since the day Derek died.

The soft warmth of Eleanor against him, the low sound of her adorable snoring, and the touch of her palm against his chest soothed him and his lion, and he'd fallen asleep in less than half an hour.

He reached carefully for his phone, trying not to disturb Eleanor because she needed her sleep, not because he wanted her body against his for even a little longer, and checked the time. Shit, it was almost nine. He hadn't slept in this late in years.

He settled back against the pillow, staring at the light filtering in through the crack in the drapes, ignoring his morning wood and his temptation to wake Eleanor up by burying his face between her thighs.

Goosebumps skittered to life when Eleanor stretched and then buried her face between his shoulder blades. Her hand rubbed lazy circles across his flat abdomen, and precum dripped from his cock. Fuck, she was killing him.

"Eleanor, wake up," he said.

"Mmm." She made a muffled noise against his back as her finger circled his navel before tracing the waistband of his briefs. "I'm awake. Let's have a quickie before I go to work."

He cleared his throat. "Eleanor, time to wake up."

She stretched again before tugging playfully at his waist-band. "C'mon, handsome, don't you want a.... oh crap."

She pushed away from him like he was on fire and sat up in the bed, shoving her hair away from her face as he eased into a sitting position.

"You broke the pillow barrier to cuddle," she said with an accusing look as she rubbed gingerly around the sutures in her arm.

"It wasn't me. You did," he said.

"I did not. I hate cuddling, and I certainly wouldn't cuddle with you, not after…"

Wes's face flushed as Eleanor's voice died out, and she stared at the way his cock tented the quilt. Her cheeks were red, and when she glanced up at him with a hungry look that made his lion purr, Wes slid out of bed in a hurry.

Evelyn looked away as Wes grabbed his clothes and headed toward the bathroom. "It's almost nine. We need to get going."

CHAPTER 10

Evelyn stared with real apprehension at the locker in front of her. They were at the last bus station on her list. If this wasn't the locker, she'd have to widen her search to the rest of the bus stations in the city and be stuck here another night at the very least. Her rapidly dwindling savings account would only give her one more night in a motel, so she needed to find the right locker today or tomorrow.

"You okay?" Wes stood close, his big body comforting her rather than crowding her.

They hadn't talked much this morning, which, frankly, was killing her because even when she was kind of pissed at him, she still loved the sound of his voice.

"Yeah. Just hoping this is the right one," she said.

Wes scanned the people around them. "Only one way to find out."

Her hand shaking slightly, she stuck the key in the lock and turned it, expecting the same resistance as all the other locks she'd tried. When it turned smoothly, she said, "Holy shit. This is the one."

She grinned at Wes. "This is the one!"

He returned her smile, the relief on his face mirroring hers. "Great. Open it up, Butterfly."

She opened the locker, grabbed the manilla envelope in it, and shut the locker. Before she could open the envelope, Wes took her hand. "Not here. We'll open it in the car."

She followed him out of the bus station, clutching the envelope to her chest as she stared suspiciously at the people around them. No one gave them a second look, but she didn't take a deep breath until they were in her car with the doors locked.

She tore open the envelope and slid the contents out into Wes's cupped hands. A silver flash drive and a small rectangular video tape.

"What the hell is this?" Eleanor picked up the video tape. It reminded her of the old VHS tapes she'd seen in pawn shops, but it was much smaller.

"It's a video tape," Wes said. "It's how us old folks used to watch movies. Be kind, please rewind, and all that shit."

She scowled at him. "Call yourself old again, and I'll make you walk back to Bridgedale. I realize this is a video tape, but I've never seen such a small one before. This wouldn't fit in a VCR."

"It's camcorder video tape," Wes said. "Before cell phones, people had to use video cameras to record themselves doing stupid shit. These cassettes fit in the camcorders. Your dad must have recorded something with a camcorder. Did he not have a cell phone?"

"He did, and he used it. He was good with technology." Eleanor ran her finger along the front of the video cassette. "I don't remember Mom or Dad using anything but a cell phone to record stuff."

"Well, we'll either need to have it digitized into a new format or find a camcorder to watch it," Wes said.

"It might not be anything to do with why someone tried to kill me," Eleanor said. "For all I know, it's just, like, a home-made porno starring Dad and some random chick. Ugh."

"Maybe, but I don't think the same can be said about this." He held up the flash drive.

"Agreed." Eleanor slid the cassette and the flash drive back into the envelope and set it on the back seat. She buckled her seat belt and checked the time. "I know it's close to lunch, but are you good with just hitting a drive-thru or something? I want to get back home as soon as possible."

"That's fine with me," Wes said.

As she drove out of the bus station, Wes said, "I want to apologize again for last night, Eleanor."

"It's fine," she said. "I'm sorry too. It sucks that we fought, but at least we both know where we stand now, right? We can go back to being friends."

"Right," he said.

"Great," she said with a cheeriness she didn't feel. "I'm glad we're friends, Wes."

He made a half-nod and stared out the passenger window.

WES STARED WORRIEDLY AT ELEANOR AS SHE PARKED IN front of his house, leaned her head against the headrest, and closed her eyes. Even in the dim light from the streetlights, he could see the dark circles under her eyes and the pinched look of exhaustion on her face.

As if she sensed his worry, she smiled without opening her eyes and said, "I'm fine, Wes. Don't be a worrywart."

"You're not fine. You're worn out," he said.

"Man, that was some delay, huh?" She glanced at the

clock on the dashboard. It was nearly one in the morning. "Almost five extra hours to get home."

"It was a bad accident," Wes said.

"Yeah." She rubbed at her forehead. "It's a miracle no one died. That car was crunched like an accordion."

They sat in silence for a few seconds before Eleanor cleared her throat. "Anyway, thanks for coming with me. I really appreciate it." She gave him a 'get out of my car now, please' smile.

"You're welcome. Will you text me when you get to Cooper's?"

"Yeah, sure, of course." She suddenly found something very interesting to look at on the car's dashboard.

"Eleanor," he said. "You can't go back home. It isn't safe."

"I can't go to Cooper's," she said. "It's super late, and I don't have a key, and I'm not waking Cooper and Daisy at one in the morning to let me into their house. And before you ask, no, I can't afford another night in a motel, not even a murder one. So, my choices are sleeping in my car or sleeping in my bed with a baseball bat. I'm going with the bunking with a baseball bat option."

"You can stay at my house tonight," Wes said.

His lion growled his approval as Eleanor stared at him in surprise. "There's no way you're letting me into your house, Wes."

"Why wouldn't I?" he said.

"Oh, I don't know… maybe because you flinch whenever I get close to you? You think I'll try to fuck you without your permission."

He scowled. "I don't think that. And I don't flinch when you're close to me."

She reached for his leg, and he shifted away on impulse. Eleanor sighed, and his lion called him an idiot.

"I hate that you're afraid of me," Eleanor said.

He couldn't help but laugh. "I'm not afraid of you, Butterfly."

"Hey, I can be scary. I have a pocketknife, and I never shut up. One of those things always scares men away."

"It has nothing to do with you and everything to do with me," Wes said. "It's my lack of control that scares me."

Eleanor stared at him. "You really wanna fuck me, huh?"

"Yeah, I really do," he said. "C'mon, let's get in the house. I have a guest bedroom you can use."

He opened the car door and stepped out, first inhaling deeply and then scanning the darkness for any sign of the man who'd attacked Eleanor earlier. There was no sign or smell of him, and Wes grabbed their bags from the trunk. Eleanor followed him up the sidewalk, and he unlocked the door and ushered her inside.

She toed off her shoes as he set their bags down and flipped on the lights. She walked down the narrow hallway that opened up into the living room and kitchen. "This is lovely, Wes. I like open-concept homes."

"Thanks," he said. "The living space and kitchen used to be separate, but me and Boone tore down the wall a few years ago when we remodeled the kitchen."

"Ooh, I love me a handy guy," she said. "You should give me Boone's number."

The growl slipped out before he could stop it, and she grinned teasingly at him. "Kidding, big guy. You know you're the only handyman I want to fuck."

His purring was so loud, it was embarrassing. But it made the pinched look disappear from Eleanor's face, so it was worth it.

"Do you have a laptop I can borrow?" Eleanor said. "I want to see what's on the flash drive."

"Yes, but we can check it in the morning if you're too tired," Wes said.

"I'd rather look at it now. If I don't, I'll just lie awake all night wondering what's on it."

"Okay. Follow me." Wes headed down the hallway just off the kitchen, opening the first door on the left.

"Combination office and workout room. I like it," Eleanor said as she studied the bookshelf stuffed full of books and the small desk on the right side of the room. The left side had a heavy bag hung from the ceiling, a small rack of free weights, and an exercise bike.

"Thanks," Wes said as he opened the laptop sitting on the desk. He punched in his password and pulled out the chair. "All yours."

"Thank you." She sank into the chair and plugged the flash drive into the computer before glancing at the book-shelf. "I read a lot too. Almost two books a week."

"My record is five books in three days," Wes said.

"Show off," she said with a grin before turning back to the computer screen. "Okay, let's see what this is."

She opened up the flash drive folder. There was a single pdf document labeled with her father's name, and she double-clicked the document. "Man, I hope you have a good virus protection program. My dad doesn't seem like the type to infect a document with a virus, but I don't know him that well. Or maybe a computer virus is what they're after. Maybe this thing is going to, like, take down the city's power grid through your computer or -"

She closed her mouth with a snap and said, "Sorry, Wes."

"For what?" he said.

"I'm yammering away like I always do."

"I don't mind," he said.

She studied him. "You actually don't. Do you?"

Before he could reply, the document opened. He leaned over her shoulder to study it, his lion purring happily at Eleanor's scent and the light touch of her shoulder against his chest.

They looked at the document in silence for a few minutes before Eleanor stared up at him. "It's a formula, right?"

"Yes, I think so," he said.

"But a formula for what?" Eleanor scrolled through the document, but there were no clues to what it was for, just, as far as Wes could tell, the formula itself.

"What did you say your dad did for a living?" Wes asked.

"He's a biochemist." Eleanor read through the formula again. "The last time we spoke, he said he was working for a company that studied the effects that a certain medication had on DNA. Maybe this has something to do with that? Like, maybe they found out the meds are killing us or something, and that's why the bad guys are after this? Maybe this formula proves the medication is deadly?"

"Maybe," Wes said. "But I don't even know what half these words mean."

"Ditto," Eleanor said. She sat back in the chair, tugging thoughtfully at her bottom lip, making Wes's cock stiffen and his desire to take Eleanor directly to his bed increase tenfold.

Too busy picturing exactly how Eleanor would look naked in his bed with her legs spread wide and her hands buried in his hair while he ate her out, he didn't pay attention when she spoke.

Maybe he should ask her if she wanted her pretty pussy eaten. It would help her sleep, right? She was tired but also on edge, and an orgasm would be just the thing to -

"Wes? Hey, are you falling asleep on me?"

He took a deep breath, shoving his need for Eleanor to the back of his brain. "No, sorry. What did you say?"

"I asked if you knew any other biochemists who could tell us what the formula is."

"I don't."

"Me neither," she said before yawning. Wes straightened and moved away as she closed the document and removed the flash drive.

"Here, give me the flash drive," he said.

She handed it over, and he crossed the room to a painting that hung on the wall. He took it down and grinned a little at Eleanor's soft squeal of excitement. "Oh my God, you have a secret wall safe. That's so cool."

She joined him at the safe as he entered the combination on the keypad.

"I didn't look," she said as the safe clicked open.

"What do you mean?" he said.

"At the password. I looked away, so you don't have to worry about me breaking into the safe or -"

"The password is 6411," Wes said as he pulled open the safe door. "I trust you, Eleanor."

"Thanks, Wes, that means a lot… holy shit." Her voice turned uncharacteristically quiet as she studied the stacks of cash in the safe. "That's a lot of money."

He set the flash drive next to his passport before closing the safe and replacing the painting.

"Are you a millionaire, Wes?" she said.

"It's only about seventy-five grand," he said.

"Only," she snorted. "Do you know what I could do with seventy-five grand?"

"What would you do with it?" he said.

"I would… well, I could go on a nice vacation," she said.

"Somewhere warm with a beach with white sand and turquoise-coloured water. Doesn't that sound nice?"

"It does," he said. "Have you travelled much, Eleanor?"

"Nope," she said. "I've never even been out of the country. I want to travel, I'm confident I would love it, but anytime I've saved up enough to travel, something happens – my car needs repairs, or I need my appendix removed, and my insurance doesn't cover all the hospital bills. Just life, you know?"

He nodded, and she smiled at him. "How about you? Do you like to travel?"

"I do. I've been fortunate to see a lot of the world."

"Probably some pretty nice beaches, huh?"

He nodded, and she smiled wistfully. "I'm going to make it happen one day. I mean, have you even lived if you haven't gone swimming in turquoise-coloured water?"

He purred to her, and her smile widened. "I really like your purring. It's nice."

He wanted to kiss her. He wanted to pick her up, take her to his bed, and hold her in his arms while she slept. His lion agreed wholeheartedly with him, but Wes took a step back and cleared his throat. "It's late. I'll show you the guest room so you can get some sleep."

"Yeah, okay." That soft smile still on her face, Eleanor followed him out of the office.

CHAPTER 11

"Alfie, I swear to God, if you shit in the house one more time, I'm gonna make you into a mincemeat pie, you little asshole."

The miniature poodle stared up at Boone before turning and trotting down the hallway toward Nan's bedroom.

"I mean it, you little shit!" Boone called. "Mincemeat pie!"

"Stop threatening Alfie," his grandmother hollered. "Or I'll tell him to poop in your shoe."

"He already pooped in my shoe!" Boone said. "Twice!"

His grandmother laughed, and Boone muttered a curse under his breath before finishing loading the dishwasher. Chase's cousin was due to arrive any minute for the interview, and while he didn't hold out any hope that she'd last more than a day with his grandmother, he didn't have much choice. Apparently, the local private nurses in the city had a network, and the word was out about his grandmother. He couldn't get a single one to even interview with him.

Panic stirred at his insides, and his tiger paced restlessly back and forth. While Cooper was a great boss and hadn't said a word about all the work Boone had missed, he couldn't take the next six weeks off while his grandmother healed. He didn't have that much vacation time, and he'd be screwing over Coop and the rest of the team even if he could take off the entire six weeks. More panic churned his guts. He loved his nan, but he also loved his job and didn't want to lose it.

He wiped down the counters and set a fresh pot of coffee to brew. If this Hedra chick could last even a couple of days, that would give Boone time to contact some private nurses outside of the city.

It's not gonna work, his tiger grumbled. *She's a human. Nan will eat her alive.*

She has a shifter father. She's human, but she has some shifter in her. It'll be fine, Boone replied.

Boone thought he sounded confident enough, but it wasn't like he could lie to his tiger. The damn thing could feel his anxiety, and it only heightened his tiger's nervousness.

The doorbell rang, prompting Alfie to break out into a chorus of high-pitched barking that made Boone want to stick a fork in his ear. He took a deep breath and smoothed back his dark hair. He caught a glimpse of himself in the mirror in the hallway. Fuck, he needed a haircut and a shave in the worse way. At least his t-shirt and jeans were clean. That was a minor miracle as of late.

This is a bad idea, his tiger growled as Boone reached for the door. *She's human.*

She has some shifter in her, Boone repeated and opened the door.

He stared at the human standing on the doorstep. His tiger took one look and then sat up and trilled happily. *Ask her if she wants a little more shifter in her. Ask her!*

Shut up, you idiot! Boone couldn't take his eyes off the woman. She had bright blue shoulder-length hair and dark

118

brown eyes framed by long lashes. A smattering of freckles crossed the bridge of her perfect nose, and her septum piercing had a tiny blue opal in the middle of the silver ring. His gaze lingered on her mouth before moving to her body. She was curvy with gorgeous smooth skin, and even the loose scrub top she wore couldn't disguise the fullness of her breasts. He could easily imagine cupping those lush tits of hers while her soft body made the perfect cushion for his.

One perfectly painted fingernail tapped him on the forehead. He jerked his head up, tearing his gaze from her beautiful tits as his face turned bright red. Holy fuck, he had just ogled his potential new employee like a gross pervert.

"Boone Jameson?" the woman said.

"Yes. I'm sorry, I didn't mean to, uh…" Fuck. Why couldn't he stop staring at her lips?

Because they would look incredible wrapped around your dick?

His inner voice was not fucking helping.

"I'm used to it," she said. "My tits are pretty awesome. Although, if you're going to drool on them every time you see me, we should probably not bother with the interview."

"Sorry," he said again as he stared directly into her pretty brown eyes. "I'm not usually, I mean… I have no excuse beyond that was incredibly rude, and it won't happen again."

She grinned at him and held out her hand. "Let's start over. I'm Hedra Miller."

He shook her hand, his tiger purring like a kitten at the feel of her soft skin. "Boone Jameson. It's nice to meet you."

"You as well."

"Please come in." Feeling like the world's biggest idiot, he stepped back so Hedra could come inside. She followed him to the kitchen, and he pointed to the closest chair. "Please, have a seat. Would you like a coffee?"

"Sure, thank you."

He poured them both a coffee and set the sugar and creamer set on the table.

She studied the delicate bone china set decorated with light pink flowers. "This doesn't seem like something a bachelor would own."

"It's my nan's," he said. "She insisted I bring over a few things from her house to make her feel more at home."

"Ah," she said as she poured some creamer into her coffee. "So, is your grandmother living with you permanently now, or just while she heals?"

"Just while she heals. She doesn't have a downstairs bedroom or full bathroom at her house, which is why she's staying with me."

"It's a nice place." Hedra sipped at her coffee and studied the kitchen. "I like the backsplash tile."

"Thanks," Boone said as his tiger purred like an idiot. "I did it myself."

"Chase mentioned you were good with home repairs and stuff like that. He said you renovated your place and a co-worker's house."

"I enjoy working with my hands," he said. "It's a fun side hobby."

"Right," she said.

Holy fuckballs. Why are you being such an idiot? His tiger growled so loudly, it nearly deafened Boone.

I'm not being an idiot. Just shut up and let me talk to her.

His tiger growled again. *She'll never mate with us if you keep talking. Let me speak to her. I'll convince her to fuck us.*

His tiger made a push for control, and Boone shoved him back. *Are you kidding me? I'm already lucky she's even agreeing to the interview after the way I leered at her. You are not asking her to fuck us.*

His tiger sulked like a little kid but retreated. Boone cleared his throat, smiling uncomfortably at Hedra. "Uh, sorry about that."

"It's fine. Chase says your tiger is a talker."

"What else has Chase told you about me?" he said.

"Not much," she said.

Was she lying? He didn't know her well enough to tell.

She reached into her oversized bag and pulled out her resume, setting it on the table in front of Boone. He scanned it quickly as she drank some coffee.

"So, you worked at Saint Mary's Hospital for five years," he said. "But your preference is not to work in a hospital here?"

"My favourite part of being a nurse is helping people on a more one-on-one basis," she said with the air of someone who'd practiced the speech. "In a busy hospital, that can be almost impossible. I decided becoming a private nurse was better suited to my skill sets."

"What made you decide to move here?" Boone asked. He didn't need to know that detail, but his tiger was already fascinated with the little human and pushing Boone for every bit of information he could get.

"I needed a change," she said.

He waited for her to elaborate, and when she didn't, he decided it was best to get right to the point. "My grandmother can be… difficult."

"I've heard," she said.

"Most of her private nurses have quit within twelve hours."

Are you crazy? Stop telling her that. You'll scare her away! His tiger was nearly apoplectic with rage.

"I like a challenge," Hedra said.

"She's not," Boone paused as his tiger snarled at him,

"fond of humans. And she can have a barbed tongue from time to time."

Hedra's smile could have dimmed the sun. He stared in fascination at her full lips and straight white teeth, his heart thumping away like he'd just run up ten flights of stairs and his cock stiffening against his jeans.

"I don't scare easily. I have four older cheetah siblings and, trust me, your grandmother won't say anything to me that my siblings haven't already said," Hedra said.

"She has a good heart, and she's fiercely loyal to the people she loves," Boone said. "She's just also a bit… grumpy."

Hedra's smile turned into a laugh, and Boone's tiger trilled a mating call. Boone swallowed the sound before it could escape.

Have you lost your fucking mind? We are not mating with her.

His tiger sulked worse than Alfie did when Boone wouldn't give him another of those disgusting fake pepperoni treats.

"Is she a tiger shifter like you?" Hedra asked.

Boone nodded. "She rarely shifts anymore, and she hasn't shifted at all since the accident. But she can still extend her claws when she's pissed off."

"Slashy with claws when angry… noted," Hedra said.

"She won't hurt you," Boone hastened to say. "Well, not with her claws. Her words though…"

"Sticks and stones may break my bones and all that," Hedra said before taking another swallow of coffee. "Chase mentioned you were looking for someone to start right away and that your preference is for a live-in nurse."

"Yes," he said. "My hours can be long at the security firm and don't always follow a strict nine to five schedule. So, you'd be required to be on call outside of the regular eight hours during the week. That being said, I've talked to Coop about working some of our more straightforward security work for the next six weeks, so overtime should be minimal. And I won't require you to work weekends."

"Straight forward security, huh?" Hedra eyed him over her coffee cup. "Sounds kind of boring. Chase says you're usually the first to volunteer for the more dangerous stuff."

She knows how brave I am. His tiger strutted around like a rock star.

He made a non-committal sound. Doing the stupid shit like mall security *would* be boring as hell, but what choice did he have? Even if – and this was a very big if – his nan didn't scare Hedra away in the next few hours, the less time she actually had to take care of his nan, the better. Working the boring shit meant he'd be around to help Nan in the evenings and on the weekends.

Hedra studied him silently, and feeling a little stupid, he said, "I offer twenty-five dollars an hour plus room and board. You'd have your own bedroom next to Nan's. It's on the smaller side, but it has a connected bathroom you'd share with Nan. You're welcome to whatever food is in the house, and I'm happy to shop for any special dietary requirements you might have. You will be required to make Nan breakfast and lunch. Are you good with that?"

"Yes," she said.

"She can be picky about what she eats, but I try to encourage her to eat as many vegetables as possible. She prefers a carnivore diet, but her human side needs the greens."

"I've got shifter nieces and nephews. I'm used to hiding veggies in meat smoothies," Hedra said.

Boone laughed. "Perfect. So, the next step would be to

123

meet Nan. If that goes well and you're still interested in the position, it will start, well… immediately if that works."

"It does," Hedra said. "I checked out of my hotel this morning."

At the look on his face, which he imagined practically screamed, "not a great idea", Hedra said, "Sorry, I'm being too presumptuous. I'm not expecting or assuming you'll hire me. I'll find another hotel to stay in if your grandmother doesn't like me."

"Oh, she's not going to like you," Boone said and then winced. "Shit, that came out wrong."

Hedra laughed. "Did it, though?"

"No," he admitted. "Nan won't like you. But the job is yours if after you meet her, you don't run screaming from the house."

"I'm not much of a screamer," Hedra said.

The dirty part of his mind, which frankly made up about ninety percent, immediately set to wondering just what he could do to Hedra to make her scream his name in bed. He'd start with pussy eating and go from there, he decided. He bet she tasted delicious. He bet she –

He forced his head back into the game. Despite what Hedra said, he doubted she'd last even a day with his grand-mother, and besides, sleeping with the woman he hired to look after Nan would be a huge mistake.

His tiger growled in disagreement. Boone stood and said, "Okay, ready to meet Nan?"

"I'm girding my loins as we speak," Hedra said.

Boone laughed but paused in the doorway. Hedra stared expectantly at him, and when he didn't move, she said, "What's wrong?"

"I feel like I'm leading the lamb to the slaughter," he said.

She laughed. "I'm a lot tougher than I look."

At his look of disbelief, she laughed again and said, "If my family could hear you calling me a lamb, they'd die laughing. Once you get to know me, you won't ever think of me as a lamb again, I promise."

Leaving her purse in the kitchen, Hedra followed him down the hall toward Nan's bedroom. Boone glanced back at her. "You're not allergic to dogs, are you? Nan has a miniature poodle. They're supposed to be hypo-allergenic, but I'm not sure that isn't just a bunch of bullshit."

"Not allergic, and I love dogs," she said. "Although poodles are my second least favourite dog breed."

"What's your first least favourite?" he said.

"Schnauzer."

"Why?" he said.

"They look like the type of guy who would shiv you for a pack of cigarettes from the prison canteen."

He laughed again before knocking on his nan's half-open door. "Nan? I have someone I want you to meet."

He pushed the door open and stepped into the room. His stomach churned and sweat dampened the back of his shirt. If Hedra took offense to his nan and refused to be her nurse, he was well on his way to being totally fucked.

Saying a silent prayer that his grandmother would just once be nice, he said, "Nan, this is Hedra Miller. Hedra, this is my grandmother Althea Jameson."

"Hello, Mrs. Jameson. It's nice to meet you." Hedra walked fearlessly to the bed and held out her hand.

His grandmother sniffed deeply. "You're human. I don't like humans."

"So I've heard," Hedra said.

Nan studied Hedra's hair and the piercing in her nose before peering around her at Boone. "She'd better not be my new nurse."

"Worse," Hedra said. "I'm his new girlfriend."

Boone's mouth dropped open as a startled growl escaped his grandmother's mouth. She stared wide-eyed at Hedra as Alfie, who was lying next to his grandmother on the bed, stood and cocked his head.

"Just kidding," Hedra said. "I'm not dating your grandson, but I am your new nurse."

"You're not boning my grandson?" Nan said.

"Nan!" Boone could feel the blush rising up his neck.

"Nope," Hedra said. "This is currently a boning free zone." She waved her hand back and forth in a half-circle in front of herself.

"Thank God," Nan muttered.

"See?" Hedra said. "Compared to the alternative of me boning your grandson on the regular, me being your nurse isn't that bad after all, is it?"

"I don't like humans," Nan repeated.

"I heard you the first time," Hedra said with a cheerful grin.

Alfie stalked toward her in that stiff-legged way dogs had when they were getting ready to bite or tell you off. He sniffed in Hedra's direction, and a low growl drifted from his throat. Boone groaned inwardly. The little shit was about to start barking his head off and wouldn't stop until he'd driven Hedra from the room.

Boone jerked when Hedra stared at Alfie and did a remarkably accurate imitation of a cheetah's growl. Alfie froze in place, staring uncertainly at Hedra. She growled again and bared her teeth at the poodle. He whimpered and scampered back to the safety of Nan, huddling against her side and staring silently at Hedra.

"Alfie thinks you smell," Nan said. "I think you smell too."

"You don't smell that great yourself, sweetheart," Hedra said with a grin.

His grandmother bristled, glaring at Hedra before growling. "Well, you can hardly expect me to ask my grandson to help me shower. And I certainly wasn't letting the nurses at the hospital help me. They went through my things while I showered."

"They didn't go through your stuff, Nan," Boone said.

"I could smell their gross human scent on my phone and my purse, Boone," Nan said.

"Well, let's get you in the shower now," Hedra said.

To Boone's complete shock, his grandmother sniffed and said, "Fine. But only because I have a birthday party to attend this evening and I'd like to look and smell my best."

She peered around Hedra. "You may leave, Boone."

Boone hesitated, and his grandmother rolled her eyes. "For heaven's sake, Boone, I'm not going to attack the girl in the shower. Go on back to the kitchen."

Boone glanced at Hedra, who smiled cheerfully. "We're good."

A glimmer of hope rising in his chest, Boone left the bedroom.

CHAPTER 12

"Oh my God, Wes, I'm sorry. I can't believe I slept so long." Eleanor plopped down into a kitchen chair and smoothed her damp hair self-consciously. She'd remembered to bring toiletries but not her blow dryer, and she wasn't exactly rocking the soaked rat look.

"It was a long day yesterday, and you needed your rest. Besides, it's not that late." Wes closed the dishwasher door.

"It's twelve-thirty," Eleanor said. "The shower in your guest bathroom is amazing, by the way. I think I tried every setting on the showerhead."

"Do you drink coffee?" Wes said.

"I am an enormous fan of the bitter bean juice," Eleanor said.

Wes laughed and grabbed a mug from the cupboard. "Do you take sugar and milk?"

"Just sugar, thank you."

Wes popped the coffee pod into the machine and set the sugar on the table. "You good with sandwiches for lunch?"

"Yes, but you don't have to feed me or make me meals," Eleanor said as she took her phone out of her pocket.

The coffee finished brewing, and he placed it in front of her. "I want to. Did you cancel your clients for the weekend?"

"Just trying to do it now, but my phone is being weird." Her annoyance over her phone wasn't enough to dim her rush of lust when Wes leaned over her to stare at her phone screen. God, did he smell good.

Wes stiffened and then made a weird sound that was half trill and half purr. His eyes turned golden, and the pupils narrowed to slits. He smiled at her, and the sight of his fangs brought a weird twinge of pleasure to her pussy.

"Hello, sweet human," Wes's voice was deeper, and a bit gargled. She swallowed hard when he purred to her.

"Um, hi," she said.

"Pretty little human," Wes said in that thick voice before burying his face in her damp hair and inhaling.

She gasped when his big hand cupped her jaw, and he ran his thumb over her lower lip. "My pretty human. Eleanor. Eleanor Whitman."

"Wes," Eleanor said, her voice a little shaky. "Um, you're kind of freaking me out a bit."

His golden eyes flashed in the light from the window, and he pressed a light kiss against her mouth. "Do not fear your mate, sweet human."

"Mate?" she said. "Uh oh."

Wes's nostrils flared, and his eyes returned to their normal blue. He straightened and backed up a few steps, rubbing one hand over his jaw. "Shit."

"Do we need to have sex, so you don't go crazy?" Eleanor said.

He stared blankly at her. "What? No, why?"

"Because I'm pretty sure I just talked to your lion, and he said he was my mate. But you don't think you're my mate, and Daisy said when that happened to Cooper, he started going insane. She had to bang him to snap him out of it."

"I… I'm not… that is… my lion doesn't think he's your mate."

"Pretty sure he does, dude," Eleanor said. "So, just let me know when the insanity starts to set in, and I'll give you a good boning."

The blush in Wes's cheeks was friggin' adorable. She grinned at him as he cleared his throat and grabbed some lunch meat from the fridge. "I'll get started on the sandwiches. You cancel your appointments."

She typed silently for a few minutes. "Do you think I should cancel Monday's too?"

"Yes," Wes said. "Tuesday as well."

Her rent-paying ability dwindled with every client she cancelled. Still, she didn't have much choice. She cancelled Monday's appointments but couldn't bring herself to cancel Tuesday's. "Are you sure I can't help you make lunch or -"

The doorbell rang, and she froze with her mug halfway to her mouth. Wes growled deep in his throat and left the kitchen. "Wait here, Eleanor."

She stood and followed him to the door, pulling out the pocketknife and clicking it open. Wes glanced over his shoulder. "I told you to wait in the kitchen."

"You might need my help," Eleanor said.

"I appreciate the thought, but again, that knife wouldn't cut through bread."

"As soon as we take care of whoever's at the door, I'm cutting my sandwich with this knife, just to prove you wrong," Eleanor said.

"Take care of? We're not the mafia, Eleanor," Wes said.

That made her laugh despite her anxiety. Wes looked

through the peephole, and the tension left his shoulders. "It's Coop and Chase."

He opened the door. "Hey, come on in."

The two men stepped inside. Wes said, "Eleanor, this is Chase Stover. He works at the security firm."

"Hi, Eleanor. I like your knife," Chase said with a grin.

She blushed and folded up the knife before sticking it back in her pocket. "Hi, it's nice to meet you."

Chase was cute with dark hair and hazel eyes and a smoking hot body. She was confident that there was a six pack underneath the Shadow Security golf shirt he wore. Usually, that would get her salivating, but either her lady parts were completely broken, or they were only activated by Wes and his six pack now.

"It's nice to meet you too. I've heard lots about you from Daisy," Chase said.

Wes growled deep in his throat, and the frosty look he gave Chase was enough to make the younger man take a step back.

"Wes," Cooper said, "relax, buddy." The tattooed lion shifter smiled at Eleanor. "Is that coffee I smell?"

Wes took a deep breath before jerking his head in the direction of the kitchen. "Come into the kitchen, and we'll get you caught up on what's happened."

Show him she's ours. Kiss her. Mark her.

Can you do me a favour and please stop talking?

Wes never thought the day would come where he'd be pleading with his lion to shut the fuck up. His lion had said more in the last fifteen minutes than he'd said in the previous two years. And while Wes was happy that his lion was coming out of his depression, if he didn't stop pushing Wes to mark Eleanor, Wes was gonna fucking lose it.

The cheetah wants what's ours!

She's not ours, and you have to stop thinking she is. It's fine if Chase is attracted to Eleanor – his lion's angry growl reverberated in Wes's head, making him wince - *and it's fine if Eleanor is attracted to him.*

Shit, that was the wrong thing to say. His lion was working himself up into an absolute frenzy and pushing for control.

Sweating with the effort to hold back his lion, Wes tried to soothe him. *She's not attracted to him. You know she isn't.*

That, thank fucking God, was the truth. If Eleanor lusted after Chase… Wes wouldn't be able to contain his lion.

Mark her! Mark her right now, his lion demanded.

Enough!

"Wes?" Eleanor rested her hand on his forearm, and his lion immediately calmed. Wes took a deep breath and tried to act normal.

"Yes?"

"What's wrong with your lion?"

"Nothing. Why?"

She shrugged. "I don't know. I feel like he's upset."

"He isn't. He's fine. We're fine." He forced himself to smile at her before looking across the table at Cooper.

"Thanks, Lusa. Yeah, it's not a problem. No, just tell Mr. Morrison that you'll be there at three to set up his system." Cooper set down his phone. "Sorry about that. So, Chase is going to hang out with Eleanor here at your place this afternoon."

"Why? I'm right here," Wes said.

"Yeah, about that," Cooper said. "Alanna Robertson called the office."

Wes groaned, and Eleanor glanced at him. "Who's Alanna Robertson?"

"About a thousand-year-old leopard shifter," Chase said. "With a huge crush on Wes."

Eleanor grinned. "Really?"

"She's also one of our best clients," Cooper said.

"And wealthiest," Chase added.

"She has an appointment this afternoon that she'd like you to attend with her," Cooper said. "She's convinced her granddaughter has put a hit out on her again."

"Send Chase or Grayson," Wes said. "She's not in any danger. Her granddaughter has never put a hit out on her, Cooper."

"I know that, and you know that. Hell, deep down, Alanna knows that too. But she likes the excitement of believing that she's in danger."

"She's wasting her money," Wes said.

Chase snorted. "The lady probably has a swimming pool full of cash."

"Grayson or Chase can go with her," Wes said to Cooper. "I don't need to go."

"She asked for you specifically," Cooper said.

"Eleanor can't be left alone," Wes said.

"I'm fine," Eleanor said. "I won't leave your house."

Wes shook his head. "It isn't safe."

"That's why I brought Chase," Cooper said. "He'll watch Eleanor while you're with Mrs. Robertson."

"No fucking way," Wes growled. "He doesn't have the experience to keep her safe."

"Yeah, I do," Chase said with a scowl. "Don't be a dick, Wes."

"I'm not being a dick."

"You kind of are," Eleanor said.

He frowned at her, but she shrugged. "I call it as I see it, buddy."

"I just want you to be safe," he said.

"I know, and I appreciate that. But you also need to do your actual job, the one that you get paid for," she said.

"I tried to convince Alanna to use Grayson," Cooper said. "But she's insistent it be you. You know if we refuse, she'll stop using us for security. And it isn't just about her."

"What do you mean?" Eleanor said.

"Nothing," Wes said. "Don't worry about it, Eleanor."

"What do you mean, Cooper?" Eleanor repeated.

Looking a little uncomfortable, Cooper said, "Alanna Robertson was one of our first clients when I started Shadow Security. She's never been in any real danger, but she has plenty of friends and acquaintances in the city. People who need our security services."

"We provide all the security needs for Thomas Bidler. Do you know who that is?" Chase said to Eleanor.

She nodded. "Yeah. Richest guy in the city. He created some app that made him millions."

"That's the guy. He's our client because Mrs. Robertson is friends with him, and she recommended Coop's company to him," Chase said. "If she doesn't get what she wants from us…"

"She'll tell him to stop using you for security," Eleanor said.

"Unfortunately, yes," Cooper said. "To be completely upfront with you, forty percent of our current client list is directly because of Alanna's recommendations."

"Holy shit," Eleanor turned to Wes, "you have to do it, Wes."

He scrubbed a hand across his face. Eleanor was right, but fuck did it bug him to leave her alone.

Alone? Or alone with Chase?

He ignored his inner voice. He didn't have much choice. He wouldn't be the one responsible for Cooper losing forty percent of his business, no matter how badly he wanted to keep Eleanor safe. He took a deep breath and nodded. "Yeah, okay."

"Good," Cooper said. "Chase will stay here with Eleanor until -"

"You let no one inside. Do you understand?" Wes said to Chase. "You don't open that fucking door to anyone but me. I don't care if your damn grandmother is knocking on the door."

"Relax, Wes, I know how to do my job," Chase said.

Wes swallowed down both his growl and his urge to show Chase what Wes could do to impudent little shits like him. He needed to chill the fuck out. Chase was a good guy and perfectly capable of keeping Eleanor safe.

What if he mates with her? His lion was close to losing his shit again.

He won't. Eleanor isn't attracted to him.

If his scent is on her, I'll rip out his throat.

Wes ignored his lion's threat. The best thing he could do was pretend like he didn't care if Eleanor mated with Chase. His apathy might help calm his lion. Of course, he needed to actually not care and right now, just the thought of Chase touching Eleanor made him want to punch a hole in the wall.

"Alanna needs you from two to seven, which means you'll be an hour late for your own party, but that's okay. We'll keep it low-key until you arrive," Cooper said.

"We should cancel the party," Wes said. "It's not a good time."

"We're celebrating your birthday this year, no arguing," Cooper said.

"What?" Eleanor sat up straight, staring at Wes. "It's your birthday today?"

"Tomorrow," Wes said. "But it's better to cancel the party. We can celebrate next year."

Cooper reached out and squeezed his shoulder. "No, we're not cancelling. It's been four years. You deserve to have your day celebrated. I understand why you don't want to, but I think it's important for you. For all of us."

He could smell both Eleanor and Chase's confusion as he stared at Cooper. "It doesn't feel right without him."

"I know." Cooper squeezed his shoulder again. "But he'd be pissed at the way we act like your birthday doesn't exist." He cleared his throat. "Lusa will pick you up from Alanna's and drive you over to my place."

"I can drop Wes off and pick him up after the party," Eleanor said. "I don't mind."

Cooper frowned. "You're going to the party too, Eleanor. You and Chase can come by around six."

A flush covered her cheeks. "I can't go to Wes's party just because…"

"Just because what?" Wes said.

"Just because everyone who's babysitting me is going to be there," Eleanor said.

"I want you to come," Wes said.

She studied him, the flush deepening. "You're only saying that because you have no choice but to invite me."

"No, I'm not," Wes said. "I want you at the party, and you're going. End of discussion."

She rolled her eyes, but he could smell her happiness, and it made his lion purr contently.

"Perfect. Wes, I'll drop you off at Alanna's place on my way back to the office," Cooper said.

Eleanor stood, and Wes took her hand before she could

leave. "Be careful, Eleanor. Stay close to Chase, and don't leave the house by yourself. All right?"

"All right," Eleanor said. "I'll be safe. I promise."

She squeezed his hand before following Chase out of the kitchen. Wes watched her leave, his lion growling his displeasure at Eleanor being out of their sight.

CHAPTER 13

"Wait, so you don't work for Shadow Security?" Hedra took a sip of her drink. Boone's grandmother's new nurse was super cool with her blue hair and piercings and her take-no-prisoners vibe. Eleanor knew for a fact that it didn't matter what she did, she would never be as cool as Hedra.

"No. I'm Wes's driver. I mean, I'm not just *his* driver. I drive all sorts of people to different events and places. But Wes is my best customer," Eleanor said.

"Why doesn't he drive?"

"I don't know," Eleanor said.

"And Wes is the missing guest of honour for this birthday party. Right?" Hedra said.

"That's right," Eleanor said with a laugh. "But he'll be here soon. He's at a client's."

"Ah," Hedra said before staring across the room at Grayson and his girlfriend Ryan. She pulled absently at a lock of her blue hair. "When Chase told me that one of their clients was Ryan Shepherd, I practically begged him to get her autograph for me. He refused. Said it would be weird."

"You're a big fan of *Alien Hunter*, huh?" Eleanor said.

"Yes," Hedra said. "We're talking cosplay as Ryan's character in *Alien Hunter*, go to every *Alien Con*, and own the special edition boxset of the entire series. I watch the reboot of the series starring her sister, Ryleigh, even though Ryan isn't in it. Have you ever watched the show?"

"I haven't. Not the new one or the old one. I keep meaning to catch the reruns they show on the Syfy network but haven't got around to it," Eleanor said. "But Daisy says that Ryan is super nice. I'm sure she'd sign something if you asked her."

"Better not," Hedra said before smiling at Eleanor. "I'm here tonight because I'm working. I don't think Mr. Jameson or his grandmother would appreciate me fangirling all over one of their friends."

"How's it going with her, anyway?" Eleanor said. "I heard she's… difficult."

Hedra shrugged. "It hasn't even been a day yet, but I can confidently say that she'll be my toughest client. But I love a challenge."

They both studied Boone's grandmother, who sat on the couch. She wore a red floral dress with yellow running shoes and an orange, polka-dotted silk scarf tied around her neck. Alfie, wearing a matching polka dot collar around his neck, sat on her lap.

He stared unblinkingly at Hedra before baring his teeth at her in a silent snarl. Hedra laughed. "Alfie is not a fan of me."

"Alfie doesn't like anyone." Chase joined them, a bottle of beer in one hand and a cheerful grin on his face. "Boone says he once chased the mailman up a tree. Now Boone has to pick up his grandmother's mail at the post office because she's on their 'do not deliver' list. Is that not the funniest shit you've ever heard?"

"He looks so sweet, though," Eleanor said.

"He isn't," Hedra and Chase said in unison before grinning at each other.

"You don't look half-bad for once, bud." Hedra touched Chase's shirt and eyed his hair. "Other than your hair."

"At least it's not blue," Chase said. "What did your dad say when he saw it?"

"Nothing because I'm a grown-ass woman who can do whatever she wants with her hair," Hedra said.

Chase just laughed before holding out his hand. "Eleanor, can I freshen your drink for you?"

"Sure, thank you." She handed over her wine glass, and Chase headed toward the kitchen.

"My cousin thinks you're hot," Hedra said.

Heat rose in Eleanor's cheeks. "No, he doesn't."

"Oh, trust me, he does."

"He's, uh, he's very handsome," Eleanor said.

"But he's not your type, huh?" Hedra said.

"It's not that, it's just, um…"

"Eleanor, you don't have a drink. Let me get you one." Daisy joined them. "What are you drinking?"

"Oh, Chase is getting me some more wine," Eleanor said.

"Shocker," Daisy said.

Hedra laughed. "He thinks Eleanor's hot."

"Right?" Daisy said excitedly. "I mean, I was pretty sure he did, but then I confirmed it with Cooper."

"Chase told his boss he thinks I'm cute?" Eleanor said.

"No, he would have smelled it on Chase. Cooper is a lion shifter, right?" Hedra said.

"That's right," Daisy said.

"And you two are getting married?" Hedra said.

A smile beamed across Daisy's face. "We are. So, how are you getting along with Boone's grandma?"

Eleanor said a silent prayer of thanks for the topic change. "So far, so good," Hedra said.

She continued talking, but Eleanor didn't hear a word. How could she when Wes had walked into the living room looking like a gorgeous god? He wore a burgundy Henley with tight jeans, and his dark hair was damp like he'd just had a shower.

"Huh, I guess I know why you aren't into my cousin," Hedra said.

"Sorry, uh, what?" Eleanor forced herself to focus on something other than the way Wes's jeans clung to his perfect ass.

"You're totally into that guy who just walked in," Hedra said.

"No, I'm not," Eleanor said.

"I don't need to be a shifter to smell your lust for him," Hedra said.

Daisy laughed, and Eleanor scowled at her.

"Sorry, but it is kind of obvious how much you want to bang Wes," Daisy said.

Wes scanned the room, and when his gaze landed on her, Eleanor practically combusted at the heat in his gaze. Her cheeks flushed, her nipples hardened, and just like that, her stupid panties were soaked. With everyone in jeans, she'd felt a little overdressed in her dress and heels, but seeing how Wes looked at her, she was happy she'd convinced Chase to let her make a quick stop at her place to pick up the dress.

"Wes, you gorgeous man, get your ass over here and have a birthday shot with me," Boone shouted from across the room.

With a final glance at Eleanor, Wes headed over to Boone as Cooper and Grayson joined them.

"Wow." Hedra fanned her face. "Looks like the birthday

142

boy knows exactly what present he wants to unwrap for his birthday."

Eleanor turned bright red as Daisy laughed again. "Right? He's so into Eleanor. It's adorable."

"Wes isn't, I mean, he's not…"

"You can't even say it because you're not a liar," Daisy said. She smiled at Hedra. "Don't you think Eleanor and Wes would make a cute couple?"

"The cutest," Hedra said. "You should…"

Hedra's voice died out, and Eleanor finally tore her gaze from Wes's amazing ass. She grinned at the look on Hedra's face. Ryan had joined them, and she held out a wine glass. "Eleanor, here's your drink. Chase got sucked into doing shots with Grayson and the others."

She glanced at the group – both Lusa and Chase had joined them – and a soft smile crossed her face. "I love seeing them together like this, just having fun. They all work way too much."

"Agreed," Daisy said. "Ryan, have you met Hedra? She's Mrs. Jameson's new nurse."

"Hi, Hedra. It's nice to meet you." Ryan held out her hand, and Eleanor tried not to giggle when Hedra stared blankly at it.

She elbowed Hedra, who made a soft grunt before shaking Ryan's hand. "Um, hi. I'm a huge fan. I love your show. It's so nice to meet you, Ms. Shepherd. I'm Hedra. Shit, you already know that. Fuck, I just said shit in front of Ryan Shepherd. I mean… fuck."

Ryan burst into laughter. "Grayson says I swear like a sailor, so no need to apologize, Hedra. Also, call me Ryan."

"Ryan," Hedra said faintly. "I'm calling you Ryan because you asked me to call you Ryan."

Eleanor and Daisy both laughed as Hedra groaned and finally released Ryan's hand. "Oh my God, I'm an idiot."

"You're not," Ryan said. "I'm glad you liked the show."

"I love your photography too," Hedra said. "I loved the pic you put up on Instagram yesterday. The use of light and shadow was amazing."

"Well, you've just become my favourite person in the whole world," Ryan said with a grin as Boone's grandmother waved impatiently at Hedra.

"Please excuse me," Hedra said. "I need to check on Mrs. Jameson."

"I'll come with," Ryan said.

"You sure you want to?" Daisy lowered her voice. "When I met her earlier, she told me that I smelled funny."

"Oh, she sounds like fun." Ryan linked her arm around Hedra's arm, and Eleanor wasn't sure if Hedra was about to laugh or cry.

The two women walked away, and Daisy smiled at Eleanor. "So, everything went smoothly this afternoon?"

"Yes. Chase and I took a quick trip to my place – don't tell Wes - and I picked up some more clothes, and then we watched movies at Wes's house until we came here."

"Hedra's right, you know. Chase does think you're cute," Daisy said.

"He was perfectly professional the whole afternoon," Eleanor said.

"One - there's a very strict 'no sleeping with the client' rule, and two – Chase takes his work seriously, so of course he would be a complete professional. It's not because he isn't into you."

"I'm not interested in him," Eleanor said.

"Because you're interested in Wes."

"Sadly, yes. Even though he's made it clear that we can't sleep together because he says he's too old for me."

"Ridiculous," Daisy snorted. "Age is just a number, and besides, it's so obvious how much he likes you."

"You're preaching to the choir, girl," Eleanor said. "But I don't know how to get him to change his mind."

"I think that dress you're wearing is a good start," Daisy said with a smile. "Your legs look amazing."

"Thanks," Eleanor said. She studied Wes, who clinked a shot glass of amber liquid against Boone's shot glass. "Would it make me a horrible person if I deliberately try to seduce Wes tonight? Because I think it might, but I am dying over here."

"I'm sorry. I don't have an answer for you," Daisy said.

"It's fine. Although, I kind of wish I'd grabbed my vibrator this afternoon too."

Daisy laughed, and Eleanor said, "Sorry, that's too much information. Hey, could I stay with you and Cooper again? I brought my stuff with me. If it's too much trouble, I understand."

"Of course you can," Daisy said. "But are you sure that's what you want?"

"Nope, it isn't. But if I go home with Wes, I'll do something stupid like try to convince him to have sex with me, and that's a real dick move, right? So, it's better if I stay here."

"All right," Daisy said. "Come on, let's go to the kitchen and get some food. You haven't eaten anything all night."

———

"Happy Birthday, Wesley."

"Thank you, Nan." Wes sat down and kissed Boone's

grandmother on the cheek. "You're looking beautiful tonight."

She rolled her eyes, but he could smell her happiness. "Are you enjoying your party?"

"I am," he said. It was only a partial lie.

She studied him for a few minutes before taking his hand. "I know today isn't easy, lion shifter. Not with Derek gone, but like I tell Boone, you can't hide away forever, can you?"

"No, ma'am," he said.

"But that's exactly what you're doing. You and that grandson of mine," Nan said moodily. "The four of you have never recovered from your loss, and I get it, I do, but all of you are alive." She poked him hard in the chest. "This world is for the living, and that's what the four of you are. So, you need to stop hiding and start living. Do you hear me?"

"Yes, ma'am," he said dutifully.

She growled in irritation and dropped his hand when her nails sharpened to claws. "You and my grandson, two damn peas in a pod. You say all the right things, but you think I can't tell you're lying to my face?"

He cleared his throat. "I'm not... that is, I don't mean to..."

"Never you mind," she said with a weary sigh of resignation. "There's nothing an old woman like me can say that'll get through to you or my grandson. It doesn't matter that I'm eighty-four years old and have buried three husbands. What do I know when it comes to grief, right?"

"Nan, I..." he had no idea what to say.

She sighed again before saying, "I have a camcorder."

"I'm sorry?" The sudden topic change made him feel slow and off-balance.

"I have a camcorder. Boone said you needed one, asked

146

me if I still had mine, and I do. It's back at the house, but I'll get Boone to drop it off to you."

"Thank you," Wes said.

"Ayuh. Don't break it," she said.

"I won't," he said.

She suddenly grinned at him and patted his cheek. "I know you won't. You're one of the good ones, Wesley."

"So are you, Nan."

She glanced across the room at where Eleanor stood. "That little bit of a human sure does have a thing for you. How come you're not giving her the D?"

Wes's mouth dropped open, and Nan cackled with laughter, pressing against her stomach with one hand and her healing hip with the other. "My God, the look on your face, lion shifter."

She laughed again and then winced. She waved irritably at Boone when he started to cross the room. "I'm fine, Boone. Just a little twinge."

She patted Wes's knee. "Part of not hiding is accepting love from other folks, Wesley. You're not to blame for Derek's death."

"I know," he lied.

She studied him, her faded blue eyes piercing into him. "I'll forgive you for lying to me because it's your birthday, lion shifter. But don't ever do it again."

"Yes, ma'am."

"COOP, I LOVE IT." WES HELD UP THE CROCHETED BLANKET and grinned at his boss. "It's fantastic, and it'll look great on my couch."

Cooper looked pleased, if not a little red in the face, as he slipped his arm around Daisy's waist. "I tried to match the colours to the pillows on your couch."

Boone snorted laughter, and Lusa whacked him in the gut. "Shut it, Boone."

"Hey, it's fucking awesome," Boone said. "If I don't get a granny square blanket for my birthday, I'll be pissed. I mean that, Coop."

"Language please, Boone. We're not in prison, for goodness sake," Althea said.

"Sorry, Nan," Boone said.

Wes stood and hugged Cooper before adding the blanket to the large bag that held the bottle of whiskey that Grayson and Ryan had given him, the personalized whiskey glasses from Boone, and the gift card to his favourite restaurant from Lusa and Chase.

"Speech, birthday boy!" Chase hollered.

Wes tried not to grimace. Since Derek died, his birthday was no longer something to celebrate. Derek's birthday was the same day as Wes's, and for years they'd celebrated their birthdays together. Derek should have been here, and even now, it was still a knife to the guts that he wasn't. Cooper and the others had honoured Wes's refusal to acknowledge his birthday for the past four years, and he wished like hell they would have kept doing it.

His lion was sinking into that familiar grip of depression. Desperate to keep him from spiraling, Wes glanced around the room, looking for Eleanor.

She stood near the doorway to the kitchen in that fantastic dress. His lion calmed and then purred happily when Eleanor smiled at him. Relief washed over him. Eleanor had no idea how easily she could soothe his lion, but holy fuck, did he appreciate it. His lion hadn't been this happy in years.

The others stared expectantly at him. He took a deep

breath, his gaze lingering on Eleanor. "Thank you, everyone, for being here tonight. It means a lot, and I want you to know how much I appreciate your friendship and your… love."

It was a lame speech but the best he could do. Public speaking gave him hives. He could feel his face starting to burn, and Grayson, who always seemed to know when Wes was at his limit, swooped in and saved him.

"We love you too, Wes." Grayson raised his glass. "Happy Birthday to the best man we know."

The others raised their glasses, and cheers of 'Happy Birthday' echoed through the room. Keeping the smile plastered on his face, Wes took a drink. The fiery liquid burned his throat and immediately threatened to come back up when it hit his churning guts. He swallowed hard, sweat breaking out on his back. He wasn't the best man they knew. Hell, he wasn't even a good guy. Would a good guy have gotten one of their best friends killed?

He swallowed again and cleared his throat as the others quieted. "I also want to acknowledge and remember the actual best man that we all know. For years, Derek and I celebrated our birthdays together, and I hate that he isn't here with us now."

Boone's face had gone stark, and his hand clenched around the glass he held. Wes wanted to look him in the eye, but the pain and the sorrow on Boone's face were too heartbreaking. He looked away, studying the wall behind Boone as he raised his glass and said, "To Derek. Happy Birthday, man."

"To Derek," the others echoed.

CHAPTER 14

Boone caught her scent as the front door closed behind her. He stayed perfectly still, hoping she wouldn't notice him in the far shadows of the porch. When her footsteps started toward him, he swiped at the tears on his face and cleared his throat.

"I'm getting some fresh air. I'll be inside in a minute." Fuck, he hoped she took the hint. Crying in front of his nan's new nurse would be the perfect conclusion to an already difficult fucking day.

He clenched his jaw when his tiger made a low and mournful cry. It wasn't that Derek hadn't been on his mind all day anyway, but the toast to him, the pain in Wes's voice, had flooded Boone with memories that he'd rather forget.

He closed his eyes as more tears leaked down his face. Just fucking once, he wished that the memories could be of the good times instead of the day Derek died.

Hedra stood directly behind him. "Are you all right, Mr. Jameson?"

"I'm fine. Just, uh, needed some fresh air," he said hoarsely.

There was a moment of silence, and then Hedra said, "Daisy told me who Derek is. I'm sorry for your loss."

If she didn't leave in the next thirty seconds, he was going to burst into tears and really fucking embarrass himself. "Thanks."

His tiger made another low cry of pain and sorrow as Hedra touched his back. "Mr. Jameson, I'm a good listener if -"

The loss, the raw and unbearable pain that flooded through him as if Derek had died only yesterday instead of four years ago, suffocated him. He turned around to stumble past Hedra, but she took one look at his face and stepped forward, wrapping her arms around his shoulders and pulling him into her.

He slid his arms around her waist and buried his face in the crook of her neck. His tears wetted her skin, but she didn't seem to care as she rubbed his back. He let himself sink into her softness, his body shaking and his hands digging hard into her hips.

His tiger calmed before Boone did, which was strange, but Hedra's soft purring soothed the beast faster than Boone had ever been able to comfort him. His tiger trilled to Hedra, and she trilled back before purring again.

It was nice, Boone thought absently. Typically, his tiger didn't respond to another's purrs or trills. Not since Derek died anyway. But Hedra's purring was... wait, what the fuck?

He leaned back, studying Hedra. "You're purring."

Her purring cut out abruptly, and he caught the faint scent of her embarrassment. "Sorry. My sister is... well, she needs a lot of comforting sometimes, so I learned to imitate purring and trilling. I usually only do it for her, though. I hope it didn't upset your tiger."

"Why would it?"

She shrugged. "It drives my brothers crazy. They say it always sounds a little off."

"It does," he said and then grimaced at the look on her face. "Sorry, I didn't mean... that is, I liked it. My tiger liked it."

She smiled at him. "I'm sorry about your friend."

"Thanks," he said. "Sorry I'm bawling like a baby."

"Never apologize for your emotions," she said.

"I just really miss him," he said. "Derek was special, and I..."

He was close to tears again, and despite what she'd said, he blinked rapidly to hold them back.

Hedra smoothed her thumbs over his cheeks, wiping away the tears that still lingered. "Can I tell you a secret?"

"Sure," he said, his voice still hoarse.

"Girls dig guys who aren't afraid to show their emotions."

"That hasn't been my experience in the past," Boone said.

She grinned at him. "You obviously haven't been dating the right kind of girl."

He didn't plan to kiss her. He really didn't. But she was still in his arms, and her gorgeous mouth was only inches from his, and then her gaze dropped to his mouth, and the scent of her arousal drifted between them.

It sent his tiger into a frenzy of need and want, and, like he so often did no matter the consequences, Boone gave in to his deeper instincts and pressed his mouth against Hedra's. She returned his kiss eagerly, making his tiger purr with pleasure. When Hedra parted her lips, Boone slid his tongue into her mouth. She tasted sweet, like vanilla birthday cake, and the low moan she made and the way she pressed her perfect curves against him hardened his dick.

He pushed her up against the side of the house, swallowing the sound she made when her head bounced against the siding. He slid his hands into her hair, angling her head so he could deepen the kiss, tasting every part of her as she clung to his hips and ground her pussy against his erection.

He cupped her breast through her scrub shirt, rubbing his thumb over her hardening nipple. He growled happily when she moaned and arched her back. He pulled her head back and tasted the soft skin of her throat.

He kissed his way to her ear and sucked lightly on the lobe. She moaned again, and he nuzzled the soft spot behind her ear. "Spread your legs for me, little lamb."

She did what he asked, and he pressed this throbbing dick against her core before reaching down and gripping her thigh. He lifted her leg to his hip and pressed rhythmically against her. She gasped and moaned, meeting each of his thrusts as he kissed his way up her neck and claimed her mouth again.

Fuck, she tasted so good.

He sucked on her bottom lip before releasing it with a soft pop. He stared into her ocean coloured eyes, looking for any sign that she wanted him to stop. They were filled with warmth and lust, and he groaned. "Tell me to stop, sweet lamb, or I'll fuck you right here."

She didn't say anything. Instead, she rubbed her pussy against his cock, skimmed a kiss across his mouth, and unbuckled his belt.

He purred to her and reached for the waistband of her scrub pants. Before he could push her pants down her legs, the front door opened, and Grayson stepped out onto the porch. "Boone? You okay? You've been out here for..."

Grayson stopped, staring at him and Hedra before stepping into the house. "Sorry," he said and shut the door.

Hedra pushed away from him, backing up until her ass hit the porch railing. "Fuck me, I did it again."

His tiger growled and then settled into a pout. Boone

buckled his belt, his hands shaking and his cock still hard as a fucking stone. "Again? You've kissed an employer before?"

"Don't get all judgmental on me," she said.

"I'm not," he said. "It's just a question."

"A question said in a very judgy tone," she said.

"Is judgy even a word?"

She glared at him before smoothing her scrub top. "Look, am I fired or not?"

"No, of course not," he said. "This is my fault, and I apologize. You were trying to be nice, and I turned it sexual."

"We both turned it sexual," she said. "I know you smelled my lust for you, and that's why you kissed me."

Not used to a woman being so upfront, he said, "I wanted you before I smelled your lust."

Her gaze dropped to his mouth and then to the front of his jeans. He grimaced and adjusted himself, trying to relieve the pressure. "Please stop staring at my dick. You're not helping the situation."

She blushed and then folded her arms over her amazing tits that he really, really wished he'd at least seen before Grayson interrupted them. "We're attracted to each other, but this was a terrible mistake. Agreed?"

"Agreed," he said. "I'd prefer to have a professional only relationship with you."

"Same," she said. "So, you stop staring at my tits, and I'll stop staring at your dick, and we'll be... friendly but not familiar. Deal?"

"Deal," he said.

"Good." She brushed past him and walked into the house.

His dick still hard, Boone leaned against the railing and tried to think of anything other than the sound of Hedra's soft moans and the sweet taste of her mouth.

WES NEEDED TO LEAVE BEFORE HIS LION DID SOMETHING insane, like murder Chase. The cheetah shifter's interest in Eleanor became increasingly apparent the longer the night went on, and the more Chase drank.

He couldn't blame the kid, and if Wes stopped and tried to be fucking rational about it, he would give Chase a chance to date Eleanor. They were around the same age and Chase –

No! If he goes anywhere near Eleanor, I'll tear him apart.

Wes winced and rubbed at his temple. His lion had been freaking out all night every time Chase even got close to Eleanor. Wes honestly wasn't sure how much longer he could maintain control. His lion wanted to be free, wanted to show Chase and every other male in the room that Eleanor belonged to them.

He should have marked Eleanor before the party. Then maybe his lion would stop losing his shit, and Wes could have a moment of peace.

You can't mark her. She doesn't belong to you.

His inner voice was right, but his lion growled and stalked back and forth with real anger.

"Wes?" Grayson stood beside him. "You okay?"

He nodded. "Yeah, my lion is being… difficult."

"Because Chase is flirting with Eleanor?"

Wes sighed. "Is it that fucking obvious?"

Grayson just shrugged. "You should just ask her out."

"I can't, and you know that."

"Why not?" Grayson said. "She's not really a client. Plus, she's attracted to you. We can all smell it."

"I'm too old for her," Wes said. "Christ, Grayson, it's all kinds of inappropriate."

"That's a bullshit excuse, and you know it," Grayson said. "People don't give a fuck about age anymore."

"Yeah, well, I do."

"What's the actual reason you're hesitating?" Grayson said.

"I told you. I'm too old for her."

"We've been friends for how long, Wes?" Grayson said. "You've never lied to me before. Are you really going to start now?"

Wes growled at him, but Grayson didn't back off. He stared calmly at him, and annoyed by his friend's inability to butt the fuck out of his personal life, Wes said, "I'm too fucking broken for her."

"You're not broken," Grayson said. "Just because you can't have kids doesn't mean -"

"I'm not talking about that," Wes said. "But it's another reason why Eleanor and I wouldn't work out. I'm too much. My life is too... I can barely stand under the weight of my own baggage. I'm not asking Eleanor to carry some of it too. She doesn't deserve to be forced into my fucked-up life, okay?"

Grayson frowned. "Wes, your life isn't fucked up. You have a great career, friends who love you, and you're loyal and kind to the people you love. Any woman would be lucky to have you. And that includes Eleanor."

"You're wrong," Wes said as his anger grew.

"Explain to me why I'm wrong."

What the fuck? Was Grayson really going to make him say it? Especially today when the raw pain of missing Derek made him feel like a thousand bees stung his insides? "Are you fucking kidding me, Gray? You know why you're wrong, but you want to hear me fucking say it? Fine, I'll fucking say it. Eleanor deserves someone who didn't -"

His lion roared so loudly that Wes grimaced and grabbed at his head before looking up to see what had his lion so pissed off. Grayson's voice faded as the same anger infusing his lion settled over Wes.

Chase was touching Eleanor. The little pissant had his hand on Eleanor's arm, and now he was about to lose *his* fucking arm. Wes would rip it off at the shoulder and feed it to him.

He pushed past Grayson, stomping toward the younger cheetah shifter. Chase's back was to him, and Eleanor glanced over Chase's shoulder. Her eyes widened, and she shook off Chase's hand before stepping around him and blocking Wes's path.

"Wes, stop," she said.

He growled at her, and she said, "Stop growling and calm down. You know I'm not attracted to him. Don't be a dick."

"He touched you," Wes said as Chase turned around. "He touched you, Eleanor."

"Yes, and I was fine with it," Eleanor said. "Leave Chase alone."

Wes glared at Chance over Eleanor's head. "You need a woman to fight your battles?"

Chase rolled his eyes. "Christ, Wes, chill the fuck out. I'm not hitting on Eleanor. Besides, she's not your property, so stop acting like she is. Women hate that shit."

Eleanor touched Wes's chest before rubbing in small circles. "I'm not attracted to Chase. He's not my type, and I don't even find him good looking."

"Ouch," Chase said with a wry grin. "Don't hold back, Eleanor. Tell the entire room how you really feel."

Boone's grandmother cackled laughter from her spot on the couch. "If it makes you feel any better, cheetah shifter, I'd bone you if I didn't have a broken hip."

There was complete silence for about five seconds before Cooper roared with laughter. It didn't take long for the others to join in. Chase grinned at Nan and sat on the couch beside her.

"Mrs. Jameson, are you trying to seduce me?" he said.

"Chase, knock it off," Boone said as Nan laughed.

"Get me another Dr. Pepper please, and stop ruining my fun, would you, Boone?" Nan said before patting Chase's knee. "Cheetah shifter, you just might become my favourite of Boone's friends."

Wes sucked in a deep breath as Eleanor continued to rub his chest. Her touch helped soothe his lion like it always did, and as the anger faded, his embarrassment grew.

"Fuck," he muttered, "I can't believe I just did that to you. I'm sorry."

"It's fine," she said. "Shifters are possessive of their mates. Everyone knows that."

He swallowed hard. "We're not mates."

"Your lion thinks we are. Do I need to take you upstairs for a quickie to settle him down?" she asked with a teasing grin. "Because I'm willing to take one for the team if I have to. Especially if it saves poor Chase from being ripped into tiny pieces."

His lion purred happily – Wes honestly wasn't sure if it was the offer of the quickie or the idea of Chase being torn apart that made him happy – and then pushed him to mark Eleanor.

"Stop it," he said under his breath.

Eleanor leaned closer. "Stop what?"

"I was talking to my lion," he said. "He wants me to…"

"To what?" she said.

"Mark you." He probably shouldn't have told her that.

Her slow and sexy smile made him want to find the

nearest empty room and bury himself to the hilt in her pussy. "Is that right?"

"Yes," he said hoarsely.

"If I let you mark me, will it stop you from trying to kill any shifter who comes near me?"

"Probably," he said.

"Probably?" She arched an eyebrow at him and took a step closer until her breasts brushed against him. The conversation from the others dimmed to meaningless babble, and he suddenly didn't give one fuck that they weren't alone.

He slid his arm around her waist, pulling her up tight against him. "It will."

She smiled up at him. "Then I guess you'd better mark me, Wesley."

"Not here," he said.

"I guess it is a bit crowded," she said with another one of those sexy smiles. "Come upstairs to the spare bedroom."

"No." He studied her mouth and then her tits. "I'll mark you at my house."

He knew once he started marking her, he wouldn't stop until she was naked. Until she was on her back with her legs spread wide and her hands buried in his hair as he ate her out. He wanted to taste her pussy so bad, his mouth was fucking watering.

Hesitation crossed her face, and that sexy smile faltered. "I thought it might be best if I stay with Daisy and Cooper tonight."

"No," he said.

"Wes, if I go home with you," she looked around and lowered her voice, "if I go home with you, I won't be able to stop from, uh, doing things to you."

"What kind of things?" he said.

She blushed but said, "Mouth things."

"That's quite the coincidence because I planned on doing… mouth things to you," he said.

His lion purred at the scent of her lust. Her sexy vixen persona had disappeared, leaving his sweet and slightly awkward Eleanor again. "What kind of mouth things?"

He lowered his mouth to her ear and nipped the lobe before saying, "Licking your pussy clean of all your sweet cream, sucking on your clit until you're begging me to let you come."

"Wes," Eleanor said in a soft moan. "Wes, please, I -"

"Hey! Get a room, you two."

Wes lifted his head, staring blankly at Cooper, who grinned at them from across the room.

"I know it's your birthday party, but I have a strict no nudity rule in the living room," Cooper said.

Eleanor blushed as the others laughed, and Cooper's grin widened. Wes took Eleanor's hand, tugging her toward the door. "Good night, everyone. Thank you for a wonderful party."

He hustled Eleanor out of the living room and down the hallway toward the front door. Her overnight bag sat in front of the hall closet, and he scooped it up and slung it over his shoulder before opening the front door.

When Eleanor hesitated in the doorway, he tugged on her hand. She chewed on her lip and said, "Wes, are you sure?"

He brought her hand to his mouth and kissed her soft palm. "Yes. Let's go home, Butterfly."

CHAPTER 15

Eleanor's nerves sang higher than a soprano as she stepped inside the house. Wes closed the door behind her and dropped her bag on the floor. She'd taken only two steps when Wes took her arm and pushed her up against the wall. With a strangely fierce look on his face, he wound his hand in her hair, pulled her head back, and swiped his jaw across her throat.

She shivered at the rough stubble, goosebumps prickling to life across her skin as Wes purred before marking her throat twice more.

"Better?" she said shakily.

"Hmm," he muttered before kissing her throat. "Not enough, but I'll mark you some more later. Right now, I have something much more pressing to do to you."

"Oh yeah? What's that?" She clutched at his head, waves of lust radiating throughout her nerve endings when he kissed her breasts through her dress and skimmed his hands over her hips.

"Mouth stuff," he said with a sexy grin that made her already damp panties turn soaking wet.

Oh God, she was so turned on, it was entirely possible she'd just come right here in his damn hallway. It hadn't helped that Wes kept one hand on her thigh the entire drive home, not stroking or caressing, just a steady weight right above her knee. That warm, unmoving pressure against her skin had driven her crazier than if he'd slid his hand up her dress and touched her pussy. She was honestly surprised she hadn't crashed the damn car.

"Wes," she breathed when he knelt in front of her and kissed her flat stomach, "we should go to the bedroom."

"Nah," he said before biting her hipbone. He tugged on her dress with his teeth as his hands slid up under her dress and caressed both her thighs. "Spread your legs, Butterfly."

She glanced at the front door and the long narrow windows that flanked it before spreading her legs shamefully wide. Wes purred his approval, and she moaned when he kissed her pussy through her dress, his thumbs kneading the crease between her legs and her pussy.

"Pull up your dress," he said.

"Wes," she glanced again at the windows, "someone might see us."

"Maybe," he said and pulled on her dress again with his teeth. "Pull your dress up around your waist, Eleanor."

Oh fuck. She shouldn't. She really shouldn't. But Wes was impossible to resist. Not when he stared up at her with that intense look of need while his hands caressed her skin.

She pulled her dress up, bunching it around her waist. Wes growled happily as he stared at the barely-there thong she wore.

She'd told herself that she hadn't worn her skimpiest underwear in the hopes that Wes might see them, but she couldn't deny the heady rush of pleasure she got from the way Wes stared at the scrap of fabric.

She gasped in surprise when his fangs descended, and he leaned in and hooked the side string of her thong with his fangs. One quick twist of his head and the sliced string laid limply against her outer thigh. He moved to her left and sliced through the remaining string with another twist of his head. Her thong fell to the floor, and Wes's purring kicked up a notch in sound and vibration.

"Your pussy is beautiful, Butterfly," he said with something that almost sounded like reverence. "I can't wait to taste it."

"Wes, I… oh God." She clutched at his head as he pressed a kiss against the small patch of hair at the top of her pussy before lifting her left leg and draping it over his shoulder.

"Oh God," she repeated when his warm breath washed over her wet pussy lips. "Wes, the bedroom, we should go to the… oh fuck!"

Her voice ended in a strangled cry as Wes licked her pussy with a flat stroke of his tongue. She leaned against the wall, her body trembling and her pelvis arching as Wes licked her again. His tongue probed along her slit, and when he finally reached her aching, throbbing clit, she cried his name and buried one hand into his hair, the other clutching at her dress. She ground her pussy against his face, staring with wild eyes at the top of Wes's dark head.

He purred continuously as he sucked on her clit. Her low cries turned shrill, the pleasure already building into something hot and unstoppable. She dug her heel into Wes's broad back, pulled his hair, and moaned his name as her climax washed over her.

Wes purred again before lifting his head and pressing a kiss just above her pussy. He eased her leg down and stood gracefully. Afraid she might simply collapse like a broken toy, she clutched at his shoulders as he smiled at her.

"I love the way you taste, Butterfly."

"Thank you," she said as she heaved in another lungful of air. "I love the way you eat pussy."

He laughed and then picked her up. She used the fabric of her dress to wipe off his face. "The amount of liquid on your face is kind of embarrassing."

He nuzzled her throat as he carried her to his bedroom. "It's not."

"Says you," she said as he set her on her feet before clicking on the bedside lamp. She eased out of her heels, shivering when Wes slipped his arm around her waist and brought her back against his chest. "I really want to fuck you now, Wes."

"Soon, Butterfly." He brushed her hair forward across her shoulder and kissed the daisies tattooed on the back of her neck. "I love your tattoo."

"Thank you," she said. Her voice was unsteady again, but Wes's big hand had cupped her breast, and his thumb circled her nipple. She couldn't be blamed for how needy she sounded. Not when her pussy throbbed like she hadn't just had the best orgasm of her life not two minutes ago. "Oh God, Wes."

He kissed her tattoo again before grasping the zipper on the back of her dress and tugging it down an inch or two. "Do you have any idea how long I've wanted to see where your tattoo ends?"

"Um, a couple of weeks?" she said.

He growled and squeezed her breast. "Since the third time you drove me to work."

"Why the third time?" she asked, her back arching when he pinched her nipple.

He kissed the line of daisies exposed on her back as he

166

tugged her zipper down another inch. "That was the first time you wore your hair up, and I saw the tattoo."

"You've been into me for that long?" she said.

"Butterfly, I wanted you from the first moment I saw you," Wes said.

Her heart did this weird fluttering thing as warmth blossomed throughout her entire body. She knew Wes wouldn't agree to anything beyond sex, so why did his words make her feel so gooey inside?

She reached behind her, groping blindly for Wes's dick. He hissed out on a breath when she brushed across the front of his jeans before he pushed her hand away.

"Hey, I want to touch too," she said.

He pulled the zipper to the middle of her back. "Not yet."

"That's not fair," she said.

He unhooked her bra and then licked up her spine, following the daisy vine back up to her neck. "If you touch me, I'll have you on your knees with that pretty mouth wrapped around my dick. You'll have to wait longer to be fucked."

"Not necessarily," she said as Wes pulled on the zipper. "I could just have a taste."

He groaned, the sound turning into a low purr as he eased her dress down until it pooled at her feet. "I don't have that type of control right now."

"Because you've thought before about what it would be like to get a blowjob from me?" She wanted to hear him say it.

"Yes. Every fucking day," he said.

"Me too," she said as Wes took off her bra.

He pressed a light kiss against the sutures in her arm and then dropped her bra next to her dress on the floor. "Your arm okay?"

She nodded. "Still sore as hell, but better than it was."

"Good," Wes said.

Eleanor leaned back against him. "I had so many fantasies about driving somewhere quiet and secluded and then… oh!"

Wes cupped both her tits and the feel of his rough fingers teasing her nipples made it hard to think beyond how it might feel to have his mouth on her nipples too.

"And then what, Butterfly?" Wes kissed the back of her shoulder before marking along her back with a rough swipe of his cheek.

"Then climbing into the back seat with you and… oh, that feels so good, Wes." She arched her back when he tugged on her nipples.

"Back seat and then… finish your story." Wes gave her shoulder a sharp nip.

"Then sucking your dick," she said. "Fuck me, Wes."

His low chuckle brought fresh wetness to her pussy. "That seemed like an abrupt end to the story."

"Maybe because if you don't fuck me in the next five minutes, I'm gonna lose it," she said.

His hands kneaded her breasts before one slipped down and cupped her ass cheek. "Patience, Eleanor."

"I've been patient enough," she said. "Time to give me the goods."

His laughter washed over her. God, she loved it when he laughed. She needed to make it her mission to get him to laugh every day.

"Soon," he said as he cupped her hips and turned her slightly, so she faced the light from the lamp. He traced his finger down the daisy vine to where it ended just above her right hip.

She glanced at him over her shoulder. "It's not finished."

"Your tattoo?"

She nodded. "I want it to go over my hip and across my stomach and end in a circle around my belly button. But I had to use the money I'd saved to finish it to pay for car repairs instead."

He slipped his hand around her to trace a circle around her navel. "It'll hurt to get your stomach tattooed."

"Tattooed along your spine isn't exactly a walk in the park," she said. "I'm tougher than I look, Wes."

"I know, Butterfly." He kissed her shoulder and palmed her ass before pushing her gently toward the bed.

"Finally." She climbed onto the bed and laid on her back. "We're getting to the good stuff."

"Good stuff?" he said before pulling his shirt over his head. "What I just did to you in the hallway wasn't good?"

Her gaze narrowed in on his perfect, beautiful chest. "It was incredible, but I really want to fuck you, Wes."

He grinned and pulled off his socks, then reached for the button on his jeans. She sat up on her elbows, watching with studious concentration as Wes unbuttoned and unzipped. He shoved his jeans and briefs down his legs and stepped out of them.

She loved his lack of self-consciousness as he stood naked in front of her. She studied the gloriously thick shaft of his erect cock and the precum that slicked the head. Wes gripped his cock, and jealousy went through her when he gave himself a few long, slow pumps.

"That's my job," she said.

He just grinned and opened the bedside drawer to grab a condom. As he opened the package, she said, "Are you sure I can't have a small taste, Wes?"

His nostrils flared, and he growled deep in his throat. "Later, Butterfly."

She ignored her disappointment. She only felt this way

because she was certain tonight would be it for them. Confident that Wes would come to his senses tomorrow morning and insist they were better off as friends only. She'd never have her chance to taste him.

"Are you sure?" she said. "I'm really good at it. Not to brag, but I have serious dick sucking skills. I'm like a Hoover."

He laughed so hard, he had to stop rolling on the condom. "I'm sure you do, but I need to be buried in your sweet pussy, Eleanor." He paused, his pupils narrowing to slits for a few seconds. "We both need that."

He was talking about his lion, and a little shiver went through her. Not that she thought Wes was on the verge of insanity just because he wanted to fuck her so bad, but a small part of her liked how attached his lion was to her. Sure, it made her a bad person, but she wasn't above using his lion's obsession with her to her advantage. Not if it meant being with Wes.

You're getting a little obsessed with him too. You know that, right? Not good, Eleanor. Wes isn't into you the way his lion is, and if he convinces his lion that you're not their mate, you'll be left with a broken heart.

Wes knelt between her thighs, and she pushed away the negative thoughts. There would be plenty of time for those later. If this was her only time with Wes, she wanted to be fully present.

He studied her, his hands on her knees and a worried look on his face. "Are you all right?"

"Never better," she said with a smile. "Let's get this party started."

He stayed where he was, that worried look deepening as he inhaled. "Butterfly, if this isn't what you want -"

"It is," she said. "Trust me."

She cupped her tits, circling her nipples with her thumbs and smiling to herself when the worry dropped from Wes's face, and naked hunger took its place. He growled and leaned down, pushing aside her hands and echoing her words from before. "That's my job."

"Then do your job, Wesley," she said with a playful poke to his ribs.

He growled again, but her admonishment about growling was forgotten when his hot mouth latched onto her left nipple and sucked hard. She buried her hands in his hair, her back arching as he teased and tormented.

"Wes, please," she moaned when he turned his attention to her right nipple. He licked a slow circle around her throbbing nipple then nipped at the underside of her breast.

"Soon," he said. He marked just above her breasts with a slow swipe of his jaw and then marked her throat. "I've waited a long time to touch your perfect tits, and I'm going to enjoy it."

She shifted slightly beneath him and arched up, letting her pussy brush against his cock. He groaned and gave her a sharp nip where her shoulder met her throat. She cried out, and he soothed the sting with his tongue. "Behave, Butterfly."

"Fuck me," she demanded.

He grinned and marked her shoulder with another swipe of his jaw. She loved the intoxicating combo of pain and pleasure from his rough stubble, and she rubbed her pussy across his dick again.

"Fuck," he breathed and kissed her hard on the mouth. She sucked on his tongue and ran her hands up his ribs and across the light layer of hair on his chest before she pinched one flat nipple.

He jerked against her and released her mouth, staring

down at her with a small grin as he smoothed his hand over her inner thigh and pressed. "Open for me, Butterfly."

"Finally," she said and let her legs fall apart without a lick of shame.

His grin widened, and he stroked her thigh with his fingertips. "Can you come from being fucked?"

"Sometimes," she said. "Depends on how you work your equipment. If you know what I mean."

He laughed as he gripped his dick, guiding it to her entrance. "If I'm not working the equipment right, just let me know."

"I'll keep you updated," she said.

He pressed the head of his cock against her, and they both groaned when he slid into her warmth. When he pushed again, she squeezed him with her thighs, her hands clutching at his waist.

He stopped and pressed a kiss against her collarbone. "Okay, Butterfly?"

"Yeah," she said as she adjusted her hips. "You're on the thick side."

"I am," he said with a hint of uncharacteristic arrogance, "but your little pussy is going to take all of it."

Hot desire flashed through her at his words. Her suspicion that her pussy had just gotten a lot wetter was confirmed when Wes smiled and pushed all the way into her with one hard thrust.

"Fuck," he said with a low groan. "You're so wet and tight."

She braced her feet on the bed and squeezed his hips. "Show me what you've got, big guy."

He purred to her and nuzzled her neck before marking her throat a couple of times. He pumped slowly in and out, peppering soft kisses across her collarbone as he made an intoxicating mixture of purrs and growls.

She shifted her hips again, moaning when the position change made Wes's cock press exactly where she wanted it... needed it. She thrust her hips to meet his strokes, encouraging him to move harder and faster, the warmth coiling in her belly, her need for relief already singing a sweet song of urgency.

"My equipment hitting the right spot, Butterfly?" he said with a soft grin.

"Yes," she moaned, sliding her hands around him to dig her fingers into his firm ass. "Move faster, Wes."

He propped himself up on his hands above her and slid in and out of her in a hard, quick rhythm that had her panting for more. She moaned his name and met him stroke for stroke. She stared in fascination as his eyes turned yellow, and the dark stubble on his jaw lightened to gold.

His purring grew deafening in the room, the sound heightening her need and her desire. He drove in and out of her, and she cried his name as her climax washed over her, just as intense as the first one.

He growled her name, his head falling back and his beard thickening as he pushed deep and his body first stiffened and then trembled rapidly. She lifted her head and kissed his chest, smiling when he moaned and bent his head to kiss her hard on the mouth.

He rolled off of her, collapsing on his back for a moment before sitting up and sliding off the condom. "Be right back, Butterfly."

He walked to the bathroom, and she curled on her side and tucked her hand under the pillow. Wes returned a few minutes later with a glass of water. She sat up and drank a few swallows before handing it back. He drank some water and set the glass on the nightstand before climbing into bed and pulling the sheet and quilt over them.

Feeling awkward, Eleanor said, "I can go to the guest room if -"

"No," he said and then pulled her into his arms like he thought she might jump out of bed. "Stay here with me."

She smiled happily and burrowed up against him, yawning as she rested her cheek on his chest. "That was amazing, Wes."

"For me too, Butterfly."

She kissed his chest before squinting at the clock. "Hey, it's after midnight. Happy Birthday."

He chuckled and kissed her forehead. "Thank you. Go to sleep, Eleanor."

"Hmm," she said and closed her eyes, the sound of Wes's heartbeat lulling her into sleep.

CHAPTER 16

"Christ, there has to be something you can do for them."

Hoyt's voice behind him was a mixture of disgust and pity. Chad moved away from Barkwell's door, bumping Hoyt's shoulder as he did so. "Step back, Hoyt. You're nearly up my fucking ass."

Hoyt backed away, his gaze still on the small window at the top of the thick steel door. "They're dying, Chad."

"They're not dying," Chad said. "They're going through withdrawal."

"Sounds like they're dying," Hoyt said as Barkwell let out another scream that was audible even through the thick door. Robinson echoed it in the room next to his, and Hoyt winced. "You can't give them something?"

Chad walked down the hallway, hiding his annoyance when Hoyt followed him. The security head wasn't the chatty type, so he obviously had something to tell him. Despite the empty hallway, he didn't give in to his temptation to ask Hoyt to share the information while they walked. It was better to speak in his office.

Hoyt stepped into the elevator with him, and as the doors closed, finally cutting off the screams of the enhanced, he ran a hand over his face. It didn't shake - you didn't get to the position Hoyt held by having shaky hands, but Chad had never seen him so rattled before.

"Can you give them something?" Hoyt repeated.

"We're trying to ease the symptoms, but coming off the serum cold turkey is proving to be more difficult than Dr. Lowenstein anticipated," Chad said.

"Once they're through withdrawals, will they be back to normal?" Hoyt asked as the elevator carried them up the seventeen floors to Chad's office.

Chad shrugged. "Dr. Lowenstein believes so, but right now, it's hard to tell. All of them are weak and nauseous with tremors and muscle ticks. They can't shift."

Hoyt's face paled. "They can't shift? Is that permanent?"

"It's hard to tell," Chad said. The elevator doors opened, and they walked swiftly to Chad's office. He sank into his chair, rubbing at his temples. He had a fuck of a headache starting, and he had no idea what day it was. Too many nights of sleeping on the couch in his office.

"What day is it?" he asked.

"Saturday," Hoyt said.

Chad groaned and opened the desk drawer to grab the bottle of aspirin. He shook out four and crunched them down, the bitter taste in his mouth making him grimace.

"You keep taking them that way, and it's gonna fuck up your stomach," Hoyt said.

"You think I give a shit about that right now?" Chad said. "Bradmore is breathing down my neck over the loss of the formula, and if we don't get it back in the next seventy-two hours, I guarantee that you and I will be sharing a shallow fucking grave in the desert. So, give me some good fucking news, would you, Hoyt?"

The flash of fear in the ordinarily unflappable Hoyt's eyes wasn't a good sign.

"Kirkman hasn't had a chance to get the formula yet."

"Hasn't had a chance," Chad repeated. "What the fuck does that even mean? We know she has it. Her little trip to the fucking bus station proved that Whitman sent it to her. And don't you even try to tell me that maybe it was just a letter to her in that envelope because I am in no fucking mood for games, Hoyt."

Hoyt scowled at him. "Obviously, it's the formula."

"Kirkman should have taken it from her in the bus station," Chad said. "Before she even had a chance to look at the flash drive. We can only fucking hope that she's as dumb as we believe she is. If she figures out what the formula is for..."

He grimaced as his head ached and throbbed. "Fucking Kirkman. He's useless. Your best man, my ass."

Hoyt stiffened. "Kirkman is my best, and considering that the daughter has twenty-four/seven security from a firm of shifters, it's not all that surprising that he hasn't gotten the formula. He's lucky that lion shifter didn't kill him."

"This is what I get for sending a human," Chad muttered as he scanned his laptop screen. The words were blurry, and he rubbed at his gritty eyes as Hoyt grunted in annoyance.

"If you actually thought a shifter would be better than Kirkman, you would have already pulled him and sent someone else to retrieve the drive. But you know it won't make a difference. You read the file I gave you on this Shadow Security firm. All of the employees are shifters, and most of them are former military. Fuck, four of them were in special ops. This isn't just a typical security firm watching her back, Chad, and you fucking know it."

Chad muttered a curse and sat back in his chair. Hoyt leaned forward. "We need to send in a team. She's staying at an employee's house, Wesley Masters, the lion shifter that nearly killed Kirkman. The team hits them middle of the night. They kill Masters, get the drive from Whitman's kid, and then clean her too. We make it look like a simple home invasion."

Chad shook his head. "Bradmore and the others won't approve sending in a team. They think it increases the chance of exposure."

"For fuck's sake," Hoyt said. "If we don't get that drive back from the daughter, this whole program could be blown wide open. Do they not fucking get that?"

"I'm sending in Rourke," Chad said. "He leaves today."

"That's a bad fucking idea, Chad," Hoyt said. "You want them cleaned without a mess. Rourke's gonna leave a mess."

"He'll be fine," Chad said.

"Fine? You saw what he did to those people. They weren't even part of the mission. Hell, they weren't even fucking shifters. He tore them apart without a single hesitation or any remorse afterward. Whitman rabbited because of what Rourke and the others did. You can't trust him to take back the formula and clean Whitman's daughter without leaving a trail of fucking carnage behind him."

"We tweaked the formula, remember? The aggression is lowered, and the impulse control is better. "

"Whitman said it didn't work," Hoyt said.

Chad sucked in a deep breath. "Hey, Hoyt? Do me a favour? Stay in your fucking lane. Your job as security head was to keep the formula here in the facility. You failed. You're lucky your head isn't on a fucking pole right now."

Hoyt's face reddened, and his big hands clenched into fists. He stood and headed for the door. "Fine. But don't you fucking look to me for help when Rourke gets himself splashed all over the six o'clock news."

He stalked out of Chad's office, slamming the door shut so hard, the frame cracked. Chad rubbed at his throbbing head, wished he had a regular job like a fucking accountant, and then picked up the phone.

"Yeah, it's me. We're sending Rourke in. Get him ready. I'll be downstairs to speak to him in an hour."

SATURDAY MORNING, WES FOUND ELEANOR IN THE KITCHEN, flipping pancakes with her hair still wet from the shower and wearing a cotton pajama set with tiny pink turtles printed on the shirt and pants.

He grinned at how adorable she was. He'd woken alone in the bed but heard Eleanor in the kitchen before panic could set in. He'd brushed his teeth and showered, then pulled on a pair of jeans and a t-shirt.

He slid his arm around Eleanor's waist and nuzzled her neck before marking it. He loved that his scent covered her, and his lion was positively giddy about it. She relaxed against him, smiling when he kissed the tip of her nose. "Happy Birthday, Wes. I hope you like pancakes."

"I love pancakes. Thank you." He pressed a kiss against her mouth. "I like your pajamas."

She laughed. "Honestly, if I'd known that we'd hook up, I would have brought sexier ones."

He marked her neck again before cupping her breast through her shirt. "I think these are sexy."

Her low moan as he teased her nipple with his thumb

made him purr happily. But she took his wrist when he started to slip his other hand inside her pajama bottoms.

"What's wrong, Butterfly?" he said.

She smiled at him. "The pancakes will burn if I let you distract me."

He sensed this was about more than the pancakes burning, so he kissed her throat a final time and stepped away. "I'll set the table."

He put the plates and the cutlery on the table and grabbed the syrup and butter. Eleanor set the plate of pancakes in the middle of the table, and they both sat down. She put a couple of pancakes on her plate and smothered them with an obscene amount of syrup. Wes took two pancakes as well, but his appetite had disappeared, and his lion whined like a tiny cub.

What if Eleanor regretted last night? What if she hated that she let him mark her? What if she -

"Wes," Eleanor said. "I don't regret last night, so stop looking like I'm stomping on your balls, would you?"

He twitched and nearly dropped his fork. "Since when did you become a mind reader?"

She laughed. "I'm not. But when you're into a guy who doesn't talk much, you become an expert at reading his facial expressions and body language."

He poked at the pancake with his fork. "Will you tell me what's wrong?"

"Nothing's wrong, exactly," she said. "It's more of a... we need to be clear on some particulars type of thing."

He knew they needed to have this conversation, so why did he feel so sick to his stomach about it?

Maybe because it's your birthday. A day that used to be good but now sucks, and there's a big part of you that wanted to spend all of today with Eleanor in your bed, so you don't have to think about how it's your fault Derek isn't here on his own fucking birthday.

He set his fork on the table so Eleanor wouldn't see the way his hands trembled. He was a selfish asshole, and thinking he could use Eleanor today to forget how fucked up he now was, was repulsive.

Eleanor means more to you than that, and you know it. Stop denying it, asshole.

He ignored his inner voice. Eleanor couldn't be more to him than a distraction. He wouldn't fuck up her life the way he'd fucked his. She deserved to be happy, and he would never make her happy.

"Your continuing silence suggests I'm freaking you out," Eleanor said before shoving a healthy forkful of pancakes into her mouth.

"You're not freaking me out," he said. "I'm worried about upsetting you, but I also want to be honest with you and be confident that what I'm about to say is clear and not misleading."

She made a face and swallowed her bite of pancakes. "I know this is a fuck buddies situation. I won't start crying because you say the words out loud, Wes."

His mouth dropped open, and his lion made a startled growl. Eleanor took a sip of coffee and sat back in her chair. "Why do you look so surprised that I'm all right with a sex-only relationship?"

"I don't… I guess I thought you wouldn't be into it."

"I had the best sex of my life last night, Wesley. Why wouldn't I be into it?"

"Because you like me," he said, then grimaced. "Shit, that sounded more arrogant than I meant."

She shrugged. "I do like you, but I'm also an adult who

knows when a guy isn't into me the same way I'm into him. Normally, I'd move on, but since you're stuck with me until I figure out what my father sent me that people are willing to kill for, why shouldn't we enjoy the bonus of banging each other's brains out?"

"I'm not stuck with you," he said irritably. "I want to help you, Eleanor."

"I know," she said, "and I appreciate it more than you know."

"You want to be in a relationship," he said, "and I can't give that to you."

"You've made that clear. But I won't exactly be looking for my Prince Charming while someone's actively trying to kill me. Once the danger is over, you and I can go back to friends only, and I'll keep looking for," Eleanor smiled, but it looked forced and unnatural, "the love of my life."

His lion had a lot of very loud things to say about Eleanor being with anyone else but them. Wes poked at his pancakes again. He needed to say no, but he couldn't resist being with Eleanor for even a little longer. One night with her wasn't enough.

"Push your chair back, Wes."

He glanced at Eleanor before wordlessly pushing his chair away from the table. His breath hitched in his throat when Eleanor straddled him and rubbed her pussy against his growing erection. "You aren't eating your pancakes."

"Not hungry." He gripped her hips and stared into her sweet face. "Eleanor, are you sure about this? I feel like I'm taking advantage of you."

"Actually," she bent her head and kissed his throat before nipping at his jaw, "I'm the one taking advantage of you."

"Is that right?" He squeezed her firm ass, pressing her harder against his dick.

"Yep," she said before pressing feathery light kisses across his cheek. "Using you for my filthy urges."

"I like your filthy urges," he said and then moaned when her tongue traced the shell of his ear.

"I didn't get you a birthday present." Her hands slipped under his shirt and stroked along his stomach.

"You don't need to get me one." He kneaded her ass and then rubbed her thighs.

"You sure? Because I thought maybe I'd take you back to your bedroom and suck your cock as my birthday gift."

He stood up so abruptly that Eleanor shrieked in surprise, her legs clamping around his waist as he used his hands on her ass to keep her snug against him. He started toward the bedroom without a word. Eleanor giggled and kissed his throat again. "I take it you want my birthday gift?"

"Hell, yes," he said. He stepped into his bedroom and tossed Eleanor onto the bed. She bounced a couple of times, giggling wildly as he stripped off his t-shirt, jeans, and briefs. The giggles died in her throat, and she sat up, scooting to the side of the bed and letting her legs dangle over the edge.

"Come here, Wes," she said, her gaze arrowed in on his aching cock. He stroked his dick a couple of times, squeezing the base to help control his need when Eleanor licked her lips.

"Take off your shirt, Butterfly," he said.

She pulled it over her head and tossed it aside. He stared at her gorgeous breasts. Their pink-coloured nipples hardened in the cool air, and he growled deep in his throat when Eleanor squeezed her breasts and teased her nipples with her thumbs.

"Come here, Wes," she repeated with a soft smile.

He stood in front of her, groaning when she leaned forward and licked the head of his dick. She smiled up at him, and he palmed the back of her skull, urging her forward as he purred to her. He watched her perfect lips slide down around his dick and fought hard not to shove his cock straight down her throat.

When she sucked, he moaned and couldn't stop from making two hard thrusts into her mouth as his hand fisted in her hair. He pulled back, afraid he'd scared her or upset her, but when his dick popped out of her mouth, she pouted up at him. "Why are you stopping?"

"Fuck," he said hoarsely.

She grinned and licked his dick like a fucking lollipop. "So, I should keep going?"

"Fuck, yes," he groaned, his hand tightening in her soft hair.

Her grin turned into a laugh, and he cried her name when she fisted the base of him and sucked on just the sensitive head. Her tongue cleaned away the precum at the slit before she bobbed her head up and down his dick.

His free hand clenched at his side. He ached to slide his hands into Eleanor's hair, hold her steady, and fuck her face. Instead, he fought for control, his gaze glued to the way her lips glided over his hot, aching skin.

She released him and stared up at him before pressing a kiss against the throbbing vein on the underside of his dick. "I won't break, Wes."

"What?" he rasped, his hips bucking when she stroked his balls with gentle fingers.

"I can take what you give me," she said. "Stop holding back."

"Butterfly, I…"

"Don't hold back." She stared up at him, her dark eyes filled with warm trust. "Give us what we both want."

She took him into her mouth again, and with a low growl, he slid his other hand into her hair, his fingers wrapping around the silky strands. Purring loudly, he thrust in and out of her mouth, pushing deeper with every stroke until he pressed against the back of her throat. He pulled back and let her take a few breaths before pressing forward again.

"Good, Butterfly, so good," he praised when she sucked eagerly. He used his thumb to wipe away the mix of precum and saliva on her chin before cupping the back of her skull and thrusting hard and fast.

His head fell back, and he moaned her name as pleasure washed over him. He was so fucking close. It would only take a few more strokes of Eleanor's hot mouth and tongue to bring him to his climax. Before he could give in to the temptation to come in her mouth, he pulled away.

She pouted again as she licked her swollen lips. "Hey, come back here."

He pushed her onto her back, and she squeaked in surprise when he grabbed her pajama bottoms and yanked them down her legs. As he'd hoped, she was naked beneath them, and he stared appreciatively at her pussy. "Are you wet enough for me, Butterfly?"

She smiled lazily at him and spread her legs wide before rubbing her clit with her fingers. "More than enough, handsome." She showed him the moisture on her fingertips, and he growled happily.

"Get on your hands and knees," he demanded.

She rolled to her stomach and onto her hands and knees. Wes smoothed his hand over her ass before rubbing the back of her thighs. When she spread her legs, he purred and ran a finger over her wet slit.

She moaned and arched her back. His cock throbbing, he lined it up at her opening before pausing. She stared at him over her shoulder. "Why are you stopping?"

"Condom," he said. "Can you reach the nightstand drawer?"

She bit at her bottom lip. "My last tests were negative, and I've had the birth control shot. If your tests are negative, I'm good with no condom."

"My tests are negative," he said and then slid into her with a low purr. Her slick heat surrounded him like a glove, and his balls immediately tightened as the base of his spine tingled. Fuck, he was so close already.

Determined to last longer than a couple of fucking minutes, he gripped Eleanor's hips and held her still when she immediately started rocking on his dick.

"Wes, fuck me," she moaned.

"Give me a minute," he said.

She wiggled in his grip, and he groaned out a curse before giving her ass a light slap. "Behave, Eleanor."

"You behave," she muttered.

He grinned and reached under her to rub lightly at her clit.

She arched her back again, letting her head fall back as she moaned his name. "Oh, that feels so nice."

He thrust slowly in and out of her wet pussy, gripping one ass cheek with his hand as he rubbed at her clit with the other hand. She met each of his thrusts with reckless enthusiasm, her soft cries spurring him on to move harder and faster.

"Rub your clit, Butterfly," he said and moved both his hands to her hips. She reached under her body and stroked her clit, those soft cries growing progressively louder as he held her tight and pounded into her.

When her pussy tightened around him at the moment of her climax, he roared her name and sunk deep inside of her, his hands clamping onto her hips. He pumped back and forth, the pleasure flooding through his body as Eleanor's pussy squeezed and released him.

Her legs shook as he pulled out of her perfect warmth. She collapsed on her face on the bed. His hands trembling as much as her legs, he rearranged her limp body until she was tucked under the sheet and climbed in beside her. She rolled to her side to face him, her usually pale face flushed with colour and her dark hair sticking to her face.

He brushed her hair away from her face and kissed her forehead. "You okay?"

"I want to do that again," she said.

He laughed. "I'm gonna need at least ten minutes, Butterfly."

"Fine," she said before throwing her arm around his waist and snuggling into him. "You can have a birthday nap, and then I'll give you part two of your birthday gift."

"What's part two?"

"All this," she waved tiredly at her body, "riding you like a crazed cowgirl."

He laughed, and she smiled but kept her eyes closed. "I love your laugh."

"Thank you."

"Hey, Wes?"

"Yeah?"

"I have to tell you something important."

"What?" his stomach tightened, and he automatically pulled her closer. He told himself that she wasn't ending their time together, so he needed to just fucking cool it.

"The riding you like a crazed cowgirl is more of a gift to me. I definitely don't have to rub my clit to have an orgasm when I'm on top."

He laughed and slid his hand down her back to squeeze her ass. "Is that right?"

"Hmm," she said sleepily. "I hope you don't mind if your mate uses you for her own filthy pleasure."

His lion purred happily, and the beast's contentment infused Wes with a warmth he hadn't felt since before Derek died. He pulled Eleanor in tight against his body as her head thunked down on his chest, and she snored softly.

He kissed the top of her head and kept his voice low. "No, my beautiful mate, I don't mind."

CHAPTER 17

He had sand in his mouth again. He swiped his gloved hand across his lips, knowing it was a useless gesture, but, fuck, did he hate that gritty feeling. Boone and Grayson were forever bitching about the heat, but it was the sand that got to Wes.

It was everywhere and in everything. A fine layer of grit that never really washed away no matter how many showers he took. It got in his hair and under his nails, in his ears and up his nose. Hell, he'd find it in his fucking underwear, despite his layer of clothes.

There was nothing quite like the maddening itch of sand in your underwear.

Wes squinted out the windshield as he drove through the operating base toward the outer gate. His sunglasses provided little help against the glare of the desert sun. He glanced over at Derek sitting in the passenger seat. He studied the map and, like always when he concentrated, the tip of his tongue stuck out from between his lips.

"Let me get this straight, Coop," Boone's voice drawled from the middle of the backseat of the armoured Humvee.

"You thought sending us out on a new patrol was better than relaxing on base? Where I might remind you, there's a kiddie pool full of water waiting for my hot and sweaty feet to be dunked in and a DVD of *Back to the Future* waiting to be watched."

"You and that fucking movie," Grayson grumbled. He sat directly behind Wes, and Wes glanced at him in the rear-view mirror. Grayson's dark hair needed a haircut, Wes could see it curling against his neck below his helmet, and he hadn't shaved this morning. He looked tired and out of sorts.

"What's that supposed to mean?" Boone said with a grin.

"It means," Cooper sat directly behind Derek, "that it's a stupid movie, and we're all fucking tired of watching it."

"You've cut me deep, Coop," Boone said. "It's like you don't even want to be a part of the Michael J. Fox fan club anymore. I, for one, will not stand to hear you besmirch the name of the beloved Canadian icon known as Michael J. Fox."

Cooper laughed. "Says the guy who refuses to watch one rerun of *Family Ties*."

"Because I have taste," Boone said.

"Since when?" Derek said without looking up from the map.

"Watch it, buddy," Boone said with a mock growl.

"I'm just saying that a grown-ass man who owns a pair of adult-sized Batman Underoos may have questionable taste, that's all," Derek said.

"I'm wearing them right now," Boone said proudly.

Grayson and Cooper both laughed, and Wes grinned at Derek. Derek returned his grin and folded the map. The gate ahead of them opened, and Wes drove through, his stomach tensing the way it always did when they left the relative safety of the base. He glanced at the speedometer before decreasing his speed a little. The roads weren't exactly in great shape and -

"Fuck! Wes, look out!"

His gaze shot to the road, and he stomped on the brakes. The vehicle lurched to a stop. Wes's seatbelt cut into his chest, and Derek made a painful grunt as his seatbelt locked up.

"Fucking hell, Wes. Where'd you get your driver's license? A fucking gumball machine?" Boone said.

His heart beating in his chest, Wes stared at the lizard sitting in the middle of the road. It had green spots on its torso and a black head. Its tongue flicked out lazily to taste the air as Wes glared at Derek. "A fucking lizard, Derek?"

"It's a Timon princeps," Derek said. "Also known as the Siirt lizard."

"I don't care," Wes said.

Derek peered through the windshield. "Doesn't mean you should just drive right over him."

"Yeah, Wes, you fucking monster. He probably has a little lizard wife and a couple of lizard kids at home. Maybe even a lizard mistress on the side," Boone said.

Grayson laughed as Wes's lion growled in annoyance at Boone.

"Go on, little buddy." Derek tapped the windshield.

"Derek's got a soft spot for the reptiles," Boone said to Grayson. "Probably reminds him of his last girlfriend. She was one cold-blooded -"

"Cut it out, Boone," Derek said before tapping on the windshield again. "Get moving, lizard. Go home to your family."

"Or your mistress," Boone said.

Wes glanced in the side mirror at the two vehicles stopped behind them. The second vehicle idled just outside the open gate, while the third hadn't even made it out of the base yet. The radio crackled, and Jorgens, the second vehicle driver, said, "Everything good, Masters?"

He grabbed the mic and pressed the button. "Yeah, all clear. Just waiting for a lizard to cross the road."

"Of course, you fucking are," Jorgens said. "It ain't like we got somewhere to be, right?"

Wes ignored him as Derek tapped on the windshield a third time.

"Maybe you should get out and carry him to safety," Boone suggested. "I can take your picture if you want. Post it on Twitter. Hero soldier saves lizard from certain squashing."

"It'll go viral for sure," Grayson said.

Boone laughed as Cooper said, "Wes, keep moving."

"Yes, sir," Wes said.

Derek made a pained expression, and Wes hesitated before tapping the horn. The short beep was enough to get the lizard moving. It scampered across the road, climbing over a pile of jagged rocks and disappearing into the shadows formed by them.

Wes stepped on the gas, and Derek relaxed in his seat. He braced his arm against the window, his fingers tapping at the top of the windowsill as he said, "They're also called the Zagrosian lizard. They're in the family Lacertidae, which means wall lizards."

"Fascinating," Cooper said dryly.

"Hey, someday, we'll be in a situation where obscure lizard facts will save our asses, and Derek will become the hero he was meant to be that day," Boone said.

"Thanks, I think?" Derek said.

The road led them through the desert to a town whose inhabitants had long since fled. Wes had driven through its deserted streets numerous times before on their way to different patrol areas.

Abandoned buildings lined either side of the road they drove down. Burned and blackened cars sat on flat tires in front of the buildings. Most of the buildings were crumbling from mortar rounds, with chunks of rock and brick perched precariously on caved-in roofs and deep cracks lining what walls had managed to remain upright.

A flicker of light to Wes's left caught his attention. He glanced out the window, searching for the source as his heart beat a little faster. The reflection of the sun off the scope of a sniper rifle, maybe?

"Wes, the intersection is coming up. Turn left," Derek said, tapping his fingers again at the top of the windowsill.

"It's a right," Wes said as he glanced at the road and then studied the building roofs.

"It's a left," Derek said.

Wes slowed down, still sweeping his gaze over the charred landscape beside him. It was probably just the sun catching on a shard of glass that caught his attention.

"I checked the map before we left. I'm sure it was a right," Wes said with another glance at the road.

"It's left, asshole. I know how to read a fucking map," Derek said. "Christ, Wes, you're gonna miss the fucking turn. Take a left, for fuck's sake."

Wes turned left. The two cars behind him followed dutifully, and Wes took a final look in the rear view mirror. There! The light flashed again, and Wes relaxed against the seat. Just like he thought, nothing more than the sun hitting some broken glass.

"Do you know what I'm going to do when we get back from patrol?" Boone said.

"Soak your feet and watch *Back to the Future*?" Grayson said.

"Nah, I'm gonna -"

Derek's window shattered, and Wes jerked the steering wheel to the left, his heart accelerating nearly as quickly as the Humvee as his seat jolted.

"What the fuck?" Boone said. He leaned forward and examined the hole in the side of Wes's seat.

"Wes?" Derek's voice was low and surprised.

Wes turned his head, his gaze widening as the world slowed to an agonizing crawl. Derek's face lost all its colour, and he reached under his right armpit before showing Wes the bright red blood on his fingers.

"Fuck!" Wes shouted. His heart a frantic knock against his ribcage, he blasted the Humvee down the road, turning left at the first side street and careening down it before slamming on the brakes.

"Masters, what the fuck?" Jorgens voice crackled over the radio.

He grabbed the mic as Derek slumped forward against his seatbelt. "Derek's been shot. There's a goddamn sniper. You and Rodriguez circle back, see if you can spot him. Watch your fucking backs."

The two other vehicles backed down the narrow road and disappeared. Wes slid out of the Humvee. Gray and Cooper were already out of the vehicle, their guns out and their gazes scanning the area around them. Boone yanked open Derek's door and undid his seat belt before easing him onto the ground. "Get the fucking kit, Wes!"

"Oh fuck, oh fuck, oh fuck," Boone chanted as he ripped open Derek's vest. "Wes, I need that fucking kit."

Wes grabbed the first-aid kit from the Humvee and dropped to his knees beside Derek's prone body. He stared at the gaping exit wound in Derek's left side just above his ribcage, his hand clenching around the kit.

"Wes, I need the fucking QuikClot!" Boone roared.

Wes pulled the QuickClot gauze from the kit, tearing them open and handing them to Boone, who slapped them down on the exit wound. Derek groaned as blood soaked the gauze immediately and then splashed to the ground, darkening the sand.

Wes ripped open more QuikClot gauze, pressing it down hard on the wound, as Boone placed a bloody hand on Derek's forehead. "Hang in there, buddy. We're calling for a medic. You'll be fine, okay? Don't move."

Derek stared up at him, his eyes dark holes in his pale face. He purred softly before making a low trill. Boone returned his trill before glancing at Grayson. "Call for a medic. Hurry."

"Boone." Cooper crouched beside Boone, his hand resting on his shoulder. "Boone, he's losing too much blood."

Grayson knelt next to Wes and pulled Derek's helmet off before he took his hand. Tears slid down his face as he smiled at Derek. "Hey, buddy."

"Don't leave," Derek whispered before drawing in a laboured, whistling breath. "Don't wanna die alone."

"You're not dying," Boone said fiercely. He shook off Cooper's hand and laid down next to Derek, sliding his arm under Derek's head, so it didn't rest in the hot sand. "You're going to be just fine, Derek. Do you fucking hear me? You're going to be fine."

"Terrible... liar," Derek said before spitting out a mouthful of blood.

Boone wiped the blood from Derek's chin and roughly kissed his forehead. "I'm not lying. You just need to stay awake, okay?"

Wes pressed harder against Derek's side, making him groan. The QuikClot wasn't enough. He could practically hear Derek's life blood pattering into the sand.

Boone glanced at Cooper and then at Wes. Wes's lion whined and retreated at the pure agony on Boone's face.

"Do something!" Boone snarled as his pupils turned to slits. "Don't just fucking stand there, you cunts. Do something, get on the motherfucking radio and call -"

"Boone," Derek wheezed, "stop."

Boone stared down at him and stroked his sweaty hair back from his forehead. "Don't talk. Conserve your strength until the medic gets here."

Derek smiled at him, his teeth coated in bright red blood. "Love you, man."

"I love you too," Boone said. "Please don't leave me, Derek. Okay? Don't leave me."

He took Derek's hand and kissed the palm of it before purring to Derek. "Please."

He rested his forehead against Derek's, purring and trilling. After a moment, Cooper rested his hand on Boone's back. "He's gone, Boone."

Wes's lion roared in pain and sorrow. He stood and staggered back, staring blankly at Derek and the others. This wasn't happening. Derek couldn't be fucking dead. This was a bad fucking dream, and he'd wake up any minute now.

He backed away until his ass hit the Humvee. He stared at Derek's body, at the dark pool of blood seeping into the sand below him, as his lion snarled and growled. Derek couldn't be dead because Wes made the wrong fucking turn.

Sand blew in his face, blinding him and clogging his throat, and he choked and coughed, brushing at his mouth and his eyes.

"It's your fault, Wes."

He looked up, terror icing his veins. Boone, Cooper, and Grayson were gone. Derek sat alone in the dusty sand, slumped over with blood drooling from his mouth.

"Derek?" he whispered.

Derek lifted his gaze, and Wes shrieked at the decay on his face. Derek's dark eyes were milky white, and the tip of his nose had rotted away. Worms squirmed in and out of the rotting holes in his cheeks, and when Derek grinned, Wes could see the nest of worms wiggling on Derek's tongue.

"I'm dead because of you, Wes. You knew we shouldn't have gone left, didn't you? You knew it. But you went left anyway, and now I'm fucking dead. Because of you." Derek climbed to his feet and shuffled toward him, golden tufts of fur stuck awkwardly to his degrading skin like thick tumbleweeds.

Wes held his hands out in front of him. "Derek, I'm sorry. I didn't mean for this to happen. I was... I was distracted, and I -"

"Dead because of you," Derek growled as his fangs, once white but now a dull mustard yellow, appeared. They sliced through a worm squirming near his lips, and half of its wriggling, squiggling body fell to the sand at Derek's feet. The other half slid back into his mouth.

"I didn't mean it, Derek," Wes moaned. "I'm so sorry."

Wes, wake up. Honey, please wake up.

"Dead because of you," Derek's voice was like a ghost in the wind.

"I'm sorry," Wes moaned again.

Wes, baby, open your eyes.

Her soft voice rang in his head. His lion cried mournfully and strained toward the sound of her voice. Wes wanted to follow him, oh how he wanted that, but he was frozen against the Humvee, mesmerized by the hate in Derek's milky gaze.

His lion made a low whimper. *Our mate calls us. Please.*

"This is your fault." Derek's cold finger reached out and traced Wes's cheek. "All your fault, Wesley."

He opened his mouth to scream, he had no choice *but* to scream, and then she was there in the desert. Her worried face, her warm brown eyes, the welcome scent of his mate obliterating the stench of decay and death.

"Wes!" Warm hands touched his chest and then stroked his face. "Please wake up, honey. Please."

Her voice and her touch pulled him entirely from the depths of his nightmare. He blinked groggily, staring up at Eleanor's face as she rubbed his chest again. "You had a bad dream."

"I'm okay," he rasped as he pushed himself into a sitting position. His hands shook wildly, but Eleanor took his hands and squeezed them before he could hide them under the quilt.

"You're not okay," she said. "You're shaking and," her fingertips traced his cheek, and she showed him the moisture on them, "crying."

He sucked in a deep and shuddering breath. "What time is it?"

"Just after nine," she said.

"In the evening?" He stared at her in confusion.

"No, the morning. It's Sunday morning." Eleanor cupped his face and pressed a kiss against his mouth. "You were moaning in your sleep, and then you - you made this awful cry and…"

"I'm sorry," he said.

"It's all right." She pressed her forehead against his. He pulled her into his lap and clung to her with panicky tightness until his breathing evened out.

"Wes?" she said.

"Yeah?"

"You were dreaming about Derek, weren't you?"

His hands tightened around her waist. "How do you know that?"

"You said his name in your sleep," she said. "Will you tell me what the dream was about?"

He didn't want to tell her, not when the nightmare of his death was so fresh, but when she pressed a kiss against his mouth and said, "Please tell me, honey," he couldn't resist her soft request.

"We were out on patrol…"

CHAPTER 18

Eleanor rubbed Wes's chest and pressed a kiss against his mouth. "I'm so sorry that happened, Wes."

She still sat on his lap. Halfway through his sharing about Derek, she'd tried to slide off his lap, worried that she was getting too heavy. He'd immediately pulled her closer and held her with an almost panicky tightness.

He brushed a kiss across her collarbone. "I worry about Boone a lot. He and Derek were the closest, and... he uses humour to hide his pain. I don't think he's completely processed Derek's death even now."

"Neither have you," she said, then winced at her bluntness. Shit, just once, she wished she had a filter.

He shrugged. "I've tried, okay? But nothing works."

"A trauma like the one you all went through needs therapy and -"

"I did therapy," he said. "We all did. It helped Gray and Coop."

"That's good." She stroked his thick, dark hair. "Are you still doing therapy?"

"There's no point. It didn't work. I'm managing it on my own."

"Are you? I saw the way you looked when you spoke about Derek at your birthday party, honey."

"Because we share the same birthday, and it's difficult to celebrate without him," Wes said.

"I think it's more than that," she said. "Daisy mentioned to me at the party that Cooper told her it's the first time you'd let them celebrate your birthday since Derek died."

"So what?" Wes said. "Can you blame me? What kind of asshole wants to celebrate his birthday when it's also the birthday of the guy he got killed?"

"Wes, it wasn't your fault." She hated that he thought it was his fault. Obviously, Wes felt guilty about what happened, but she assumed he felt survivor guilt, not… this.

"Yes, it is," he said. "I was driving. I turned down that fucking road."

"Is this why you don't drive anymore?" she said.

He tried to look away, and she cupped his face, turning him back to her. "Is it?"

"Yes," he said. "I've tried a million times to get behind the wheel since that day, and I can't. I have a panic attack every fucking time."

"Okay, that's understandable," she said. She hesitated, trying to be tactful but also kind with her words. "But you weren't the one who wanted to go left, right? Derek told you to go left."

"Exactly," he said as his face flushed. "I'd read the fucking map before we started the patrol, I knew Derek was shit at reading maps, but I still went left anyway because I let myself get distracted by something else. That distraction killed Derek."

"No, a sniper killed Derek. And, from the sounds of it, nearly killed you too. The bullet was in your seat."

His body was stiff beneath hers, and she could hear the agitation in his voice. "If I hadn't turned left, I would never have driven past that sniper, and Derek would have lived."

"Honey, I know it feels that way, but I promise you that isn't true. It was an accident."

He growled and lifted her off his lap, dumping her on the bed before climbing out and pacing back and forth. "Don't call it a fucking accident. It wasn't an accident."

"Okay," she said. "I apologize. That was the wrong terminology to use. But it wasn't your fault."

"Stop it," he said. "You weren't there, and you have no fucking idea what it's like to watch…"

He sucked in a deep breath, raking both hands through his hair. "It was my fault, and I have to live with that. End of story, Eleanor."

She could feel anger creeping under her skin. She tried to ignore it. Wes wasn't being deliberately bullheaded, she reminded herself. He really believed it was his fault.

"No, not end of story," she said. "I know this is difficult, but you have to go back to therapy, Wes. You need to find someone who will help you understand it isn't your fault. Please."

"Why do you care?" he snapped.

"Why do I… Wes, why would you ask me that?" she said. Hurt mixed in with the anger. "I care because I care about you."

"You shouldn't," he said. "I know you're lying about being okay with a sex-only relationship, Eleanor. It's written all over your face."

"So what if I am?" she said.

"I can't give you more," he said.

"Can't or won't?"

He growled again before glaring at her. "You shouldn't want to be with me. Why don't you understand that? I've told you what I did to my best friend. I am broken, Eleanor. I have so much fucking baggage that I can barely stand under its weight. I won't make you carry it too."

"What if I want to?" she said.

"You're crazy," he said with a jagged and bitter laugh that made her heart hurt.

"No, I just want to be with you. I'm not perfect either, Wes. But being in a relationship means we help each other with -"

"It isn't just this," he said.

"What do you mean?" she asked.

"I'm too old for you, and I can't give you what you want."

She stared at him. "What I want?"

"Do you remember when I told you I knew I wasn't the father of Juliet's baby?"

"Yes," she said as confusion loomed large. "Because the timing wasn't right."

"That's only the partial truth," he said. "I knew I wasn't the father because I can't medically have kids, Eleanor. I had never bothered to tell Juliet because she was adamant that she didn't want children."

"Okay," she said, "but what does that have to do with me?"

"I can't give you babies," he said. "If you and I become mates, you'll never have biological children. Is that what you want?"

"Yes," she said.

"And yeah, I know there's adoption, but forgetting that I

can't have them, I don't want them. And I'm not - wait, what?"

"I don't want kids, Wes," Eleanor said. "I never have."

He stared blankly at her before shaking his head. "Bullshit."

"Excuse me?" Her temper, always so close to the surface, flashed brightly. "What did you just say?"

"Juliet didn't want kids either. Now she has seven," he said.

"Are you seriously comparing me to her?" Eleanor said.

"No, but... look, you're young. You'll change your mind about wanting kids," he said dismissively.

Her anger washed over her like a flash flood, drowning everything in its path. "What the fuck, Wes!"

She climbed out of his bed and stalked out of his room. "You asshole."

He pulled on his jeans and followed her to the guest room, standing in the doorway as she dressed. "Eleanor, all I'm saying is -"

"Don't," she said. "I know exactly what you're saying, Wesley." To her dismay, tears slid down her cheeks. "I knew I didn't want kids by the time I was twelve years old. But since the very fucking moment I could physically have them, people have said that shit to me. Alluding that I'm too dumb to know what I want. That no real woman wants a life without kids, and in a few years when I *mature*, when I settle down with the right fucking man, I'll finally realize that my life couldn't possibly be complete without a kid or two."

She grabbed her overnight bag from the floor and stuffed her phone and her purse into it on top of the neatly folded clothes. "Do you know the only person who ever believed me was my mom? She never thought that I would change my mind. She loved me exactly the way I was. And then she died, and I had no one who understood me or accepted me just as I was."

She zipped up her bag. "But then I met you and you… you accepted me for who I was too. You didn't care that I talked all the time, or that I was too blunt, or too awkward, or too… Eleanor. You liked me the way I was. At least I thought you did. But I know better now. You're no different from the others, Wes. You think I'm stupid."

"Eleanor, I don't think you're stupid," he said. He purred to her, but she ignored it and threw her bag over her shoulder before grabbing her car keys from the nightstand.

"I'm sorry," he said. "I shouldn't have said that. Where are you going?"

"Back to my house," she said. "I can't stay here with you anymore."

"You can't leave," he said. "It isn't safe for you."

"It isn't safe for me here," she said.

Hurt flooded his face, but she told herself she didn't care. She couldn't stay here a minute longer.

"Butterfly, I can't let you leave," he said.

She reached into the side pocket of her overnight bag and pulled out the can of Mace, popping the lid off with her thumb and letting her finger hover over the button. "Get out of my way, Wes."

"Eleanor, you won't Mace me," he said.

"The fuck I won't," she said. "What you just said to me proves that you don't know me at all. So, let me be perfectly clear - I will Mace you if you try to stop me from leaving."

He growled low in his throat, and his pupils turned to slits as he talked to his lion. When he returned to her, she said, "Get out of my way."

He stepped aside so she could brush past him. "You're

letting your anger get the best of you, Eleanor. You're making stupid decisions."

"Well," she said as she yanked open the front door, "I guess that's not all that surprising since I'm so young and stupid, right?"

He growled. "I didn't say that."

"You didn't have to," she said. "It's written all over your damn face. Goodbye, Wes."

She walked out of the house, slamming the door behind her and stomping toward her car parked on the street as she shoved the Mace back into the side pocket of her bag.

Eleanor! What are you doing? Stop it right now. Get your ass back into Wes's house. You really are being so fucking stupid right now.

She muttered a curse but fuck if her inner voice wasn't right. She *was* being fucking stupid. Leaving Wes's house because he'd hurt her feelings was a goddamn too stupid to live move. She'd be damned if she was murdered because Wes thought she was young and dumb and made some shitty comment about the kid thing. Besides, she might not want to admit it, but she'd immediately overblown the situation because she was sensitive about it.

She took a deep breath as she stopped a few feet from her car. Okay, she would go back inside the house, and while she wasn't quite ready to talk to Wes or even look at him, she could sit in the guest room and sulk like a moody teenager, right? That would absolutely show him just how fucking mature she was.

With another soft curse, she turned and started back toward the house. She'd only taken a step or two when the man stepped out from between the shadows of Wes's house and his neighbour's house to the left.

She froze, staring cautiously at the man as he grinned at

her. He was the biggest man she'd ever seen with dark blue eyes, thick blond hair that hung in a tangled mess down his back, and a bushy blond beard sprouting on his jaw like an alpaca in desperate need of a grooming.

His massive body took a few steps closer. His neck was almost non-existent, hidden beneath the heavy muscles that rose above his shoulders. His arms were thick with corded muscle, and he had thighs so wide they needed their own damn zip code.

"Hello, Eleanor Whitman." His gravel-like voice sent horror scraping across her nerve endings. "You have something I want."

"Oh fuck," Eleanor said and ran for her car.

CHAPTER 19

Eleanor didn't even make it close to her car. The guy was scarily fast, and when his big meaty hand landed on her shoulder and whipped her around, she screamed piercingly.

His hand immediately closed around her throat, cutting off both her scream and her ability to breathe. Her bag slid off her shoulder, landing in the grass with a heavy thump, taking the precious Mace with it.

She clawed at his hands as he lifted her easily into the air, her feet dangling, black roses blooming in her vision, and her head feeling like it was about to pop off like a cork. She kicked at his groin, but he twisted away and grinned at her.

"Now, now, Eleanor Whitman, no being naughty. I want the flash drive. And if you give it to me without any fuss, I'll kill you quick. How about that? Would you like that?"

He leaned closer and pressed a kiss against the throbbing vein in her forehead. "Poor little human. So weak, so fragile. I can smell your fear, and it," he inhaled deeply as his pupils turned to slits and his fangs dropped, "smells delicious."

She kicked again at his groin, this time the toe of her

sneaker connecting, and he growled before shaking her. "Stop that, I said! Don't be naughty. Naughty girls get their guts torn out, and their eyeballs eaten. Do you understand, Eleanor Whitman?"

Her lungs screamed at her for air, but the man's grip didn't loosen, even when she dug her nails into his flesh.

He growled again. "As soon as I have that flash drive, I'm going to fuck you up so bad, you'll wish your momma had never given birth to you. You'll wish..."

He lifted his head and sniffed the air, a grin crossing his face as Wes's voice rang out. "Get the fuck away from her."

The man dropped Eleanor, and she collapsed on the ground. She sucked a whistling breath of air into her screaming lungs and then immediately coughed and gagged. Her eyes watering, she tried to get to her feet, but her trembling legs refused to hold her weight. She fell on her butt, still gasping in air through her swollen throat, still coughing and gagging.

"Lion shifter," the man said with a low growl as his body swelled. The back of his shirt tore, revealing rippling muscles covered in thick gold fur. "Give me what I want, or I'll kill the girl slow and make you watch."

Wes roared so loudly it made Eleanor's ears hurt. She stared in wide-eyed shock as both Wes and the man shifted abruptly. The stranger was a lion shifter like Wes, but he was... holy fuck, he was twice the size of Wes's lion. As he bounded toward Wes, she tried to scream Wes's name, but her ravaged throat immediately rebelled, and she doubled over with another coughing fit that made her dizzy.

She watched in horror as the two lions leaped at each other. Wes was sent flying by the heavier weight of the man, his lithe body slamming into the side of the house before dropping to the ground. He was on his feet in an instant, rising onto his hind legs and swiping one claw tipped paw at the bigger lion.

The lion roared with rage when Wes's claws raked across his face, drawing bright red blood. He crouched and leaped onto Wes, their bodies writhing and rolling on the ground. Eleanor staggered to her feet when Wes screamed. His attacker had sunk his fangs deep into Wes's shoulder. Eleanor stumbled forward, grabbing her bag and fumbling the Mace out of the pocket.

Wes twisted away from the larger lion, his tail lashing back and forth and his golden eyes glowing with anger. Bleeding heavily from his bitten shoulder, he didn't hesitate to charge forward and attack again. The lion swiped at him, barely missing Wes's face. Wes leaped onto him, using his weight to drive the lion to the ground.

Before he could bury his fangs into the lion's throat, the massive lion heaved Wes off like he weighed no more than a bug and quickly pinned him to the ground.

"Wes!" Eleanor screamed as the lion roared in triumph.

"No!" she screamed again and ran across the lawn toward the two lions. She wouldn't make it in time. She was too fucking slow. The man would rip out Wes's throat, and she'd have to watch the man she loved die. Her heartbeat tripled, sending a frantic rush of blood through her veins as she continued to run forward anyway, the Mace can held out in front of her.

Heavy footsteps thudded behind her, and a large, sleek tiger ran by her and leaped at the lion about to kill Wes. He landed on the lion with a meaty roar, knocking him off of Wes and driving him into the ground.

A second tiger ran past, his tail flicking out to snap around her legs and trip her. She hit the ground, her teeth snapping together and her knee screaming at her when it slammed into the ground.

Wes jumped to his feet as the two tigers fearlessly attacked the lion. He joined in, snarling and growling as the three of them tore at the lion with their teeth and their claws. The lion fought back savagely, his big body twisting and turning and his claws slicing through the air.

He howled in pain when one of the tigers danced forward and snapped his front leg with a hard bite of his immense jaws. Wes raked his claws down the lion's back, and the lion howled again, saliva dripping from his fangs as blood poured out of the wounds on his back.

Sirens wailed in the distance, and the lion swiped his paw across the bigger tiger's back, drawing a roar of outrage from the striped beast. The lion darted past the tiger and, with one final baleful glare at Eleanor, ran down the street and leaped over a neighbour's fence, his broken front leg dangling uselessly.

She climbed to her feet again, lurching forward as Wes shifted to his human form. He tore across the lawn, pulling her into his embrace and cupping her face. "Eleanor, baby, are you all right?"

"Are you?" she rasped as the sirens wailed and the neighbours stood on front porches and lawns, staring wide-eyed at them.

She touched his bitten shoulder, the bright red liquid making her stomach churn. "You're bleeding so much."

"It's fine," Wes said dismissively as he tilted her head up and examined her throat. "Your throat is bruised and swollen. You need to go to the hospital."

She swallowed, ignoring the sharp pain. "So do you."

"Everyone okay?" Grayson asked. He was naked, as was Boone when he joined them. Eleanor looked away - holy fuck, this was a weird time to be blushing over naked dudes - as Wes nodded.

"Who the fuck was that?" Boone examined the relatively shallow claw marks on Grayson's back.

"I don't know," Wes said as he glanced at Grayson. "I've never seen a shifter like that, have you?"

"No," Grayson said.

"The guy was on fucking 'roids or something," Boone said. "Did you see how strong he was? I can't believe I even broke his leg. It was like biting through steel."

Eleanor took a shuddering breath, and Wes stroked her back as a fire truck, and an ambulance turned onto the street, followed by a cop car.

"Shit," Boone said. "Looks like the neighbours called in the entire fucking calvary." He waved at a woman standing on the lawn of the house to their right and staring unabashedly at his crotch. "Hello, ma'am. Beautiful morning, isn't it?"

"Get Cooper on the phone," Grayson said to Boone. "Tell him we need him here now. And maybe a Council rep. The cops will probably be human."

"Fucking Council is gonna lose their shit over this mess," Boone said.

"No one says a word about what's going on with Eleanor," Grayson said. "As far as we know, the shifter is a complete stranger who just randomly attacked Eleanor. Got it?"

Wes and Boone nodded. Feeling like she might barf, Eleanor buried her face in Wes's thick neck and closed her eyes.

"I WISH YOU WOULD CHANGE YOUR MIND, BUTTERFLY." WES took Eleanor's hand, squeezing it lightly as she sat at the kitchen table nursing a cup of hot tea that Boone had made for her. He desperately wanted to pick up his mate and carry her kicking and screaming to the hospital if he had to, but he was afraid to do anything more than touch her hand. She'd almost died today because of him. He was shocked that she would even let him hold her hand.

"I'm not going to the hospital," she said, her voice hoarse. "The paramedics said I was fine."

"No, they said it didn't look like there was permanent damage, but you should probably have it checked out by a doctor," Boone said.

She made a face at Boone, who grinned. "Hey, it's what they said."

"My knee hurts worse than my throat," she said with another scowl at Boone. "Why did you trip me, anyway?"

"Well," Boone drawled as he leaned against the counter, "while I appreciate your bravery in trying to go after the biggest fucking lion shifter I've ever seen in my life with nothing but a can of Mace, it wouldn't have ended well for you."

She flushed, staring at hers and Wes's linked fingers. "Wes needed my help."

Wes wanted to argue, but it was true. He had needed help. He'd been about ten seconds from getting his throat ripped out. If Grayson and Boone hadn't shown up when they did, he'd be dead, and so would his mate.

His lion growled unhappily, but underneath that growl, he could feel the beast's unease at what happened. He'd never been bested in a fight, and it wasn't the near-death experience that his lion wasn't taking well, but rather the defeat in battle.

"Why did you show up at my place this morning?" he said.

"Grayson and I met for a sparring match," Boone said. "I asked him to swing by here afterward so I could drop off Nan's video camera for you."

"Thank God," Eleanor said, her voice breaking a little. "If you hadn't…"

She swallowed hard, wincing and then sipping some more tea as the tears leaked down her face. Wes wanted to wipe them away, he wanted to pull her into his lap and tell her everything would be okay, but he was still frozen by the idea that Eleanor would never speak to him again after this.

"Why didn't you just shoot him?" Eleanor asked abruptly. Her gaze levelled out on Wes. "I know you carry a gun. You all do." She stared at Boone and then at Grayson. "Why didn't any of you just shoot him in the head?"

"It's against the code," Cooper said as he walked into the kitchen. "The Council rep just left. She has your number and mine, Wes, and she said she'd call if the officers on scene needed to question the three of you again. Or if they catch the shifter who attacked you and Eleanor."

"They're not gonna catch him," Boone said. "You see how fast he fucking moved even with a broken leg? He was almost as fast as Chase. Do you think he's some sort of lion cheetah hybrid?"

"Hybrids don't exist," Cooper said with a frown. "You know that, Boone."

Boone shrugged. "Who the fuck knows what scientists are cooking up now in labs."

"What do you mean code?" Eleanor said.

"Shifters don't fight other shifters with guns," Grayson said. "It's considered weak, or a dishonour, to use a human's weapon against another shifter. We fight each other as we're meant to."

Confusion crossed Eleanor's face. "But… Daisy told me that a shifter shot Cooper in the shoulder and Chase in the stomach."

Cooper cleared his throat. "She was a female shifter."

"What does that have to do with anything?" Eleanor said.

"The code is primarily a male shifter thing," Grayson said.

"Are you kidding me?" Eleanor said. "Wes almost died because of some fucked-up honour code between asshole macho shifters? That lion was the size of a fucking dinosaur! He's obviously on something like Boone said. It was already an unfair fight the minute the guy shifted. One of you should have just fucking shot him!"

She trembled in her seat, her mug of tea forgotten, hot tears flowing down her cheeks. "Wes almost died. Do you get that? He was five fucking seconds from dying, and you're talking about some stupid honour code!"

She burst into sobs. Wes pulled her chair over to him and lifted her out of it, ignoring the throb of pain in his bitten shoulder. He held her on his lap, relief rushing through him when she flung her arms around him and clung tight, burying her face in his neck as she cried.

"Shh, Butterfly, it's all right," he murmured before purring to her. The others waited patiently as he purred to his mate and rubbed her back. After only a few minutes, her crying tapered off into the occasional watery sniff.

Cooper handed Wes the box of tissues from the counter, and Wes gave Eleanor a couple. She wiped her face and blew her nose before saying, "I'm sorry."

"Don't apologize," Grayson said. "You've had a terrible morning."

"That's the fucking understatement of the year," Boone said.

"What do we do now?" Eleanor said.

"You and Wes come back to my place," Cooper said.

"No," Wes and Eleanor said in unison.

Cooper scowled at them. "Yes. Gray and Ryan's place is too small, and Boone has Nan at his house. You're staying with me until -"

"I won't put you and Daisy in danger," Eleanor said. "It's bad enough that I almost got Wes killed. In fact, I'm leaving here and staying in a motel."

"Oh, no fucking way is that happening," Wes said. His lion pushed forward, and Wes let him take control.

"No," his lion growled at Eleanor. "You stay by my side, my mate."

"Wes," Coop said, "control."

"Holy shit," Boone said. "How long has it been since we've heard Wes's lion talk? I kind of figured he'd gone mute."

Wes pushed his lion back, taking a deep breath as his arm tightened around Eleanor's slender waist. "You're not staying in a motel, Eleanor."

"Wes, I…"

"No," he said. "We are not arguing about this. The answer is no. Full fucking stop."

She took a deep breath, and he could smell her frustration, but under that, there was relief. She was terrified, and he hated that his mate was afraid, hated that he had failed at protecting her.

He swallowed down his self-loathing as Cooper leaned against the counter next to Grayson. "Fine, you don't want to stay at my place, then we post two men outside the house in case this asshole decides to come back."

"It'll take him a while to heal from the broken arm and the wounds we gave him," Wes said.

"I'm not taking any chances," Cooper said. "Leaving you and Eleanor alone without protection is not an option."

Wes's lion grumbled, but Wes ignored him. They did need the added protection. His earlier failure proved that.

"I'll take the first shift," Grayson said.

Boone shook his head. "I'll do it. Go home and get some rest. Those slashes on your back will heal faster if you're taking it easy."

"They're shallow," Grayson said. "It's fine."

"Go home and get Ryan to pour some alcohol over them," Boone said with a grin. "Those medicated wipes the paramedics used probably don't do shit. Who knows what the fuck that dude has in his claws. You really want to get a bacterial infection?"

Gray grimaced as Boone said, "I just need to text Hedra and let her know I won't be home." Boone's face reddened, but Wes didn't have the spoons to wonder what that was about. He was bone tired and still worried that Eleanor would try to leave him again.

"I've just texted Chase," Cooper said. "He's on his way over. He and Boone can take the first shift, and then, if he's feeling up to it, Grayson and Adam will cover overnight."

Eleanor slid off his lap, and Wes swallowed his lion's grumble of protest. She carried her tea mug to the sink as Wes stood.

"Thanks, Coop," Wes said. "I appreciate this."

Cooper clapped him on the uninjured shoulder. "You know we have your back, man. Always."

CHAPTER 20

"I could stay at a motel, and Boone and Chase could watch me there," Eleanor said. Cooper and Grayson had left as soon as Chase arrived, and she and Wes sat silently in the kitchen for nearly five minutes before she couldn't take the silence anymore.

Wes grimaced. "No, Eleanor. Look, I get that you have your doubts about me protecting you now, but I promise that _"

"What? No, that isn't it," she said. "Wes, you saved my life this morning."

A look of guilt and regret, and anger crossed his face. "If Grayson and Boone hadn't shown up, we'd both be dead."

He stood and stalked to the counter, staring moodily out the window over the sink. She joined him and reached up to cup his face, turning it toward hers. "Wes, that guy wasn't just some crazy big shifter... he was insane too. He wanted the flash drive, yeah, but he also had no control. I could see it in his face. He was about to kill me, just... just choke the life out of me. If you hadn't come outside..."

She shuddered all over, and Wes pulled her up against

him. He showered her face with soft kisses before resting his forehead against hers. "I'm sorry, Butterfly. I'm so fucking sorry."

"It's not your fault," she said.

"I shouldn't have compared you to Juliet, and I shouldn't have dismissed your feelings on having kids. I upset you so much that you left the safety of the house," he said.

"That's on me," she said. "I was the stupid asshole who left. I could have just gone to the guest room to pout. I should never have left, and I knew the minute I walked out the door that I was making a too stupid to live move. I only got halfway to my car before I turned around to go back to the house, but the guy was there."

Wes kissed her forehead again. "When I came outside and saw you dangling in his grip, I…"

"What?" she whispered, staring up at him. Her stomach clenched, and she willed him to say he loved her. She loved him - she knew that now - and even though he'd been clear about what she meant to him, a small part of her couldn't give up hope that he loved her too.

"What, Wes?" she said.

"I was terrified I would lose you," he said.

Disappointment crashed over her. She tried to mask it with a smile as she squeezed Wes's waist and pressed a kiss against his jaw. "You didn't. I'm safe. But also exhausted. I'm going to lie down in the guest room for a while."

She pulled away and turned around before he could see her crying. She wouldn't make him feel bad or guilty for not feeling the same way she felt about him. His lion might think of her as his mate, but Wes didn't, and he wasn't going insane over it like Cooper had almost done with Daisy. Wes would convince his lion that she wasn't his mate and she'd never -

"Eleanor." Wes's low voice stopped her in the doorway of the kitchen.

"Yeah?" She scrubbed the tears from her face but didn't turn around.

"I'm all in."

Her hand clenched around the door frame, her fingers digging into the wood. "Wh-what did you say?"

"I'm all in, Butterfly."

She turned to stare at him, and his sweet smile brought fresh tears to her eyes. "I love you, Eleanor. You're my mate, and whatever you want from me, I'll give you. You want just to date, we'll date. You want to live together, I'll hire a moving truck tomorrow. You want to get married... just say when and where and I'll be there. I love you."

"You love me," she said.

"Yes."

"You want to marry me."

"Yes," he said.

She walked slowly toward him, taking his hands and staring up at him. "Wes, does this have something to do with your near-death experience? Are you declaring your love because of some messed up 'I almost died' high you have going on?"

He burst out laughing and pulled her close, kissing her until she was breathless. "No. I love you because I love you. Almost losing you made me finally pull my head out of my ass and realize that all that matters is being with you, my mate."

"You did totally have your head right up your ass about this whole thing," she said.

He laughed again before purring to her. "Does that mean you love me too?"

"You know I do," she said. "But, just so we're clear - I

love you, Wesley Masters. I love you to the fucking moon and back, as the saying goes."

His purring grew louder, and she grinned at him. "I love that sound."

"Good, because you'll hear it a lot. My lion is obsessed with you," he said.

"I know," she said with a smug grin.

He smiled before his face sobered. "Eleanor, I meant what I said. I'll do whatever you want to make this relationship work. But you need to know that it may not be a smooth ride for us. Derek's death is still… it's something I struggle with, and I don't know if I'll ever truly be free of the guilt. I'll go back to therapy, I will, but I can't shake the feeling that it won't work."

She traced her fingers along his jawline. "I know. But being willing to go back into therapy is the first step. And I promise I will be with you no matter what. I have baggage too, Wes. You don't have to be perfect… neither of us does, right?"

"Right," he said.

He kissed her again, and she reached around to squeeze his ass. "Why don't we go back to the bedroom?"

"You did say you were tired," he said as he trailed a path of kisses down her throat, being infinitely gentle on the bruised skin. "We could probably both use a nap."

"True, but I was thinking first you eat my pussy and then fuck me until I can't see straight, and then we'll nap," Eleanor said.

"I think that can be arranged, Butterfly," Wes said with a slow grin.

"Maybe this isn't such a good idea." Eleanor ghosted her fingertips over the bandage covering Wes's shoulder. "The paramedic said no big movements or strenuous exercise, remember?"

"I don't need my shoulder to eat your pussy," Wes said as he unbuttoned his jeans.

Eleanor laughed. "I'm now picturing you trying to muscle your shoulder up inside my lady bits."

Wes grinned as he kicked off his jeans and his briefs. "No shoulder, only tongue."

He reached out and hooked his finger around her belt loop, tugging her closer. "Take off your clothes, Butterfly."

She chewed at her bottom lip. She wanted to fuck Wes. She was already halfway to soaking her panties just thinking about being with him - apparently, declarations of love really got her excited - but despite what he said, she could see the pain lines around his eyes, and his face was pale.

"I don't think we should," she said.

"I disagree." He bent his head and pressed a soft kiss against her mouth. "It's not that painful."

"How about we compromise," she said. "You lie on your back on the bed, and I'll do all the work."

"I have been meaning to ask you to sit on my face," he said before nipping her earlobe.

Her face flushed red, and he grinned. "I'm getting a sunburn from the glow of your blush."

"I've never had a guy ask me to sit on his face before," she said. "You're, like, kind of kinky."

He laughed. "If that's your idea of kinky, be prepared to be shocked by the stuff I'll do to you."

Her throat went dry, and she dug her fingers into Wes's waist when he cupped her breast and squeezed lightly. Her pussy was throbbing, and any hesitation about fucking Wes had deserted her. "What kind of stuff?"

He sucked on her bottom lip before releasing it with a soft pop. "Get undressed, and I'll show you."

She undressed so fast she was surprised her panties didn't start a fire when she raked them down her legs.

"You're so beautiful, Butterfly," Wes said when she stood naked in front of him.

"So, are you." She palmed his cock, rubbing lightly before wrapping her fingers around him and stroking with long, deep pulls.

He moaned and made a motion toward the bed. "Fuck, Eleanor, we need to be on the bed. Right now."

She ran her fingers around the head of his cock and kissed his chest. "Agreed."

Wes headed toward the bed, and Eleanor's eager footsteps slowed when he grimaced as he sat on the bed.

"Wes -"

"I'm fine," he said. "Come here, Eleanor."

"Let's table the kinky stuff for now," she said.

"I need to be with you," he said, the raw emotion in his eyes making her throat tighten again. "I almost lost you today, Butterfly."

"I know," she said. "I feel the same way. I'm not saying we shouldn't bang each other's brains out. I'm just saying that we'll save the kink for later. Lie on your back, Wes."

He gave in faster than she expected, which told her he was in more pain than he would admit. Moving carefully, he relaxed on his back on the bed before stroking his cock with one rough hand.

Fresh desire rampaged through her body, and she quickly straddled him, knocking his hand away and gripping the base of his dick.

She positioned her slender body over him, pressing the head of his dick against her opening. Wes frowned. "Wait, let me make sure you're wet enough to -"

She pushed down, taking all of Wes's cock in one delicious, wet slide that had her gasping and him groaning out a tortured "Fuuuuuck."

She grinned, resting her hands on his flat abdomen as his eyes glowed and his fangs dropped. "I'm wet enough."

"Fuck yes, you are," he said as he gripped her hip with one hand. "Ride me, Eleanor."

"Whatever you say, Wes," she said.

He thrust up, and she clamped her knees around his hips like he was a bucking bronco. "Ooh, you liked that."

"I might have a small - *minuscule* - dominant streak in the bedroom," he said.

"Minuscule, huh?" she said. "So, if I tell you that one of my favourite things in the bedroom is to be handcuffed to the bed while being fucked, you won't judge me?"

He jerked again, she could almost feel his cock swelling inside of her, and her grin widened.

"And you call me the kinky one," he said.

She made a few experimental bounces, watching the way his face flooded with pleasure and need. "That's the kinkiest thing I've ever done. But I'm interested in trying other stuff."

"Like what?" he said as she braced her hands on his chest and started a slow up and down rhythm.

Suddenly feeling shy, she said, "I don't know. Um... would you spank me?"

His hand squeezed her hip hard as he grinned at her. "If you ask me nicely."

She laughed and leaned over him to brush her lips across his. "I won't call you 'sir' in the bedroom. Don't even ask."

He cupped her ass and rubbed lightly. "I wouldn't dream of it, Butterfly. Fuck, you feel so good on my dick."

She moved a little faster, watching the play of emotions cross his face, studying the way his fangs seemed to grow longer with every thrust. He slid his hand between them, and his fingers brushed over her aching clit.

"Oh," she breathed, her fingers pressing into his hard chest. "Do that again."

He used his thumb to rub her clit in firm circles, and she lost a bit of her rhythm as she ground against him. She slowed to a stop and concentrated on chasing her orgasm, reaching for her peak as she rocked against Wes's thumb.

She stared at Wes as her climax grew closer, her body shuddering and her pussy clenching around his cock. He smiled at her, his eyes a beautiful gold and his pupils narrow slits.

As her orgasm washed over her, she gasped, "I love you, Wes."

He purred to her, the sound draping over her like a warm blanket as she rocked back and forth, squeezing and releasing his dick.

"I love you too, Eleanor." He purred to her again, his hand rubbing her hip as she braced her trembling hands on his chest and sat up.

"Your turn," she said.

Her body still shaking, she concentrated on her movements, trying to keep them slow and controlled as Wes met each of her thrusts. He made a low growl, staring intently at her breasts, and then gave her a light slap on the ass that did weird things to her insides.

"Harder, Butterfly."

She did what he asked, and he purred to her. "Good mate. You're so wet and tight. I love being in your pussy."

She shuddered with new pleasure and reached for her clit. She didn't have to touch herself to come, but the look on Wes's face when she did, made it even hotter. He purred again, making soft sounds of praise as she rubbed at the swollen bundle of nerves.

"Good mate," he said. "Show me how gorgeous you look when you're coming all over my cock."

"Oh my God, Wes," she moaned before letting her head drop back. She rode each of his thrusts, barely hearing the low growls and groans of pleasure he made as she grew close to her second orgasm. With a low cry, she came again, grinding herself against Wes.

Wes's purring filled the room, and he made two final hard thrusts. Wetness flooded her pussy, and she collapsed against his chest, breathing hard and listening to the wild beat of Wes's heart beneath her ear.

He stroked her sweaty back, his body trembling lightly under hers.

"That was so good," she said.

"Hmm," he said.

She rolled off of him, collapsing on her back beside him. He took her hand, and they stared silently at the ceiling before he squeezed her hand and smiled at her. "I love you."

"I love you too."

"Good." He purred to her before pulling up the quilt. "Let's nap."

She laughed and curled into Wes's warm, hard body. "Yes, let's."

CHAPTER 21

"What the hell?" Chad maximized the video screen on his monitor, staring in horror at Rourke's upper body. "What the fuck happened to you?"

"Two tigers and a lion," Rourke said with a low growl. He left his phone propped up on the hotel desk, and Chad watched as he limped to the bed and sank onto it with a low groan. The slashes and bite marks on his upper body were raw and swollen, and Rourke grimaced when a bite on his abdomen started bleeding again.

His left arm dangled uselessly at his side, and Chad leaned in closer to the screen. "Is your arm broken?"

"Yeah," Rourke grunted. "Fucker bit through and snapped the bone."

Using one hand, he unfolded a leather pouch and withdrew one fluid-filled syringe. Grimacing, he injected it into his broken arm before removing a second syringe.

"Just one," Chad said sharply. "You don't need both."

"Fuck you," Rourke snarled, flipping his long hair out of his face.

"One is enough to heal you," Chad said.

Ignoring him, Rourke injected the second syringe before dropping it on the bed next to the first one. He closed his eyes, his nostrils flaring, and rolled his head from side to side.

"For fuck's sake, you asshole," Chad said. "You remember that we have a limited quantity of serum, right? There's only three more, and based on how you look like you just got your ass kicked, I assume you didn't get the formula."

"You watch your fucking mouth," Rourke growled as his eyes popped open. Their normal dark brown had gone a golden yellow, and his body was swelling. "You think because you're in your office and I'm here in this buttfuck city in a second-rate motel, that you're safe from me? I will tear your head from your fucking body and nail it to the goddamn wall for everyone to see if you keep mouthing off to me."

Cold fear ran down Chad's spine, but he didn't allow it to show on his face. "Did you get the formula or not?"

"Does it look like I got the fucking formula?" Rourke roared.

Chad flinched back when Rourke stood and turned toward the wall. He drove his right fist through the wall, roaring again as he pulled his hand out. Drywall dust and blood coated it, and Rourke licked at his knuckles before glaring at Chad. "I'm getting fucking tired of your dumb questions, Chad."

"I'm still your superior," Chad said. "So, you'll answer those stupid questions without losing your fucking shit, or you'll find yourself going through withdrawal just like the rest of the team."

Rourke's face paled, and the fur that was growing on his body faded slowly away. "Are you threatening me?"

"No," Chad said. He was playing a dangerous game, one

that could very easily get him killed, but if Rourke thought he had all the power, they were in big fucking trouble. "But it's a reminder that you work for me, not the other way around. We need that formula."

"I know," Rourke sank onto the bed again, rubbing gingerly at the claw marks that covered most of his upper body. "I would have had it today, but that lion shifter's asshole buddies showed up."

Chad took a deep breath. "I'm sending a team of six to you. We'll keep an eye on them, make sure they don't move her to some secret location where we'll never fucking find her. In a couple of days, you and the team will hit them again. This time, you'll - "

"I don't need any fucking help," Rourke growled.

"You do, or you'd have the formula right now," Chad said. "We've underestimated this security firm, and we need -"

"I don't need shit!" Rourke shouted. "I'll be back tomorrow night with the fucking formula. You send anyone here to help, and I'll send them back to you in a fucking card-board box. You hear me, asshole?"

"I'm in charge, not you," Chad said. "I make the decisions about -"

"I'll get the formula tomorrow," Rourke said and ended the call.

"Fuck!" Chad slammed his hands down on the desk, barely able to restrain his urge to throw his laptop through the window behind him.

"Still think it was a good idea to send Rourke?"

"Fuck off, Hoyt," Chad said, glaring at the man standing in his doorway.

"You sending the others to help or not?"

"Keep listening in on my private calls, and I'll have you cleaned," Chad said.

"I'm the least of your fucking problems right now, buddy. You need to clean Rourke," Hoyt said.

"You're insane," Chad said with a tired laugh. "He's the only one of the enhanced we have left. Even if we get the formula back and make more juice, Doc doesn't think the others can handle it. Says their bodies are too weak now and that it'll most likely kill them. Which means we gotta find more recruits and -"

"You can't keep using it," Hoyt said. "Look what it's done to Rourke. Hell, the others were just as bad, he's just the most unstable. There's something wrong with the formula, Chad. You know it. Tell the Board -"

"Tell the Board what? That the thirty million they've invested in this little project was for nothing?" Chad said. "That, sure we can enhance shifters, but it makes them lose their fucking minds? If I go to the Board and tell them it's not working, do you know what will happen? They'll fucking clean all of us and start the fuck again. Do you understand, Hoyt? All of us are fucking dead if we can't make this work. So, tell me again that I should go to the Board and admit the serum isn't perfect."

Hoyt swallowed hard before scrubbing his hand across his face. "So, the alternative is to have insane shifters with super strength on the payroll?"

"We'll fix it," Chad said. "But first, we need the formula."

"You send anyone to Rourke, and he'll kill them," Hoyt said. "You know that."

"Yeah." Chad took out a bottle of aspirin and chewed four of them. "Send eight. Tell them to stay off of Rourke's radar. Tomorrow night, assuming they don't move her out of the lion shifter's house, our guys will clean any security and this

Masters guy. Once they have the formula from Eleanor, they'll kill her and torch the house. It'll be quick and quiet."

"And if Rourke tries again before tomorrow night?" Hoyt said.

"He won't. He was badly injured. Even with the serum, it'll take him a couple of days to heal."

"You sure?"

Chad opened the bottom drawer and grabbed the bottle of bourbon. "No, I'm not fucking sure." He poured himself a shot and swallowed, the taste chasing away the chalkiness of the aspirin that lingered in his mouth. "But we'll have to hope I'm right."

"You sure you want to do this?" Wes said.

Eleanor nodded. "We have to. It could tell us what the hell that formula is on the flash drive, right?"

"Or it could be a homemade porn video," Wes said.

Despite her trepidation, Eleanor laughed. "Thanks for reminding me of that. If we hear any *bow-chicka-bow-wow* music, we immediately burn the video, deal?"

He grinned and kissed her forehead. "Deal."

She watched, tapping her fingers in a nervous rhythm against the couch arm, as Wes loaded the cassette into Boone's grandmother's camcorder. He'd hooked up the camcorder to his television, and she stared at the TV screen and held her breath when he hit play on the camcorder.

She didn't release it until her father appeared, dishevelled and sweaty but fully dressed, thank God.

"Eleanor, I need you to do something for me." Her father stared directly into the camera before mopping at his forehead with a checkered handkerchief.

The sight of his handkerchief brought on a pang of loss so deep, it felt like she'd been cut straight to the bone. She clutched at the couch arm as all the air disappeared from the room and the TV first wavered and then blurred.

"Eleanor!" Wes's voice came from a distance, and she clung to his arm when he wrapped it around her waist. "Take a breath, Eleanor."

"No air," she gasped out.

"There is." His voice was calm but firm. "Take a breath, Butterfly."

She breathed in, shocked when her burning lungs inflated with air. She let it out in a hard rush as Wes rubbed her back. "Good, take another one."

She took another and then another and then another, clinging tightly to Wes's arm until the world stopped being so weirdly blurry.

"You okay?" Wes cupped her face, his thumb rubbing her cheekbone, his fingers kneading the back of her neck.

"Yes, I… his handkerchief… it just brought on a lot of memories. He always had one in his pocket, and they were always checkered and…"

She paused, sucked in another breath, centred herself. "Sorry. I sound stupid."

"No, you don't," Wes said. "Memories are powerful." He pressed a kiss against her mouth. "Maybe we should do this later."

"No, I'm good now. Let's keep watching," Eleanor said.

"Are you sure?"

She didn't know if she was or not. Her stomach churned, and her hands and feet were cold while her cheeks burned. But she couldn't just sit here like a crybaby. She needed to know why she was being hunted.

"I'm sure," she said.

She stared at the screen as Wes hit the play button again.

"What I need from you is easy but important," her father said. "Take the bus locker key I've given you and put it in a safe place. Do you understand, Eleanor? You need to keep it hidden and don't tell anyone I sent it to you."

Her cheeks burned brighter as the loss and the sorrow slowly dissipated. Here was the father she remembered, the guy who always acted like she was no brighter than a burnt-out light bulb. The guy who could never seem to speak to her without that look on his face - the one that practically screamed, *why are you so stupid?*

"Don't forget where you put it," he said sharply as he rubbed at his chest. "This is too important to be another victim of your forgetful mind."

She sighed and glanced at Wes. "Once when I was seven, I put my new crayons in a safe place to keep the dog from eating them and then forgot where they were. Dad wouldn't buy me new ones and never let me forget what an airhead I was."

Wes growled deep in his throat as her father leaned forward and adjusted the view on the camera. "I need to disappear for a few months, but I'll contact you when I get back so you can deliver the key to me. This is incredibly important, Eleanor. My life's work depends on you keeping it safe. Do you understand?"

He paused for a moment, rubbing absently at his chest again as indecision crossed his face. "Shit, I need to tell you what it is in case... in case something happens."

He glanced to the right and then the left before clearing his throat. "I've worked tirelessly for the last decade to create a serum that enhances shifter's abilities."

"Oh fuck," Eleanor said.

"The company who funded my research is Dynasty Labs.

They found me twelve test subjects. Six lions, four tigers, two cougars. The serum made all of them stronger and faster. Not just that… it helps them heal faster too. The possibilities for what this means are endless. We can use the enhanced to help us win wars and make sure the good guys are in charge. I did that, Eleanor. I made that possible. You're looking at a future Nobel prize winner."

She glanced at Wes. He stared at her father with a combination of disgust and disbelief. Her father had always been arrogant. She wasn't surprised that he believed what he was doing was for the greater good.

"But there's an issue," her father said. "The formula isn't just making them stronger and faster. It's also affecting their emotions. It's upping their anger and urge to dominate while reducing their capacity to feel love or empathy. I warned the Board this could happen, but they wouldn't listen to me."

His face paled, the arrogance fading away to leave a look of sick regret. "They sent them on missions, even after it was obvious they were getting worse. The last mission, it… it went bad, Eleanor. Horribly bad. They killed innocent people, innocent *humans*, and they didn't even care. Rourke is the worst of them, but all twelve of them are affected to some degree."

He reached off camera for a glass of water, drinking half of it and then wiping his mouth with his handkerchief. "That's when I knew I had to do something. The formula will work. It just needs some tweaking. But the Board, they don't care. The aggression doesn't bother them, and they don't see the danger. But I do. I needed more time to fix it, but they refused. They were about to start mass-producing it, Eleanor. There were plans to start distributing it to the military as is."

He wiped his face again, staring blankly at the handkerchief. "I couldn't let that happen. So, I destroyed the serum at the lab, and I took the formula before they could send it out of the lab. I put it on a flash drive, and it's safe in a bus locker. The enhanced require a dose of the serum every twelve hours. Without regular dosing, they lose their abilities, go through withdrawal like an addict."

He sucked in a harsh breath. "I destroyed all of the serum. At least, I think I did. That bastard Chad might have some squirreled away. But even if he did... it wouldn't be enough for all twelve. I have to believe that they're no longer a threat."

He sighed and stared into the camera again. "I have to disappear for a while. I've destroyed my phone. It's bugged, and they can track me with it. They'll be looking for me and if they find me... I'm dead."

His face twisted. "Honestly, the probability that they find me is rather high. I'm a biochemist, not some sort of spy. It's too much of a risk to keep the formula with me, the people I work for are incredibly dangerous, but they don't know about you, Eleanor. I've never mentioned a daughter. I've cut you out of every part of my life so they wouldn't find out about you."

He winced and rubbed at his upper arm. "You'll keep the formula safe until I've found others who will protect me and allow me to continue my work until it's perfect. But, if something happens to me, if they... find me, destroy it. Do you hear me, Eleanor? Destroy the flash drive. We can't risk the formula falling back into their hands, or worse, into the hands of someone who doesn't understand how extraordinary my creation is."

He reached for the camera before pausing. "Goodbye, Eleanor. I'll be in touch soon." He fumbled for the button, and she had one last glimpse of his sweaty face before the recording ended.

Wes shut off the television and the camcorder before sitting back on the couch and staring at her. "You okay, Butterfly?"

"Yes, why?" She gave him a puzzled look.

"I don't know… maybe because your father deliberately put you in danger without even thinking twice about it. Or because he's a shit dad who couldn't even say he loved you in what turned out to be his last message to you?"

"He doesn't love me," she said. "Why would he say it?"

He grimaced and reached for her hand. "He's an idiot."

"He was quite brilliant. Brilliant enough to create a formula that enhances shifters, but stupid enough to think it was a good idea." Eleanor sat back on the couch, staring blankly at the television. "So, there are potentially another eleven shifters like that insane lion this morning. Fantastic."

"Maybe not," Wes said. "You heard your dad. He destroyed the serum."

"Yeah, but obviously, there was some he didn't destroy," Eleanor said. "What if there was enough for all of them."

"If there were, we'd know by now," Wes said.

Fear ate at Eleanor's insides. "Because all of them would have attacked us a second time."

Wes nodded. Eleanor reached for his hand. "I'm so sorry, Wes. I hate that I've dragged you into this and -"

"You didn't," he said. "Besides, you're my mate, and I will do whatever is necessary to protect you."

She squeezed his hand. "How's the bite on your shoulder?"

"Already starting to heal," he said.

She frowned. "Seriously? I know shifters can heal faster than humans, but that seems quick."

He shrugged. "We heal faster from wounds we receive from other shifters than we do from regular injuries."

"Man, there's so much I need to learn about shifters," Eleanor said. She paused and then said, "I think I should destroy the formula."

"I don't think that's a good idea. If you destroy it, the men who are looking for you will kill you," Wes said.

"They're gonna kill me anyway," Eleanor said.

"Not if we expose what they're doing," Wes said. "We know the name of the lab your father worked for, and we have the formula as proof. Cooper has a journalist friend, Mariana, who works for The Bridgedale Daily. We'll ask him to contact her and see if she can meet with us. We'll tell her about the formula and what the lab's been doing."

"That seems like a bad idea," Eleanor said.

"Exposing them is the only way to stop them from hunting you," Wes said. "You can't live your life constantly looking over your shoulder. This is our best chance at ending this, I promise."

Wes glanced at his watch. "I'll call Cooper and update him on what we've found out from your dad's video and ask him to call Mariana. Then we'll make some dinner. Okay?"

"Sure," she said. "It felt weird to do mundane things like make dinner when there was a crazed lion shifter after her for a formula her father created, but maybe this was her life now. She'd finally found her person, just in time for the rest of her life to go to shit.

Wes rested his forehead against hers and slid his arms around her waist. "Everything will be fine, Butterfly. I'll keep you safe. I promise."

CHAPTER 22

"I feel stupid." Eleanor pitched her voice low, so she didn't disturb Boone or Chase, who were in the cubicles on either side of Wes's.

Wes looked up from his laptop. "Why?"

"Because I'm sitting in your cubicle with you while you work," Eleanor said.

She'd driven Wes to work this morning. Grayson and Adam, another shifter from the security firm, were on watch overnight, and they'd followed Eleanor in their car to the office. Grayson had stuck around while Wes filled the others in on what her father told them in the video recording, then gone home to get some sleep.

"You're safest with me," Wes said.

"You know, when you said you'd keep me safe, I didn't realize that meant being ten inches from you at all times," Eleanor said.

"You weren't complaining last night," Wes said with a wicked grin.

She blushed when Boone said through the cubicle wall,

"Keep it in your pants, Wesley. There's a strict 'no sex at the office' rule, remember?"

"I thought it was a 'no sex with the clients' rule," Chase said from the other side.

"It's both," Boone said.

"Was the first rule created because someone had sex at the office?" Eleanor said.

"No," Boone said.

"Yes," Wes said.

"Was it you?" Eleanor said to Wes.

He gave her a look, and she giggled as Chase said, "Obviously, it was Boone."

"Hey, why am I the immediate suspect? Maybe it was Grayson," Boone said.

"You're lucky Cooper didn't fire you for banging that cougar on the boardroom table," Wes said.

"Wait, was it like a cougar, cougar, or an older woman, cougar?" Eleanor said.

"Both," Boone said.

"Right. Anyway, I could sit in the staff room," Eleanor said. "I feel like I'm a distraction."

"You're fine," Wes said. "I like having you in my cubicle."

She shifted on the small office chair Wes had rolled into his cubicle for her. "Well, is there something I could be doing? Some filing for you, maybe?"

He shook his head and pointed at the book she'd opened on her phone. "Enjoy your book and just relax, Eleanor. You deserve to relax and not worry about working."

"Reading a book doesn't pay rent," she said.

"My house is fully paid for, and I'm not charging you rent to live with me, my mate," Wes said absently. He'd already turned back to his laptop.

A little thrill went through Eleanor. "You want me to move in with you?"

"Yes," Wes said. "I'm all in, remember? That includes living together. Unless you don't want to?"

"Uh oh," Boone said. "Are we about to witness your first fight?"

"No," Eleanor said with a laugh. "I want to live with Wes."

"At least he doesn't sleep purr like Grayson. Fuck, how Ryan hasn't kicked him out of her bed yet, I'll never know," Boone said. "He's like a fucking tractor."

"You're one to talk," Wes said. "You sleep purr too."

"Yeah, but it's a delicate sleep purr," Boone said. "Some might even call it soothing."

"Wes? Mariana is here. You ready to talk?" Cooper stuck his head into Wes's cubicle.

"We are," Wes said.

"Perfect. Meet us in the boardroom."

Cooper left, and Wes stood, holding his hand out to Eleanor. She stood and muttered a curse when her pocketknife slipped out of her pocket and fell to the floor. Wes picked it up as she said, "I seriously hate these pants."

"I like them," Wes said, his free hand reaching around to give her ass a quick squeeze.

She grinned. The skinny jeans she wore might make her ass look amazing, but the combination of how tight they were and the barely-there pockets were annoying as hell. Nearly every time she put something in her pocket, it eventually worked its way to the top of the pocket and fell out.

"You hold onto it," she said when Wes tried to give her the pocketknife back. "It's just gonna fall out of my pocket again if I take it back."

As Wes slipped the knife into his front pocket, she made

an indignant scoff. "While I realize that now is not the time for a discussion on why men's pockets are so deep when all they have is a stupid wallet to carry, just know that I'll be bringing it up later over dinner."

"Noted," Wes said with a grin.

"I'm going to use the ladies' room," Eleanor said. "I'll meet you in the boardroom."

Wes hesitated. "I can walk you there and wait for you."

She laughed. "I think I'll be okay. I'm literally in an office full of shifters who are paid to protect people. I'll meet you in the boardroom."

She walked down the hallway and, when they reached the t-intersection, gently pushed Wes in the direction of the boardroom. "Seriously, I'll be fine. I'll be right there."

"Okay." He dropped a kiss on her lips before walking toward the boardroom.

Smiling to herself, she headed the other way to the bathroom. The bathrooms were about halfway down the hall, next to the copier room. The exit light over the door at the far end of the hall flickered on and off, the red light fading a little more with every flicker. Reception was around the corner, and as Eleanor pushed open the bathroom door, she heard the faint jingle of the door opening and Daisy's cheerful greeting.

She used the bathroom and washed her hands before studying herself in the mirror above the sink. She looked different. She looked... happy. Even though a shady corporation and an insanely strong shifter were after her, it couldn't destroy her good mood. Not when she had Wes in her life.

Still smiling, she walked out of the bathroom and almost face-first into a large bald man coming out of the copier room. He wore a brown uniform shirt with "West Coast Paper" emblazoned on the front. The sleeves were so tight across his massive biceps that the fabric had ripped a little.

"Sorry," Eleanor said, taking a step back and smiling up at the man. "I didn't see…"

Fear washed over her, stealing her breath and leaving a bitter metallic taste in her mouth. Gone was the long blond hair and the overgrown beard, replaced by a gleaming bald head and a face with pale, thin lips and a deep dimple in the middle of his chin. But the muddy brown eyes were the same as was the madness lurking in them that she'd witnessed on the front lawn of Wes's place.

"Hello, Eleanor Whitman." The lion shifter grinned, revealing his razor-sharp fangs. "You have something I want."

She tried to scream, tried to take a stumbling step back, but the lion shifter's fist hammered across her cheek, and the world went black.

———

"Thank you for meeting with us, Mariana." Cooper smiled at the pretty, blonde human.

"Sure. The story sounds interesting. Provided you have proof, of course." Mariana reached to shake Wes's hand. "Mariana Carminder."

"Wes Masters." He shook her hand. "Eleanor will be here shortly."

"Great. So, Cooper said you've seen one of these enhanced shifters?" Mariana apparently wasn't one to waste any time.

"Yes. He attacked Eleanor yesterday morning and tried to kill us both," Wes said. "If it hadn't been for Boone and Gray, he would have succeeded."

"So, it took all three of you to fight him off?" Mariana

studied Wes's body. "You look in pretty good shape for an old guy."

Cooper rolled his eyes. "Mariana, seriously?"

"What? I'm making an observation. It's what I do," she said.

"He was strong. Weirdly strong and fast. We know now that it was because he's taking a serum," Wes said.

"Right." Mariana studied her phone. "So, did -"

She was interrupted by a high-pitched shriek of "you fucking cocksucker!". Cooper and Wes froze before Cooper said, "Was that Lusa?"

Wes tore out of the conference room with Cooper right behind him. He ran down the narrow hallway, past the cubicles, and stared in horror at Lusa lying on the floor outside of the copier room. Boone knelt next to her with his hand splayed across the bleeding gashes slashed across her torso.

"Motherfuck, that hurts," Lusa snarled.

"What the fuck?" Cooper said as Boone yanked off his shirt and pressed it hard against Lusa's bleeding stomach.

"Fuck, Boone, that fucking hurts!" Lusa growled at him.

"Hold still," Boone said. "Daisy, call 9-1-1, now!"

Daisy took off for reception as Lusa stared up at Wes. "He took her. The biggest fucking lion shifter I've ever seen took Eleanor."

Panic infused every cell in Wes's body. The blood whooshed in his ears, and his lion roared with fury and fear.

Our mate! He has our mate!

"He took her out the back exit." Lusa pointed a bloody and trembling hand toward the back exit door.

Wes immediately ran for the exit. Cooper followed him, and Wes barely gave Chase a glance when he popped out of the t-intersection and joined them. Wes slammed open the exit door, adrenaline singing in his veins and his heart a jack-hammer that threatened to break his ribcage.

He could smell the lion shifter's scent in the stairwell, and the roar of his lion burst from his lips before he could stop it. He raced down set after set of stairs, the heavy footsteps of Cooper and Chase echoing behind him.

They reached the main floor and busted out into the lobby. Wes glanced around wildly. The lobby was mostly empty, and he whipped around to the left when Cooper shouted, "There!"

With Eleanor slung over his shoulder and hanging limply, the lion shifter ran down the hallway that led to the loading zone door. With another roar that made the half a dozen people in the lobby stare at him in shock and alarm, Wes shifted to his lion and took off after him.

His lion snarled when Chase zipped past him, but Wes didn't give a fuck that the younger, faster cheetah was passing him even in his human form. All that mattered was Eleanor. His fragile hope that Chase would catch up to the lion shifter before he made it out of the lobby ended when the lion shifter put on a burst of speed that rivaled Chase's astonishing speed and hit the loading door with the force of a bullet. The door opened with a loud bang, bouncing off the wall before slamming shut again.

Growling and snarling, Chase shoved it open and ran out. Wes and Cooper ran out of the building, and Cooper made a growl of surprise. A delivery truck with the words "West Coast Paper" stenciled across the roll-up door sped down the narrow alleyway. Chase, his arms pumping at his sides and his long legs eating up the distance, ran after it. His thigh muscles bunching, he leaped the last six feet, landing nimbly on the back bumper as he grabbed the narrow rail at the top of the truck.

"Holy fuck," Cooper said, his voice thick with astonishment.

Wes ran down the alley, snarling when the delivery truck made a hard right at the end of the alley, its tires squealing and the vehicle nearly tipping before gravity caught up to it. The momentum swung Chase's body sideways, and he lost his grip and flew off, slamming into the side of the building before falling to the ground.

"Chase!" Coop shouted.

Wes leaped over the fallen cheetah and onto the sidewalk. The delivery truck sped through the red light, narrowly missing a Honda Civic and forcing a silver SUV and rust-dotted Ford truck to connect with a squealing metallic crunch.

Wes ran past the startled pedestrians, but the delivery truck made another right and disappeared. Wes slowed to a stop before lifting his head and making another roar that sent the humans around him running for cover.

"Oh, for goodness sake." An old lynx shifter, her hair silver and a cane in one liver-spotted hand stopped next to him with a frosty look. "It's shifters like you that give the rest of us a bad name. Control your emotions, lion shifter."

Ignoring her, Wes turned and loped back to the alley. He shifted to his human form, not giving a shit that a crowd of humans and shifters had gathered, and they were all staring at his naked ass.

"Don't move, Chase," Cooper said.

"I'm fine." Chase climbed to his feet, wincing and rubbing at his lower back. "Nothing's broken."

"You don't know that," Cooper said as he placed a steadying hand on Chase's arm. "You need to go to the hospital."

"I don't." Chase shrugged off his concern and stared at Wes. "I'm sorry, man. I tried to hold on."

"I know," Wes said, his voice hoarse.

Cooper glanced at the people gathering around them. "C'mon, let's get back to the office."

Wes stared blankly at him when Coop took his arm. "Let's go."

"He took her," Wes said. "He has my mate, Cooper."

"I know. We'll get Eleanor back. I promise, Wes."

CHAPTER 23

"Okay. I convinced Mariana to leave, but I guarantee you she'll be back here tomorrow demanding to know what the hell is going on. If we were looking to pique her interest in this story, that worked," Cooper said as he walked into the boardroom.

He took one look at Wes and pulled out a chair. "Sit down before you fall down."

When Wes didn't sit down, Cooper said, "Wes, that's an order."

They'd long left the military, but having Cooper revert back to it, actually helped calm Wes's chaotic brain. He sat down in the chair, staring at the cup of coffee that Grayson set in front of him.

Wes could barely function since they'd returned to the office. Boone had to bring Wes's extra set of clothes from his desk drawer and practically help him get dressed. Speaking to the cops who'd been in the office was nothing but a blur to Wes.

He'd listened numbly as Cooper spun a tale about the lion shifter trying to steal some computers before being chased off. Apparently, Wes said all the right things when the officers spoke with him because they had accepted his answers without any hesitancy.

"Tell me what happened." Grayson sat down between Wes and Boone. Grayson had returned to the office just as they were loading Lusa into the ambulance. "Who the fuck attacked Lusa?"

"Lusa!" Wes gripped the table edge as fresh panic washed over him. "Is Lusa okay?"

"She's good, man." Boone squeezed his uninjured shoulder. "She's at the hospital. She needed a lot of stitches and needs to stay overnight at the hospital for observation, but she'll be all right. She's pissed as hell that he got the best of her."

"Seriously, someone needs to tell me what the fuck happened," Grayson said.

Daisy sat next to Cooper at the other end of the table and took a wavering breath. "The delivery guy from West Coast Paper came in with the four boxes of paper I ordered. Only, it was a new guy. But I didn't know it was the lion shifter who attacked Wes and Eleanor yesterday because," she swallowed hard and tears slid down her cheeks, "because he didn't look like the guy Cooper described to me. I'm so sorry, Wes. I shouldn't have let him go past reception. This is all my fault."

"Shh, my mate." Cooper pulled her into his lap and kissed her before purring softly. "It isn't your fault."

"It is," Daisy said miserably.

"No, it isn't," Wes said and then lapsed into silence. His lion's pacing and growling and fear for their mate threatened to break his damn brain.

"So, the delivery guy came in," Grayson prompted.

Boone took over. "When we saw the guy yesterday, he had hair down to his fucking waist and a beard. He shaved his head and his face and, we assume, killed the regular paper delivery guy."

"He didn't," Daisy said. "The company called about ten minutes ago. I guess the police found the delivery truck abandoned at the edge of the city, and Roger, the regular guy, was knocked out in the back. He's still unconscious, but he's alive."

"From what we can tell, he went to the copier room with the paper and then probably ran into Eleanor as she left the bathroom. He knocked her out and started to leave when Lusa showed up," Cooper said.

Boone leaned back in his chair. "Lusa said, and I quote, 'what the fuck are you doing, asshole?', and grabbed his arm. He turned, swiped her across the guts, and then took off for the back exit. Coop, Wes, and Chase went after him, and, apparently," Boone gave Chase a small smile, "old Chase here leaped onto the back of the truck like he was some kind of fucking stunt man."

Chase didn't return Boone's smile. If it was possible, he looked just as miserable as Wes felt. He stared at Wes, regret and guilt swirling on his face. "I'm sorry, Wes. So fucking sorry."

Wes shook his head, his throat burning. "You tried to save my mate. I won't ever forget that."

The phone rang, and Daisy slid off of Cooper's lap and walked over to the phone that sat on the credenza near the door. She answered it, and Wes tuned out her soft voice as Grayson said, "So, first things first, we need to find out where the Dynasty Lab is located and -"

"Wes?" Daisy said.

He turned to stare at her. Her face was pale, and she had a white-knuckle grip on the phone. "It's for you. He says," she swallowed hard, "he says he has Eleanor."

Wes's stomach flip-flopped, and his lion's eager trill made Wes's chest ache.

Cooper reached for the phone that sat on the long table. "Everyone stays quiet. Let Wes speak to him without interruption."

He glanced at Wes, who nodded. Cooper hit the speaker button, and Wes said, "Where is my mate?"

"Your mate?" The voice was low and pleasant sounding. "That's unexpected."

"Where is she?" Wes snarled.

"Relax. She's perfectly fine. At least, my man says she's fine. He's on his way here with her now, and if you -"

"You tell Rourke that I'm going to rip off his head and shit down his neck for touching my mate," Wes said.

Cooper laid a restraining hand on his arm as there was a moment of silence from the man on the phone. "How do you know his name?"

"I know your name too, Chad," Wes said. "I know exactly what you're doing to shifters with that fucking serum, and I also know that Rourke's the only science experiment you have left. So, unless you want that fucking formula splashed all over the six o'clock news, you'll give me back my mate. Now."

More silence and Wes could practically feel the man's shock oozing out of the phone. Finally, Chad said, "You're under the mistaken delusion that you're holding all the cards, Mr. Masters. Let me be clear - you are not. I don't give a fuck about Eleanor Whitman. One word from me, and Rourke will slit her throat and bury her in a shallow grave. You tell anyone else about the formula, and your mate is dead. Is that clear?"

His lion's panic was a living, breathing thing inside of

him. His hands clenched into tight fists, he said, "I'll give you the formula. Just do not hurt my mate."

"That's better," Chad said.

Wes's lion snarled at the smug tone of the man's voice.

"Now, let's get back to business." Chad's voice turned brisk. "I want the formula, and you want Eleanor. Tonight, at midnight, bring the formula to Brooks Sawmill on Highway Five. You give us the formula, and we give you Eleanor. Clean and easy."

Wes glanced at the others. They all had the same look of disbelief on their faces that he knew covered his.

"You still there, Mr. Masters?" Chad said.

"Yes," Wes said.

"Do we have a deal or not?"

"We do."

"Perfect. This probably goes without saying but come alone. You tell law enforcement or bring your security shifter friends with you, we will kill Eleanor. Do you believe me?"

"Yeah," Wes said.

"Good. See you soon."

Wes reached out and stabbed the button on the phone to end the call. His hands still shook, and he flexed them once or twice before taking a deep breath. His lion paced frantically within him. His low growls and soft whimpers amped up Wes's emotions.

"We need a plan," Cooper said. "Despite what Eleanor's father said, we have to assume that some of the twelve are getting serum, just like Rourke."

"Do we?" Boone said. "If there were more like him, wouldn't they have come with Rourke? Or attacked Eleanor again before now?"

"Yes," Wes said through numb lips. "And if they still had

more, this Chad guy would have corrected me when I said Rourke was the only one left."

"You don't know that for certain," Cooper said as the phone rang again.

"I'll answer that at reception." Daisy hurried out of the boardroom, closing the door behind her.

"There aren't any more of the enhanced," Wes said. "You know as well as I do that it's only Rourke."

"Fine," Cooper said. "But they'll have more than just Rourke and this Chad guy at the sawmill tomorrow night."

"How did you know it was Rourke who attacked you, and that guy on the phone was Chad?" Chase asked Wes.

"Lucky guess," Wes said.

"How many shifters do you think they'll have there?" Cooper said.

Grayson shrugged. "Hard to tell. If they believe Wes will come alone, there might be only half a dozen, maybe a dozen at most. Or, it could be humans with guns."

"We have to assume it'll be both," Cooper said. "Let's say ten to twelve shifters and humans - the five of us won't be enough."

"Are you forgetting something? The minute they smell us, they'll kill Eleanor," Grayson said. "I've driven past the sawmill. It was shut down about ten years ago and abandoned. It's also in the middle of nowhere. There's a wooded area directly behind the sawmill, but even if we hide there, they'll still be able to smell us. And the place is so isolated that they won't think it's just some shifters going for a midnight hike. They'll know Wes isn't alone, and they'll kill Eleanor."

"The Scent B Gone spray," Chase said.

"Fuck me, you're brilliant," Boone said with a grin. "We just got a fucking case of it delivered Friday afternoon. We spray ourselves down with that shit, and they won't smell a fucking thing."

Cooper nodded. "I'll talk to some of my contacts and get a few extra men to -"

"I don't think that's a good idea," Gray said.

Coop frowned at him. "Why?"

"It's too risky. The more men we bring in, the higher the chance of getting caught, even with the Scent B Gone spray. We'll be putting Eleanor's life at risk. You know that, Coop. The five of us can do this on our own."

"Fuck yeah, we can," Boone said. "It'll be just like Baghdad."

"Baghdad?" Chase said.

"Back in our military days," Boone said. "Combat search and rescue for a pilot that'd been shot down over enemy territory. We found him in a shithole torture camp, but twenty-six hostiles were standing between us and the bird waiting to fly us home."

"You made it out, obviously," Chase said.

"Fuck yeah, we did. There were only five of us then, too," Boone said.

"Wes, what do you think?" Cooper said. "It's your call."

"We don't need the extra men," Wes said.

Cooper nodded. "All right. Grayson, see if you can download schematics of the sawmill and a map of the surrounding area. Boone, check the -"

"No," Wes said. His panic had disappeared, leaving a false sense of calm that made his lion uneasy.

"No, what?" Coop said in confusion.

"I'm going alone," Wes said.

WES COULD SMELL HIS FRIENDS' SURPRISE AND DISBELIEF. HE clenched his jaw and held back his temper when Boone said, "Like fuck you are."

"This isn't up for discussion," Wes said.

Grayson barked out harsh laughter. "That's not how this works, Wes. We're going with you."

"No, you're fucking not."

"Yes, we fucking are," Boone said, his face turning red. "Tell him, Coop."

"We're not in the military anymore," Wes said. "I don't ask 'how high' anymore when Coop says 'jump'."

"I'm not saying that," Boone said. He stood and paced the room, his agitation showing with every step. "You're not doing this alone, and since Coop is the only one you'll fucking listen to when you get like this, I'm asking him to tell you not to be the fucking hero and accept our help."

"No," Wes said.

Boone threw his hands up in the air and stared at Cooper. "Coop, you gonna jump in here or not?"

Wes bared his fangs and growled at Boone. "Don't treat me like a fucking child, Boone."

"Stop acting like one, and I will," Boone growled back. "I know you're worried for Eleanor, but you know as well as I do that those fuckers will kill you both once they have the formula. So, don't you fucking sit there and tell me I'm not going with you. Because there is no way in hell, I'm not."

"You're not going. None of you are," Wes said.

Another loud growl burst from Boone's throat, and Grayson stood and put a hand on his arm when he started toward Wes. "Fuck you, Wes! Do you hear me? If you think for one goddamn second that I'm going to sit here on my ass while you head out on some fucking suicide mission, you're a fucking lunatic!"

Wes's temper spiked higher, his temples starting to pound. "So help me God, Boone, I will kick your ass if you -"

"If I what?" Boone shouted. "If I refuse to let you go on a suicide mission? Go ahead and try to kick my ass, old man, see how far you get."

Wes's lion roared in outrage, and Wes jumped onto the boardroom table. Before he could leap at Boone and teach the impudent little shit a well-deserved lesson, Cooper yanked him off the table and shoved him up against the wall.

"Stand down, Wes!" he snarled.

Wes growled at him, and Cooper bared his teeth at him before returning the growl. "Stand down, I said."

"Let him go, Coop. He thinks he can take me, then let him -"

"Shut the fuck up, Boone!" Cooper snapped without taking his gaze off of Wes. When Boone stayed quiet, Cooper said, "Wes, I know you're worried about your mate, but I promise that -"

"It's about more than just Eleanor," Wes said. "I can't risk - I *won't* risk - your life or anyone else's in this room. I can't be responsible for your deaths. Don't you get that? I've already killed one fucking friend. I won't do it again. I fucking won't!"

He tried to push away from Cooper, but Coop shoved him back against the wall. "What the fuck are you talking about?"

"Don't play stupid," Wes growled.

Cooper fisted his hands in Wes's shirt. "Answer the fucking question, Wes."

He wanted to punch Cooper in the face. He was supposed to be Wes's friend. Why was he making him say it?

"I killed Derek!" he shouted as his throat burned and tears slid down his cheeks. "It's my fucking fault he's dead, and

I'm not about to let history repeat itself. So, the four of you are staying right the fuck here!"

He slumped against the wall, all the fight sliding right out of him at the look of shock on Cooper's face and the realization that he'd finally admitted out loud that Derek was dead because of him.

His lion had retreated so far inward that Wes could barely feel him, and he didn't respond at all when Cooper's lion trilled softly to him.

"Chase, can you give us a minute?" Cooper said.

Chase nodded and left the boardroom. Grayson and Boone joined them, and Wes hated the looks of pity on their faces.

"Don't," he rasped, swiping at the tears on his face. "Don't fucking pity me. I don't want that. Hate me instead, just don't... don't feel fucking sorry for me."

"Wes," Cooper said, "it wasn't your fault."

"Yes, it was," Wes said dully. "I went left instead of right. If I'd gone right... if I'd gone the correct way, Derek would still be alive. It's my fault he's dead."

"Christ," Boone said. "You really believe that."

"Because it's true," Wes said.

"We weren't supposed to be on patrol that day," Cooper said. "I volunteered our unit to do patrol, and it ended with Derek dying. So, I guess it's my fucking fault Derek is dead."

"You were doing your job," Wes said. "You didn't lose focus, didn't ignore your gut about -"

"I was supposed to be sitting in the front seat." Grayson stepped closer and put his hand on Wes's shoulder. "I asked Derek to switch with me because I had a headache, and I didn't want the sun in my eyes the whole damn time. That makes it my fault Derek is dead."

"Stop it," Wes said, his anger growing again. "I know

what you're trying to do, and it's not going to work. Neither of you was driving. It wasn't either of you who turned us in the direct path of that fucking sniper by going left instead of right. If I'd gone right instead of -"

His breath escaped his lungs in a harsh whoosh when Boone shoved him up against the wall again. His face a mask of pain and sorrow, Boone said, "Derek told you to go left. Derek! You said you thought it was right, and Derek argued and told you it was left. Said he could read a fucking map, remember?"

Boone's eyes shone with unshed tears. "We all fucking knew he couldn't read a map worth shit. All of us! But we didn't argue with him. We let Derek convince you to turn left, and then he fucking died!"

He shook Wes so hard, Wes's teeth snapped together with a hard click. "Derek's death is not your fucking fault. It's not Coop's fault for putting us on that patrol, it's not Grayson's fault for switching seats, and it's not your fault for turning left down that fucking street. I won't let you go another goddamn minute believing it was your fault. Do you hear me? You fucking asshole!"

Boone shook him again, the sorrow on his face replaced with anger. "We all miss him, and we all feel responsible for his death. You can fucking play martyr all you want, but the truth is Derek died because of an asshole sniper. That's it! That's the fucking reason, Wes. He died because he was shot when we were out in the middle of the fucking desert!"

He threw his arms around Wes and hugged him hard. Wes could feel Boone's hot tears soaking into his shirt. He returned Boone's hug, trying not to cry and failing. Boone's tiger trilled to Wes's lion, and to Wes's surprise, his lion crept forward and returned the call of comfort. After a few minutes,

Boone released him and swiped at his face with the heel of his hand.

Grayson pushed tissues into Wes and Boone's hands, and Wes wiped his face as Boone did the same.

"I miss him," Wes said, his voice hoarse. "I miss him so fucking much."

"Us too." Cooper squeezed his shoulder. "But he didn't die because of you, Wes."

Wes stared at Coop, then at Grayson, and finally at Boone. Boone's eyes were red, and he looked like he'd been through a twelve-round fight, but he said, "Not your fault, asshole."

The weight that had sat on Wes's chest since Derek died in Boone's arms lifted. He touched his chest, almost giddy with relief as his lion made a low trill and then purred softly. "It's not my fault."

"It isn't," Grayson said.

For the first time in four years, Wes felt like he could take a deep breath. The pain of losing Derek was still there, and the sorrow at the part Wes had played on that day hadn't completely dissipated, but there was finally a small dim light at the end of the proverbial tunnel.

And to his immense relief, his lion's feelings of guilt and sorrow had eased as well.

Wes took another deep breath as Boone said, "Fuck, I hate crying."

"I'm sorry I tried to kill you," Wes said.

Boone smiled a little. "I'm sorry I called you an old man. Even if it's true."

"Boone," Cooper said.

"What? We just sobbed like fucking babies together. I'm not gonna start lying to him now," Boone said.

Wes huffed out a laugh as Grayson gave first him and then Boone a rough kiss on the forehead. "I love you guys."

"Leave it to Grayson to make it mushy," Boone said with a small smile on his face. "But, yeah, I fucking love the three of you too."

He stepped back, wiping at his face one last time with the tissue before balling it up and tossing it into the wastebasket. "Now, let's go save Wes's mate, kill the bad guys, and be the fucking heroes we are."

CHAPTER 24

"**Y**ou don't look much like your father."

Eleanor ignored the dark-haired man sitting next to her in the SUV. Maybe it was rude, but considering the guy pointed a gun at her, she was okay with a bit of rudeness.

"You sure he's your old man?" the man asked.

"Hoyt." The blond man sitting in the front passenger seat glanced at them in the rear-view mirror.

"What? She doesn't look like him."

"I look like my mother, asshole," Eleanor said.

"She speaks." The one named Hoyt grinned at her. "I was starting to think you were mute."

"Maybe I just prefer not to have your goon duct tape my mouth again," Eleanor said.

The giant lion shifter sitting behind the wheel growled at her. "You're lucky I didn't rip out your fucking tongue. Still might, you little bitch."

"Enough, Rourke," the blond man said.

"Fuck you, Chad," Rourke said before growling again. He opened the door and climbed out of the vehicle.

"Where are you going?" Chad said.

"I can't stand your human stink any longer." Rourke slammed the door shut and trudged across the parking lot to where a group of a dozen men stood in a loose circle. A few of them had guns, and of the ones who didn't, Eleanor suspected they were shifters.

She stared up at the decrepit building rising out of the darkness. A large sign with "Brooks Sawmill" in faded and peeling blue letters hung precariously from one rusty bolt on the metal fence surrounding the building. The sawmill was a long two-story wooden building with smashed windows and graffiti spray-painted in a thick layer along the front. To the left of the building, she could see a pile of stacked logs, the wood rotting from years of abandonment.

The whole place was creepy as hell and a terrible place to die, Eleanor decided. Her stomach churned, and she clenched her cold hands together in a tight fist. She was going to die, and, even worse, so would Wes. She had no doubt he would bring the flash drive in an attempt to save her, and she was sick to her stomach over it. She couldn't bear the thought of Wes dying because of her.

She swallowed hard and said, "We haven't told anyone about the formula. So, when Wes brings it, you can just let us go. We won't say a word."

"Of course." Chad turned sideways in his seat and stared at her over the headrest. "That's the deal, Eleanor. Wes brings the flash drive, and he gets his mate."

"And you let us live," she said.

"Absolutely."

"Liar," she said.

Hoyt snorted laughter, and Chad arched an eyebrow at him before saying, "I'm not lying. As long as your mate does what he's told, the two of you will live."

Eleanor glanced at Hoyt. "He's gonna try to sell me a bridge next, right?"

Hoyt just grinned at her. He wasn't nearly as big as Rourke, and she suspected he was human based on the guns he carried, but he scared her nearly as much as Rourke did. It was the utter lack of emotion in his gaze and the way he studied her like she was a bug he needed to squash.

Her mouth dry, she said, "I'm not a bug. I'm a butterfly."

"What?" Chad said.

"I'm a butterfly," she repeated.

"Christ, I can see why your old man cut you out of his life," Hoyt said. "You're loony."

"For your information, he cut me out of his life because I didn't want to be a biochemist like him and create serums that fucked up shifters," Eleanor said.

Chad frowned at her. "What we're doing, what we're creating, will change the world, Eleanor."

"Not for the better," Eleanor said.

"Yes, it will," Chad said.

"They killed innocent humans. How is that for the better?"

"How do you know that?" Chad said sharply.

"Does it matter? I know that Rourke and the others went crazy because of the serum, but you and the people you work for didn't give a fuck. You just want to use it for your own nefarious reasons."

"Nefarious reasons?" Hoyt laughed. "I'm starting to like this girl."

"The feeling is not mutual," Eleanor said with a glance at the gun.

"That's fair," Hoyt said.

"It's past midnight," Chad said. "Where the fuck is he?"

"It's only two minutes past," Hoyt said. "Relax, Chad."

"Maybe he doesn't care about you the way he said," Chad said to Eleanor.

She didn't reply, but a trickle of hope went through her. Maybe Wes wouldn't show up. Sure, he said she was his mate, but they'd been dating for, what, fifteen hours? She couldn't blame him if he changed his mind. Hell, she would.

No, you wouldn't.

Okay, probably not. She'd been in love with Wes for at least the last nine months, even if she hadn't said the words out loud until recently.

Fuck, she really hoped he didn't show up.

"He's not going to be alone," Hoyt said. "You know that, right?"

"I'm not an idiot," Chad said. "Why do you think we have a dozen of your team here?"

"I'm surprised Rourke let you bring me and the others," Hoyt said.

"He's not in fucking charge, I am," Chad said. "Considering that Wes and his friends almost bested him, he couldn't exactly argue when I said we were bringing a team."

Eleanor's heart slammed against her ribcage, and what little spit left in her mouth completely dried up when headlights splashed across the parking lot. She leaned forward, ignoring Hoyt when he jabbed the gun into her ribs and stared at the car idling in front of them.

When Wes stepped out from behind the wheel, her mouth dropped open, and she said, "He drove."

"What?" Chad glanced at her.

"He drove," she said again. "Oh my God, he drove the car."

"What the fuck is wrong with her?" Hoyt said to Chad.

Chad shrugged. "I don't know, and I don't fucking care. Let's get this shitshow cleaned up."

Wes's lion roared with excitement when Eleanor climbed out of the silver SUV. She looked scared to death, and he could smell her fear, but she was alive. That's all he and his lion cared about.

"Mr. Masters." A blond man wearing jeans and a pale blue dress shirt smiled frostily at him. "You're late."

Wes ignored him, staring at Eleanor. "You'll be safe soon, my mate."

"Maybe on a white sand beach with turquoise water," she said with a trembling smile that nearly broke him.

His lion trilled to her, and Wes said, "Yes. I love you."

"I love you too." Her voice was soft but steady.

"Touching," the blond man said. "But perhaps we could discuss the actual reason we're all here."

"I'm here to kill you for taking my mate," Wes said, his gaze lingering on Rourke, who stood near a group of a dozen men. Four of them were humans, and the rest were a mixture of lions, leopards, and cougars.

Rourke snarled at him. "Let me kill him now, Chad."

Chad, a dark-haired man, and Eleanor stood about six feet in front of the SUV with a massive pile of rotting logs just to the right of the vehicle. Chad held up his hand as the other men fanned out until they were in a half-circle. To their left, the sawmill loomed. Behind the mill was a wooded area, and Wes could hear the river that wound through the trees.

"No one is going to kill anyone. Wes - can I call you Wes? - will give me the flash drive, and he and his mate will leave. Assuming, of course, that you've done as instructed, Wes," Chad said.

Rourke turned and faced the sawmill. He repeatedly

inhaled, his nostrils quivering as he turned back and forth like an antenna seeking a signal.

After nearly three minutes, he turned to face Chad, who raised an eyebrow at him. "Well?"

"He's alone," Rourke said. "I don't smell any of his friends."

"Are you sure?" The dark-haired man said before pointing to the men in the half-circle. "Maybe their smell is blocking his friends' scents."

Rourke bared his fangs at him. "Fuck you, Hoyt. I can smell the fucking garlic on your shitty breath from over here. Keep suggesting I'm wrong about smelling my kind, and I'll rip your limbs off one by one."

"Enough," Chad said. "The flash drive, please, Wes."

Wes reached into his pocket and pulled out the flash drive before closing the distance between him and Chad.

One of the humans stepped forward and pointed the gun at him. Chad smiled thinly. "Please hand it to my associate, Wes."

"Give me my mate first," Wes said.

Chad shook his head. "You know that's not how this works. Give me the flash drive, and once I've confirmed it has the formula, you can have your mate."

Wes handed over the flash drive, his lion growling at him and trying to take control. He knew the plan as well as Wes did but seeing Eleanor had driven rational thought from his lion. His lion's desire to protect his mate was all-encompassing and difficult for Wes to control.

"Stop touching her," he growled to Hoyt, who held Eleanor's arm in a tight grip. His other hand pressed a gun against Eleanor's ribs.

"Excuse me?" Hoyt said.

"Stop touching my mate, I said." Wes's lion was very

close to the surface now, and the other shifters gave each other uneasy looks as Rourke grinned.

Chad took the flash drive from the human, nodding to Hoyt. "Let her go, Hoyt."

"Are you fucking kidding me?" Hoyt said.

"She won't move. Not until I tell her she can," Chad said. "Because she knows that I'll have her mate shot in the head if she does. Isn't that right, Eleanor?"

Eleanor's face paled to the point where Wes thought she might simply collapse. She took a deep breath, and his lion purred encouragingly to her when she said, "That's right."

Hoyt rolled his eyes but released Eleanor's arm. He shuffled back a little, keeping the gun pointed at Eleanor. "Anything else I can do for her, Chad? Maybe you want me to make her a fucking cup of tea or get her a fucking sweater?"

"Enough, Hoyt," Chad said.

A second human left the half-circle and retrieved a laptop from the SUV. He brought it to Chad, holding it steady as Chad plugged in the flash drive and tapped a few buttons on the keyboard. Relief washed over his face. "It's the formula."

"Give me my mate," Wes said.

Chad closed the laptop and pocketed the flash drive. "How many copies did you make?"

"I didn't," Wes said. "Give me my mate. You have your formula." He took a step forward, and the men in the half-circle raised their guns at him as Chad took a step back.

"You realize that I can't trust what you're saying, right?" Chad said. "The odds of you not making a copy of the formula are astronomically low. So, I need you to tell me the truth. How many copies did you make?"

"I didn't make any," Wes said.

Chad sighed and glanced at Hoyt. "How many of

Eleanor's fingers do you think Rourke will need to bite off before Wes admits he made copies."

Rourke grinned as rage flashed over Wes in a hot and heavy wave. He growled at Chad, his hands clenching into fists. "Harm my mate, and you'll die tonight."

"No," Chad said. "I won't. Because you foolishly came alone. The only people dying tonight are you and Eleanor."

Wes grinned, revealing his long fangs. "I'm not alone, Chad."

His grin widened when the large tiger, his sleek fur gleaming in the headlights of the car, leaped down from the top of the rotting pile of logs and landed with a heavy thud on Hoyt's back.

CHAPTER 25

Gunfire was hella loud, Eleanor decided as the brush of the tiger knocked her flying. She landed face-first on the broken and crumbling pavement, an explosive "oof" escaping from her lips when her already bruised knee slammed into a loose chunk of pavement and her bare forearms skidded across the rough concrete.

Hoyt was lying on his stomach next to her with a tiger standing on his back. As the tiger's thick claws sank into his flesh, Hoyt screamed pitifully. The scream abruptly ended when the powerful tiger bit into the back of his neck with a bone snapping crunch that Eleanor felt more than heard.

As there were more gunshots and screams of fear, she stared at Hoyt's face in numb disbelief. The tiger tore a huge chunk of flesh away from his neck, and blood gushed out in a hot rush. Hoyt fell forward, his face hitting the pavement with a wet splat as his entire body shuddered once before growing still.

"I think that guy is dead," Eleanor said as the tiger roared in triumph before bounding away. "He just got eaten by a tiger."

"Eleanor!" Wes dropped to his knees beside her as there was another piercing scream of pain. A laptop fell to the ground in front of her, and she stared numbly at the smoking bullet hole in it as Wes grabbed her arms. His hand dug into the sutures on her arm, but she barely felt the pain as she stared at him.

"Hoyt's dead," she said. "Boone ate him. Or maybe it was Grayson. I didn't get a good look. But somebody ate him. Or mostly ate him."

Wes pressed a kiss against her mouth before half-dragging and half-carrying her toward the SUV. "Behind the car, Butterfly."

"What?" she said and then flinched when a bullet pierced the front bumper of the SUV.

Wes shoved her around the SUV and pushed her onto her butt. "Stay there, Eleanor. Do not move."

Her heart pounding, she stared wide-eyed at Wes as he shifted to his lion with a low growl. His clothes burst apart at the seams and landed in a heap at her feet. She stared at him, his lovely yellow eyes and broad nose and the thick dark mane surrounding his head.

"Wes," she whispered, "be careful."

He purred to her before racing away. Swallowing hard, Eleanor peeked around the SUV. The humans were all dead, their bodies torn apart and their blood soaking into the pavement.

She clapped her hand over her mouth when her gaze slid to Chad. He was lying only a few feet from the SUV with his throat torn wide open and his eyes staring sightlessly into the night sky.

"Gross," Eleanor said in a horrified voice.

A scream of pain made her gaze swivel to the right. A cheetah and a leopard fought viciously near Wes's car. She clapped her hand over her mouth, sour-tasting vomit in the back of her throat when the cheetah raked his claws across the leopard's stomach, and its intestines fell out with a wet and gelatinous plop.

The leopard collapsed, and the cheetah roared in triumph before chasing down a second leopard. Cooper and Grayson were working as a team to take out three other shifters - two lions and a cougar. Snarling and growling, their fur splattered with blood, they fought violently with the large beasts.

"Wes... where's Wes?" Eleanor said. She searched the area frantically, her hands clutching at the smooth side of the SUV when she finally saw him. He battled a leopard, rearing up on his back legs and swiping at the beast. The leopard was fast and lean, but he was no match for Wes's powerful strength. Wes tore open the leopard's throat and roared in victory when the hot blood flowed down the leopard's chest.

A flicker of movement caught her eye, and she watched in horror as Rourke slammed into Boone. He knocked Boone into Wes's car, shattering the windshield and forcing a strangled whine of pain from the tiger's mouth. He slid down off the hood, and Boone's striped body rippled and changed into his human form.

Eleanor could already see the dark bruising forming on Boone's side as Rourke shifted to his human form and grabbed Boone around the throat. He lifted the big man into the air like he weighed nothing, grinning at him with hot glee as the unconscious Boone dangled in his grip.

"Boone, no!" Eleanor screamed as Rourke raised his other hand. The nails had already turned to claws. Before he could slash Boone open, Wes leaped onto him, knocking Boone free.

Rourke stumbled and fell. He shifted to his lion form before leaping to his feet. As Boone laid limply on the ground, Wes stood over him protectively, snarling and baring his fangs at Rourke.

Eleanor cried out when Rourke and Wes leaped at each other, their big bodies connecting with a hard thud. They fell to the ground, their claws gouging and slashing at each other as their bodies rolled across the pavement.

She looked around frantically for the others, but Chase had joined Cooper and Grayson in the fight against the other shifters, and they were paying no attention to Wes and Rourke.

"Chase! Cooper! Grayson!" Eleanor screamed, but the growling and the screams of the shifters were too loud for them to hear her. She stood and looked around desperately for a gun. Despite how fiercely Wes fought, Eleanor knew that Rourke would best him. The serum streaming through Rourke's veins made him impossibly strong.

Her gaze fell on Wes's shredded jeans lying on the ground in front of her. The handle of her pocketknife stuck out from the material, and she snatched it up, clicking open the knife as she ran toward the fighting lions.

Rourke rolled on top of Wes, pinning him down with his paws on Wes's torn and bitten shoulders. Adrenaline shrieking through her veins, the only sound in her ears the heavy, frantic beat of her own heart, Eleanor skidded to a stop next to the lions.

"Hey, asshole!" she shouted. Rourke turned his head, his teeth coated in Wes's blood and his golden eyes full of madness and rage.

With a grunt of effort, Eleanor shoved the blade of her pocketknife deep into Rourke's right eye.

He howled with pain, saliva dripping from his mouth as his body slammed into Eleanor's and knocked her off her feet. She backpedalled away, her butt dragging across the pavement and the palms of her hand getting torn up by small rocks and bits of broken glass from the shattered windshield.

His shrieks growing louder, Rourke staggered around in a circle, pawing frantically at the knife sticking out of his eye as Wes climbed to his feet. Still in his lion form, he stalked toward the wounded Rourke, his fangs gleaming and blood dripping from his matted fur.

He leaped onto Rourke's back, knocking the lion to his stomach, and Eleanor swallowed hard when Wes tore open the back of Rourke's neck. Wes bit into his neck again, severing the spinal cord and cutting off the lion's howl of agony. Rourke slumped forward, his sides heaving once, twice, and then a third time before going still.

Eleanor stared at the knife sticking out of Rourke's eye and wiped a trembling hand across her mouth as Wes shifted to his human form and limped toward her. He groaned as he sank to his knees beside her, his body covered in deep slashes and puncture wounds. "Butterfly, are you all right?"

She nodded as a final dying scream came from behind them. She craned her neck, staring at Cooper and Grayson and Chase as the three of them shifted to their human forms, leaving a pile of dead shifters behind them. Chase wiped the blood from his mouth before joining Cooper and Grayson as they crouched next to Boone.

"Boone," Cooper patted his cheek gently, "wake up, buddy. Open your eyes."

She could almost see the relief wash over Wes when Boone groaned and opened his eyes. "Fuck me. I think I got hit by a truck."

"Don't move yet," Grayson said as Boone started to sit up.

"I'm okay," Boone said. "Other than the fact that I got my ass kicked by a lion."

"A lion hopped up on drugs," Chase said. "It wasn't a fair fight."

"You're my new favourite," Boone groaned as he rubbed at the giant goose egg on the back of his skull. "Did we win?"

"Yeah," Cooper said as he stared at the bodies lying on the ground.

"Great. Fuck, I could use a beer. Maybe a burger too. You wanna get burgers and beers?" Boone said.

"Sure," Cooper said. "Wes, Eleanor… you guys okay?"

Eleanor nodded as Wes cupped her face. "Are you hurt, my mate?"

"You drove," she said.

"What?" Wes stared at her in confusion.

"You drove a car here," she said. "Without having a panic attack."

"I did. My mate needed me," he said.

Warmth rushed over her, and she smiled at him. "Promise me you'll still let me drive you to work at least twice a week."

"I promise," he said with a small smile. He hugged her hard, and she buried her face in his neck, blinking back the tears as he purred to her. "I love you, Eleanor."

"I love you too," she said.

He helped her to her feet, slipping an arm around her waist to steady her. "Are you sure you're not hurt?"

"Positive," she said. "Hey, Wes?"

"Yeah?"

"I stabbed Rourke in the eye with my pocketknife."

"I know," he said.

"That was badass, right?"

"Very," he said.

"Is this where you apologize to me for saying my knife wouldn't cut through bread?" Eleanor said.

Wes burst into laughter before pulling her into his embrace and hugging her hard. "Thank you for saving my life, my mate."

"You're welcome, my mate."

"WHAT DID COOPER SAY?" ELEANOR GLANCED AT WES, shielding her eyes from the sun as he dropped into the chair next to hers.

Wes took a sip of beer. "The Council has cleared us of any wrongdoing."

"Finally," Eleanor said. "The police cleared you a week and a half ago."

Wes shrugged. "The Council likes to be thorough. The fact that it was both humans and shifters who died made it even messier."

"It was all self-defense," Eleanor said.

"It was, and after doing their investigation, the Council agreed with local authorities and ruled it as such."

"What if they hadn't?" she said.

"It would get messy."

She waited for a beat. "Messy? That's all you're going to say… it would get messy?"

He shrugged. "It's not worth going into. They ruled it as self-defense, and we're not being charged with anything."

"What about the lab and what they were doing?" Eleanor said. "Did Cooper's cop friend say if the Board members were arrested?"

"The last Coop heard, they had six of them in custody and were still searching for the other four."

"But they've shut down the lab?" Eleanor said.

"Yes. And both the Council and the police have copies of

the formula," Wes said. "They're working together on," he hesitated, "solving the problem, I guess."

She sighed. "Do you think that means they're trying to improve it?"

"Yeah, unfortunately," Wes said.

"We should never have handed it over," Eleanor said, her good mood deflating a little despite the warm sunshine and soft breeze.

"We had to, my mate. You know that. It was the proof to back up our story."

"Yeah," she said.

"Besides, Mariana's article went live this morning," Wes said.

"Holy shit. And?"

"It's all over the Internet. They won't be able to keep what they're doing a secret. Not like before."

"I bet the head honchos are pissed we gave the details to Mariana," Eleanor said.

"Probably," Wes said with a grin, "but they have no way to prove we did it. Mariana will never reveal her sources for the story."

"Thank you for calling Cooper," Eleanor said. "I couldn't wait any longer to get news."

He reached over and ran one hand along her thigh. "You're welcome, but since this is supposed to be our vacation, what do you say we stop talking about super serums and avoiding prison time and start talking about how fucking hot you look in that bikini."

She grinned and stretched languidly on the lounger, her smile widening when Wes's gaze lingered on her barely covered tits. "You make a good point, Wesley."

Wes slipped his warm hand between her legs and rubbed her inner thigh. "You too sore from last night, Butterfly?"

She sat up and let her legs dangle over the side of the lounger, digging her toes into the hot sand. "Not even in the slightest. I keep telling you that I'm tougher than I look, Wes."

"I know."

She gazed out at the crystal clear turquoise water. The waves rolled in gently, flooding the sand in front of them with water before receding. The sun shone brightly, but the breeze blowing off of the ocean tempered the heat.

"You know," she said, "when you said you were taking me on vacation, I didn't expect to stay at a house on a private beach. This had to cost a fortune."

Wes squeezed her thigh. "I like spoiling you, my mate."

She smiled at him. "Thank you so much, Wes. This is the best vacation of my life. It's as amazing as I dreamed it would be, and having you here with me only makes it sweeter."

"I love you," Wes said.

"I love you too," she said. "I want to go swimming in the ocean again."

"Sure," Wes said. "We can go swimming in the ocean, or," his hand traced higher until he could stroke the crease between her thigh and her pussy, "I can eat your pussy right here in the sunshine on our very private beach, and then we can go swimming. What's your preference? Option A or B?"

"B," she said with a giggle before leaning over and planting a kiss against his perfect lips. "Definitely, option B."

Keep reading for an excerpt from "End of Night", Book Four in the Shadow Security Series.
"End of Night" will be available in 2022.

END OF NIGHT EXCERPT

SHADOW SECURITY SERIES, BOOK FOUR

Hedra was an animal lover. A dyed-in-the-wool, lifelong animal lover.

Which is what made her decision to kill a tiny terrorizing poodle named Alfie so shocking.

Of course, said poodle *had* just shit in her shoe for the eighth time in three days.

That was grounds for murdering him, right? A jury would take one look at the cold poop smeared all over the bottom of Hedra's bare foot and between her goddamn toes and declare her innocent.

The very victim of her murderous thoughts, the shoe pooping vigilante himself, trotted into her bedroom. He had what could only be described as a satisfied grin on his evil doggie face.

"I'm gonna murder you, Alfie," she said as she held her Croc in one hand and kept her shit-covered foot in the air. "Do you hear me, you little jackass? Your time on this earth has been cut short."

"I can hear you threatening to kill my dog, you know," Althea said from their shared bathroom. Hedra had helped her into the tub not five minutes ago and she could hear the old tiger shifter splashing around like a little kid.

"He pooped in my shoe... *again*," Hedra said. "I have poodle poop between my toes, Althea."

"Maybe you should keep your shoes on instead of going around barefoot like a hooligan," Althea said.

"I was not barefoot," Hedra said. "These are my extra pair of Crocs that I needed to change into because you deliberately splashed water onto my regular Crocs when I helped you into the tub."

"Crocs are an abomination, and I will not abide them in my house," Althea said.

"It's your grandson's house, not yours," Hedra said.

She had the old woman on that one and Althea knew it. After about thirty seconds of silence, Althea said, "Alfie also hates Crocs."

On perfect cue, Alfie growled, grabbed Hedra's Croc that wasn't currently covered in shit, and streaked out of her bedroom.

"He just stole my shoe, Althea," Hedra said.

"He's doing you a favour," Althea said. "You can't blame him for trying to save you from bad shoe choices."

Despite her irritation, a grin crossed Hedra's face. She loved spicy clients and Althea Jameson was as spicy as they came. The tiger shifter might have been in her eighties and recovering from a broken hip, but she'd kept Hedra on her toes from the moment she took the job. She hadn't been Althea's live-in nurse for very long, but every morning Hedra woke up happy and looking forward to what the day brought for the first time in a long time.

Is that because of Althea or her grandson?

She shut her inner voice down immediately. Thinking about Boone, about her *employer*, in even the vaguest of ways, always made her flashback to that slightly inappropriate moment they'd shared.

Slightly inappropriate? Girl, you were about to fuck him on his friend's porch. I'd say that's a tad more than inappropriate.

Yeah, probably. But what was done was done and she couldn't take it back. She could only pretend that the moment had never happened, and she didn't at all remember what his lips tasted like or how good it felt when he touched her.

Spread your legs for me, little lamb.

Boone's voice echoed in her head, and she shivered all over. Her nipples hardened and her pussy went wet, and dammit, why couldn't she get him out of her head? Her libido would cost her a job she really liked, not to mention free living accommodations.

She'd been standing with her foot in the air for nearly two minutes and with a grimace, she hopped her way toward the bedroom door. "Althea, I'll be back in a few minutes. I'm just going to wash my foot. Will you be okay?"

"Oh, for God's sake, human, I'm not a toddler. I think I can manage not to drown for the five minutes it takes you to clean your foot," Althea said irritably, her voice echoing in the small bathroom.

Hedra grinned again before hopping awkwardly out of the bedroom. Using the wall for support she hopped down the hallway. Her choices were the pedestal sink in the half bathroom near the front door, or Boone's ensuite bathroom.

She hesitated before heading towards Boone's bedroom. She was flexible enough to get her foot into the sink, but it would be a hell of a lot easier to wash her foot in the tub in Boone's bathroom. He'd met Chase for a sparring match this afternoon and wouldn't be home for at least another half hour. He'd never know she'd used his bathroom.

She hopped her way into his bedroom, keeping her eyes averted from his unmade bed. It would be all sorts of wrong to lie in his bed and bury her face in his pillow, even if her foot wasn't currently covered in dog shit.

Grunting and starting to sweat a little from the exertion of keeping her foot up, she made it to his bathroom, a soft 'damn' escaping her lips. In addition to a walk-in shower, Boone had one of those gorgeous old-fashioned claw tubs in his bathroom. Everything looked brand new from the hexagon shaped black and white floor tile to the gleaming white subway tile in the shower, and she had no doubt that Boone had renovated the bathroom himself. She'd discovered pretty quickly that Boone loved home renovations, and he'd purposely bought his house because it was older and required a lot of work.

She washed her foot in the tub, using Boone's body wash, and making sure to rinse the tub completely clean before swinging her legs out of the tub. She grabbed a hand towel from the rack and, sitting on the side of the tub, dried her feet.

She wondered idly if Boone would consider letting her use his tub if she cleaned it afterward. She loved nothing more than sinking into a hot bath and while the tub in her shared bathroom with Althea was perfectly serviceable, this tub was the gold standard of tubs.

It wouldn't hurt to ask. The worst that could happen was he said no, right?

"What are you doing in my bathroom?"

Boone's voice scared the hell out of her, but it was the sight of his sweaty, almost entirely naked body, that sent her ass over teakettle back into the tub, banging the back of her head on the cold porcelain.

Wedged sideways into the tub like a turtle on its back, her scrub pants soaking up the water pooled in the bottom, and her legs stuck straight up in the air, Hedra gathered what little dignity she had left and said, "I had dog poop on my foot."

"End of Night" will be available in 2022

ABOUT THE AUTHOR

Ramona Gray is a Canadian romance author. She currently lives in Alberta with her awesome husband and her super cute dog. She's addicted to home improvement shows, good coffee, and reading and writing about the steamier moments in life.

For more information about Ramona, check out her website at

www.ramonagray.ca

facebook.com/RamonaGrayBooks

twitter.com/RamonaGrayBooks

instagram.com/ramonagrayauthor

amazon.com/Ramona-Gray/e/B00OD26SAM

bookbub.com/profile/ramona-gray

The Welder

The Electrician

The Landscaper

The Firefighter

The Cop

The Paramedic

Working Men Series Bundles

Working Men Series Books One to Three

Working Men Series Books Four to Six

Working Men Series Books Seven to Nine

Other World Series

The Vampire's Kiss (Book One)

The Vampire's Love (Book Two)

The Shifter's Mate (Book Three)

Rescued By The Wolf (Book Four)

Claiming Quinn (Book Five)

Choosing Rose (Book Six)

Elena Unbound (Book Seven)

Other World Series Box Sets

Other World Series Books One to Three

Other World Series Books Four to Six